IN THE SHADOW OF THE TREES

by

Michael Schultz

Library of Congress Catalog Card Number: 97-65303

DAN RIVER PRESS
P. O. BOX 298
THOMASTON, MAINE. 04861

THIS BOOK IS DEDICATED TO THOSE CCC "BOYS" WHO STOOD THEIR FINAL RETREAT:

Clifford Alexander
Joe Barron
Robert Buck
Edward R. Clinton
Charles (Bob) Dickson
Dean Gettig
John P. Hobrat
Glenn Kopp
Edwin Kroesen
William Kresowaty
Roy (Pinky) Marker
Andy Mathews
Howard (Lefty) McClellan
Robert Nail
Mike Perrett
Dick Pierce
Harry Sharp
Edwin Zevotek

A TIP OF THE OLD CCC CAP TO THE FOLLOWING CCC "BOYS" WHO HELPED MAKE THIS BOOK POSSIBLE:

Lou Adams
Hal Bush
Robert Carson
Art Dando
Ray Haag
Martin Hansen
Henry Hobrat
James Hughes
Everett Minteer
Angelo Nocera
Steve Ocl
Don Skibinski
Bob Stevenson
Charles Varro

ACKNOWLEDGEMENTS

This book would not have been possible had it not been for the financial help of the following patrons:

Thomas M. Allegretto; Karen Baxter; Mike Blazzo; Patti Bonham; Kathleen Buck; Hal Bush; Isabelle Champlin; Arthur L. Dando; John Davis; Elizabeth Dickson; Jack and Carol Doyle; James Elinski; Jimbo Elinski; Robert Emery; Lyle Furlong; Warren and Janice George; Alice and Darrell Goodlin; Paul Gotkin; Dorothy Guaglianone; Grace Gunderman; Emma S. Hau; Henry Hobrat; Chuck and Doris Hybl; Cyrus Klingensmith; Steve Klipa; Mr. and Mrs. Edward Kramer; James V. Marzula; Madeline McMahon; James and Joan McMahon; John Melichar; Laura Mikesell; Jerry and Marlene Nelson; Everett Minteer; Angelo Nocera Sr.; John Owens; Ellen Peroski; Mary Perrett; C. Frederick Ralston; James Schultz Sr.; Kenneth Schultz; Michael and Denise Schultz; Thomas Schultz; Patrick and Joanne Skibinski; Francis J. Thompson; Charles Varro; The Wilcox Public Library; and Nadine Wilson.

I would like to thank the following people who helped me with this project whether it was reading portions of the manuscript in progress; describing their CCC experiences; advising me on medical treatments of pneumonia or treatment of eye injuries; recounting their forest fire experiences; giving me insight into boxing as a sport; sharing their knowledge about life in the Turtle Creek Valley during the 1920's and the 1930's; or just recalling their memories of that tumultuous era known as The Great Depression.

Helen Adams; Alex Badenoch; Karen Baxter; Burley Burlingame, Paul Brohn; Isabelle Champlin; Max Collins; Arlene Cull; Cozie Diaz; Lou DeBrozzi; Dr. and Mrs. Edward Duffy; Carol Doyle; Tom Esper; Ray and Julie Haag; Joe Hepinger; Jim and Joyce Hill; Lucille Gettig; Janice George; Herman Johansen; Dr. Kaj Johansen; Rosemary Macaluso; Nan McCaslin; David McFarland; Laura and Dick Mikesell; Kay Nocera; Jack Owens; Bess Pierce; Faye Pierce; Jim and Dorothy Schultz; Josephine Schultz; Robert Scott; Michael and Denise Schultz; Richard Schultz; Thomas Schultz; Pat and Joanne Skibinski; William Summers; Fred Ralston; Keith and Bunny Roessing; Dr. Roald Tweet; Dr. Adam Weiss; Judd Wilson; The

New Castle, Pennsylvania, Chapter 125 of NACCCA; and Army Zemarel.

I would like to thank Grace Gunderman, my colleague and writing mentor. She guided me over some very rough spots in the project's early phases. I could always depend on her frank appraisals whenever I gave her a part of the manuscript to read. I am fortunate to have such a friend as Grace.

I would also like to thank Jack Doyle, my patient brother-in-law, for teaching me the intracies of the computer and the word processor. Not unaware of HAL, Jack has actually revived my computer by simply speaking to it via the telephone.

Finally, I would like to acknowledge my wife, Marie. Constantly encouraging me, she has been my confidante, my friend, and for the past forty plus years, my love. I could not have done this work without her.

IN THE SHADOW OF THE TREES

CHAPTER ONE

Wynn Odum attended Union High School at Turtle Creek only because he regularly made his spending money by playing poker in the school's basement. Since the building plans of the school were as unstructured as the unruly kids who attended there, Wynn always had a place to run the game. Cutting class presented no problem. He knew that most teachers just didn't give a damn.

The lone exception was Henry Zukowski, Wynn's Twelfth Grade English Literature teacher.

So Wynn dragged himself to Zukowski's class every day, suffering through Boewulf, King Arthur, and even Shakespeare. But when Zukowski began to analyze every line of Milton's PARADISE LOST, Wynn had had it. After Zukowski launched into still another harangue on why everyone was going to Hell, Wynn exploded. "Bullshit!" he said. "That's pure bullshit!"

Turning quickly on a perfect military pivot, Henry Zukowski demanded, "Young man, explain that statement."

Nearly six feet tall and weighing one hundred and seventy pounds, Wynn was a rugged kid with quick hands and a tough jaw. His frame was muscular, but his eyes, ice-blue, were his most striking feature. Glaring fiercely at Zukowski, Wynn argued, "For a month now, you've talked about Hell. Like it's something we've got to look forward to."

"John Milton addressed man's weaknesses," preached Zukowski. "What was true then is true today, Odum!"

"He never had to stand four across in a mile-long line just to eat at a some lousy soup kitchen."

"That has nothing to do with my classroom."

Frustrated, Wynn said, "The steel mills are down, and you're getting paid in script."

"How I get paid is none of your business, young man!"

"What the hell world are you living in?" asked Wynn. He moved to a window, opened it, and pointed toward shacks that paralleled the railroad yards. "Have you ever been inside any of them?" When Zukowski remained silent, Wynn continued. "There's people living in holes in the ground, and they cover themselves with whatever they can find just to keep warm."

Manny Jenkins agreed. "Moles got a better life."

Wynn pointed to a large cardboard box. "See that big one next to the ditch?"

Jenkins asked, "The one that says Kotex?"

"An old lady and her three kids call it home."

Jenkins put his hand against his mouth to muffle a laugh. "Some kind of home, ain't it?"

"Jenkins, this is between Odum and me."

As Jenkins retreated, Wynn turned his anger once again toward Zukowski. "You and your great books! I don't have to read old farts to know about Hell. I live in it!"

Zukowski, a muscular, World War I veteran in his late thirties, glared at Wynn. "Great thinkers built an orderly world, anticipating every question from puny minds, like yours, Odum."

While some students began to form a circle around Wynn and their teacher, Zukowski asked, "Those boxing bouts your manager, Murray, got for you?"

"What about them?"

"They're fixed. And your opponents? Bought off! Everyone last one of them!" To emphasize his last point, Zukowski grabbed Wynn's shirt, but his clumsy efforts succeeded only in ripping the buttons off.

Wynn reacted instinctively. "That's a rotten lie!" he yelled, while rifling a shot to Zukowski's jaw and following it up with a solid right to his teacher's stomach. As a stunned Zukowski toppled backward into Manny Jenkins, Wynn sneered, "You think those shots were fixed?" He looked at his classmates and then pointed at Zukowski's diploma, hanging over the desk. "Who needs <u>that</u>, anyway?" Wynn asked scornfully.

While the kids helped Zukowski to a chair, Wynn opened the door and walked down the dark corridor. Pushing open the ornate double doors, he stepped out into the dirty streets where a chilly April wind greeted him. He pulled up his coat collar, hunched his shoulders inward, and began walking toward East Pittsburgh, a mile away.

Growing up in this uncompromising environment, Wynn had but two choices: to run or to fight. He never ran. As he grew older, his reputation spread. Soon his turf became the entire Turtle Creek Valley, a cluster of grimy mill and railroad towns ten miles east of Pittsburgh.

After an easy walk, he reached the chained gates of the sprawling Westinghouse plant. Moving easily among the dismissed workers, Wynn slapped some on their backs while offering others words of encouragement. Then he walked over to a cherry-red barrel that burned brightly in front of the main gate.

"Got a fight tomorrow night, kid?" asked one man who warmed his behind from the barrel.

"Yeah, I'm going to mix it up with a cat named Daily."

"I got a fin on you," shouted a disheveled man.

"Don't make no difference who you fight, right Babe?" whooped an admirer.

Wynn assumed a boxing stance while backing away from the fire. "I'll pound salt up Daily's ass. You can count on that."

A loud cheer rose which made Wynn feel good. He turned and waved to his friends before slowly walking away. A block later, Wynn still felt good, knowing that he owed it all to Murray, his manager.

CHAPTER TWO

Buoyed by his fan's support, Wynn had paid little attention to his expulsion notice from school. His mind was on boxing. While Murray (no one knew his last name) drove Wynn to the Daily bout, Wynn leaned back in the front seat, closed his eyes, and dreamed of becoming a professional boxer. He imagined appearing in the main event at Forbes Field, a Pittsburgh baseball park famous for hosting big-time fights.

The ring was located on the deepest part of the infield, right over second base. Forbes Field was packed---36,000 cheering fans, some of whom leaned precariously against the railing on the third tier, nearly a hundred feet above the infield. While most sat comfortably on folding chairs in the infield or in the first and second decks, others sat atop the vine-covered walls in left and center fields. A few had even scrambled on top of the batter's cage in deep center field.

Upon entering the ring, he heard the fans chanting, "We..in! We..in! We..in!" His name came out in two syllables, like a giant exhaling, and then, rapidly, inhaling.

This reoccurring image made Wynn smile before awaking with a start when Murray's shouted an epithet at a pedestrian.

"Sorry, about that," said Murray. "You know how I drive."

"I know," said Wynn. "You've told me before."

"I'm a graduate of the 'One Hand On The Wheel, Head Out The Window School Of Driving,'" Murray said.

"What language were you using this time?" asked Wynn.

"Italian," answered Murray. "I can cuss them out in Polish and Ukrainian, too." Then, when two children darted out into the street to retrieve a ball, Murray hit the brakes while simultaneously cursing in English. As the car picked up speed, he added, "I ain't bad with that language, either."

While Murray concentrated on the road ahead, Wynn studied his manager's puffy, short hands. One clutched the steering wheel, while the other waved a stub of a half-lit cigar. Wynn closed his eyes again and thought: your eyes bulge like an owl's and you walk like a penguin. But no one's got the guts to laugh at you. At least not to your face.

Wynn knew Murray owned Turtle Creek, and everyone in town owed Murray. Wynn learned this, because occasionally, he ran numbers for him and got to see the inside of the operations. He knew that no one crossed Murray, especially when it came to welshing on bets.

But Wynn knew there was another side of Murray.

He admired Murray's ability to oil himself into people's lives even more successfully than an alderman finding additional voters in the local cemetery. Wynn particularly enjoyed watching him operate at baptisms and weddings -- big events in Turtle Creek because everybody was always invited. At baptisms, Murray always slipped the proud new father something special for his good work, a bit more if the child were a boy.

Wynn remembered the first time he had met Murray. It was at Johnny Washkowski's wedding reception.

After watching Johnny and Suzie smear cake on each other, Wynn sampled the wedding cake. Then he took a glass of spiked fruit juice and walked toward the doorway when Murray approached him.

"You know who I am, kid?" Murray asked.

Wynn nodded and said, "Sure. Who doesn't?"

Murray went nose-to-nose to Wynn.

Wynn tried to back away when he smelled Murray's bad breath.

"I've watched you fight on the streets," Murray rasped. "You got some good moves. So let's get down to business." He pulled Wynn closer. "Do you want to fight for me? On an organized basis? Like maybe, someday, I can get you a shot at Forbes Field."

On that day, Murray took over Wynn's career and immediately began booking him into clubs and smokers. This arrangement satisfied both men. Murray made money regularly, and Wynn always won.

A loud horn from an oncoming car jolted Wynn from his reverie. He opened his eyes and repositioned himself in his seat. It was now dark, and he rubbed his eyes as the street lights of Greensburg loomed before him. "Are we there, yet?" he asked.

"Another couple of miles," Murray said. Then he nudged Wynn on his shoulder, the cigar ashes spilling down his arm. "Glad you're awake, kid. Tonight's fight is going to be...Different."

Uneasily, Wynn asked, "How so?"

"Tonight, Daily's going to win."

Wynn tugged at his hat and continued staring straight ahead. He saw his Forbes Field dream disappearing into the oncoming traffic. Finally, he blurted, "Why? I've seen Daily."

Murray flicked the cigar stub out the window and then reached into his pocket for another one. Passing it under his nose, he complained, "Some day, they're going to make a cigar taste as good as it smells." He bit off the end and spat it out the window. "Give me a light," he demanded.

Wynn reached into his pocket and pulled out a match. Lighting it with his fingernail, he held the flickering match under the cigar, while Murray took three deep drags before exhaling a massive cloud of smoke.

Murray drove another mile before he broke the uneasy silence. "I've been running a profitable game for the past six months. And I'll not forget your part." His voice became menacing, however, when he added, "Everything's in place. Understand? Babe Mancuso owns a piece of Daily, and I owe him a favor for getting a judge into my corner." Murray hesitated slightly, his voice becoming a whisper, as if he were going to share a secret. "After tonight, Babe's got his boy on the card at Forbes Field, and I walk away with a bundle."

"Now I know what the hustlers meant by finding someone fresh from the pickleboat," muttered Wynn.

When Murray stopped at a traffic light, he took his hand from the gear shift and knocked Wynn's hat from his head. "Let me see your face, kid. So I can see what's going on in your thick skull."

Although the light had changed, Murray remained at the intersection. A chorus of horns caused him to slam the car into low gear and then into second and high gears. As the car picked up speed, he said, "There ain't nothing like a fast car, Odum. Even better than a woman." When Murray slowed down for jaywalker, he asked, "Do you think you're Benny Leonard? That you knocked out those bums all by yourself? Who in hell do you...?"

Two nuns crossing the street interrupted Murray's tirade. He rolled down the window and tipped his hat in their direction "Good evening, Sisters." The big smile on his face remained until they had disappeared around the corner. "Always play the odds, kid. That salutation might be worth a little help with their Boss." Then, with the thumb and forefinger of his right hand, he grasped Wynn's left cheek, giving it a tug. "If you win tonight, we'll get your old man."

As Murray roared through the darkness, Wynn searched the floor for his hat. When he found it, he slowly put it on while trying to sort out his options. But whatever solution Wynn reached, he always came back to one sure thing: Murray never issued an idle threat.

On the west side of Greensburg, Murray pulled up to a warehouse, parking beside a loading ramp where a large, burly man motioned them inside the building. As the door closed behind them, Murray poked Wynn in his ribs and said, "Ain't this setup something?"

Wynn had never expected anything of this magnitude. His other fights had been in halls, holding fewer than a hundred fans. Amazed, he said, "This place must seat six or seven hundred people."

Smiling, Murray gave Wynn a soft tap on the jaw. "Got the big picture, kid?" Before Wynn could reply, Murray ran down the steps into the ring and began to count the house.

Wynn stopped and peered at the crowd. He watched the well-dressed men in the first three rows waving at Murray. When Wynn turned around, he counted ten rows of rickety bleachers that rose steeply to the ceiling. He listened as the fans screamed incessantly at four men in rumpled suits who took their bets. "Now I know there's one born every minute," he said. When he saw Daily and his manager, Jobe Milton, entering the ring, Wynn said aloud, "Showtime."

As Wynn crawled into the ring, Murray pointed to his watch anxiously. In a stage whisper, he said, "Let's get this thing going."

Wynn threw his shirt over the ropes and paused before he began to unbutton his pants. "I wish that just once you could get me a fight that had a dressing room." He threw his trousers onto the ring apron. His faded trunks matched the dirty shade of smoke that hung suspended beneath the ring lights. He stood upright in his corner while Murray put the gloves on his hands.

Prior to each fight, each manager frisked his opponent's man for any foreign substances that might be hidden on the fighter's body. When Milton raised Wynn's arms, Wynn asked, "What are you looking for? A rock?"

"Once I found grease taped in a guy's crotch."

"Did you turn him in to the cops?"

"He was going to rub it into my boy's eyes." After completing his thorough search, Milton shouted to Murray, "He's clean."

"Your boy's all right, too," replied Murray.

Then the managers called the boys together to explain the rules. Murray began first. "No head butting, no kicking, or tripping. And remember, it's a fight to the finish."

"If a man's knocked down," Milton said, "the other guy goes to a neutral corner and waits for his opponent to get up. If the man can't get up or his manager throws in the towel, the fight's over."

"Now get back to your corners," said Murray.

On the way back to his corner, Wynn said, "I almost believed that little speech."

"Yeah, yeah," said Murray.

While waiting for the bell, Wynn said, "I saw Daily fight at a private smoker. He had some good moves."

"Ain't smokers out of your league?"

"I got the tickets from you."

When the bell rang, the fighters moved toward each other, extended their arms, and touched gloves. After completing this ritual, Wynn threw two quick jabs at Daily, more to expend nervous energy than to hurt him. Parrying them easily, Daily countered with a right to the body that did little damage.

Wynn began with a routine body attack, waiting for an opening. When Daily lunged with a hard right, Wynn easily deflected it, but Daily's forward motion threw him into Wynn's arms. Daily

8

broke from the clinch, jabbed at Wynn's ribs, and then followed up with a left hook. Wynn rolled with the first and shook off the second easily. Stepping under a roundhouse right, Wynn moved in close and began to concentrate on the body, neutralizing Daily's long distance blows. Instinctively, Wynn pounded away at his opponent's midsection until Daily fell into a clinch.

Bulling Daily toward Murray, Wynn noticed perspiration on his manager's round face. When Wynn staggered Daily with a hard left hook, Wynn saw Murray wave his arm toward the rear of the building. Wynn unleashed a right and a left that jolted Daily. Then Wynn let go a right hook to the chin. When it connected, Daily fell to the floor.

While waiting for Daily to regain his senses, Wynn saw Murray's flunkey escorting a man down to the front row. Quickly recognizing his father, Wynn began to shake with rage. "You bastard," he screamed. "You dirty bastard, Murray!"

Unsure of his next move, Wynn watched Daily pull himself up by the ropes. Still hesitating, Wynn allowed Daily valuable time to stand unmolested against the ropes. As Wynn shuffled out to resume the attack, he was careful not to go to Daily's jaw. Then Wynn allowed Daily to fall into an extended clinch where the two men pushed and held each other. When Daily began to come around, Wynn broke the clinch and hit Daily with two jabs that looked harder than they really were.

Suddenly, Daily began to take the offensive. He lashed out with a right that caught Wynn on his left kidney. Instinctively, Wynn backpedaled, but Daily caught him with a sharp combination that knocked him to the floor.

When Wynn got up, Daily popped him with a right to the chin and a left hook to the jaw. Then Daily began to use his weight advantage, allowing him to score solidly with a left to the belly and a strong right to the jaw.

Wynn's heart was no longer in the fight, but he did not know how to lose. When Daily ripped him with a solid right hook, Wynn went down again. Slowly, he got to his hands and knees and willed himself back by focusing his eyes upon the ceiling lights. Then he slowly got up and wrestled Daily into a clinch.

As Wynn held on, he saw his father clutch his chest and collapse. The crowd noise drowned out Wynn's scream. Desperate, Wynn butted Daily, while simultaneously delivering a right jab to Daily's belly and tramping on his left foot. As Daily fell down, Wynn scrambled between the ropes and tried to grab Murray.

Murray spun around, avoiding Wynn's initial charge. Taunting him, Murray said, "Odum, you can't hurt nobody with those gloves on."

As Wynn prepared to charge again, he screamed, "You're nothing unless you have those thugs around."

With a sudden jerk of his arm, Murray yelled, "Get him, boys!"

Immediately, two men grabbed Wynn around his arms, while a third one kicked him in the groin. A fourth thug came up from behind and rabbit-punched Wynn, causing him to pitch forward, falling over his father's body.

CHAPTER THREE

When Wynn awoke, he slowly focused his eyes on the bars that surrounded him. Realizing that he was in jail, Wynn screamed, "What happened to my father?" He tried to pull himself up, but his legs would not support him. When he felt a hand on his shoulder, Wynn looked up into the face of a tall, young man whose smile revealed two missing front teeth. "And who in hell are you?" Wynn asked.

"My name's Ontek Adamcheck." He put his arms under Wynn's shoulders and lifted him to a standing position. "It seems you're a guest of the county. Just like me."

"Do you always wear that shit-eating grin on your face?"

Ontek helped Wynn over to a metal cot attached to the wall. While easing Wynn onto the cot, Ontek said, "Don't have much of a mattress, but it beats the floor."

"Where am I?"

"In the Wilmerding hoosegow."

"But I didn't do nothing."

"She...it! Not the way I look at it. Three guys dragged you in here, acting like they nabbed Al Capone!"

"Did you get any names?"

"A fella named Murray said something about an old guy who dropped dead."

"That was my father. I saw him go down just before they got me."

"They said he had a bum ticker."

"They killed him."

When Wynn sat down on the cot and buried his head into his hands, Ontek sat down beside him and put his arm around Wynn's shoulder.

This gesture caused Wynn to bolt from the cot. "What the hell are you? A queer?"

"I thought you might need a friend."

Wynn smiled sheepishly and returned to the cot.

Ontek smiled broadly. "Tell me about your old man."

"He came over from the Old Country in 1890 and got a job in the Homestead Mill."

"Was he part of the big strike?"

"Yeah."

"Did he know the guy who got his head blowed off by the cannon shell?"

"He was standing beside him when it happened."

"I bet there was blood everywhere."

"Old-timers told me that my old man sort of went crazy after that. That he talked about killing Henry Clay Frick, the guy who ran the Homestead Mill."

"Well, did he?"

"Naw," said Wynn. "But later on, a guy named Berkman did shoot Frick."

"Killed him dead?"

"Only winged him. Berkman went to jail, and Frick busted the Union. And my old man never got over the strike." Wynn got up and walked over to the small sink in the corner of the cell. Turning on the water, he slowly washed his hands. Then he returned to the cot and sat down.

"What's wrong?"

"We just sort of drifted apart."

"Where's your ma?"

"She died when I was born."

"Oh," was Ontek's only response.

"My old man wanted me to finish high school. Said it was the only way to get out of the Valley. But I never listened to him." Wynn sat quietly, thinking about their strained relationship. "When I got heaved out of high school, he actually cried."

"What did you do to get shit-canned?"

"I cold-cocked my English teacher."

12

"Jeez, I never knew anyone who did that." Ontek rubbed his chin and began to laugh.

"What's so damn funny?"

"My fourth grade teacher...That's as far as I got...Mrs. Hofmeister, she weighed three hundred and fifty pounds, and when she walked, her legs made a funny rubbing noise..."

"Shut up, you dumb galoot!" Wynn slowly rose from the cot and walked over to the window. From there, he watched two boys playing catch with a heavily taped softball while they argued over which one was going to be Lefty Grove.

The clanking open of an outer door jarred Wynn back to reality. As two men entered the cell block, Wynn said, "The old fart is Murray. He was my manager. The fat one in the monkey suit must be his pal."

"Show some respect," the man in the uniform bellowed.

"Calm down, Philip," said Murray. "Gentlemen, meet Lieutenant Philip Grabowski, my nephew."

"Should I be impressed?" snapped Wynn.

Murray winked at his nephew. "A piss ant. That's what Odum is. A piss ant!" Then, as if in prayerful deliberation, Murray closed his eyes and clasped his hands together. "You made me look bad. And in front of my business associates, too." His voice tailed off into silence. Suddenly, the cell echoed with Murray's rage. "I got friends who want to lock you up and throw away the damn keys."

Wynn spat at Murray's feet, scoring a direct hit on his manager's shiny black shoes. When Grabowski charged at Wynn, he disdainfully flicked the officer's hands away from the bars.

"Philip, we're not here to harm Wynn," Murray cautioned. "We've come to give him guidance." Pointing to the spittle running from his shoes, he ordered, "Get some paper so you can lean this up."

As Grabowski dutifully obeyed his uncle, Murray looked at Wynn. "Odum, you're going to end up dead one of these days."

"You killed my old man."

"You got it all wrong, kid." Then Murray moved closer to the bars that separated them. "If his son would have followed simple directions, like I asked, the old man would be alive."

"He had a bum heart."

"That's yesterday's news," Murray countered. "When was his last attack?"

"Two months ago."

"So he died of natural causes."

"Who said so?"

"The coroner says so!"

"When's the funeral?"

Murray slipped off his shoes and kicked them over his nephew who had reentered the room. Taking a cigar from his inside coat pocket, he waved it toward Wynn. "I got news for you. We had a nice little service for your old man."

Wynn lunged toward the bars again. "You buried him already?"

"Nope. They quicklimed him."

"You what?"

"You got twenty-twenty hearing don't you? The authorities was afraid he had a contagious disease."

Wynn let go of the bars and slid down to the floor. "I'll make you pay for this."

"Never make threats unless you can back them up," advised Murray.

After cleaning Murray's shoes, Grabowski said, "Listen, my uncle could have your ass."

Wynn spit again, but this time it missed its mark.

"How about it, Uncle Murray?" asked Grabowski, "Can't you send him to jail for causing the riot that injured seven people?"

"Philip, you've said enough." Then, turning to Wynn, Murray said, "My friend, Judge Parsons, is going to send you to the CCC's."

"That's great!" interrupted Ontek. "I got into a little fight last Friday, and Parsons gave me one year in the C's."

"What the hell's a CCC?" asked Wynn.

"The Civilian Conservation Corps," answered Ontek. "It's something started by Roosevelt that gives poor kids like us a place to live in the woods so we can fight forest fires, plant trees, and do all kind of exciting things."

"Do I have a humdinger of a place picked out for you," said Murray. Then he relit the cigar again. After exhaling a large cloud of smoke, he said, "First camp in Pennsylvania. Up near Marienville."

"Where's Marienville?"

"A place about a hundred-twenty miles north of Pittsburgh," answered Murray.

"Who's going to make me go?"

Murray pointed at Grabowski. "That's where my nephew comes in."

"What's the little tin soldier going to do?" mocked Wynn.

"The army appointed him Company Commander of Camp One."

"And you're going to serve under me," said Grabowski.

"No way in hell!"

"Then you'll go in cuffs, big shot," threatened Grabowski.

"Judge Parsons thinks you're a dangerous character," said Murray.

"Bullshit on the whole damn parade!" screamed Wynn.

"We'll handcuff you and your pal together..."

Murray interrupted his nephew. "A deputy sheriff will take you to Turtle Creek and then on to the B & O Station in Pittsburgh."

"Why stop at Turtle Creek?" asked Wynn.

"To put you on display." Murray rubbed his hands together in anticipation. "I want everybody to know what happens when a punk tries to jerk me off." Then he added, "At the B & O station, the deputy will chain you to one of the seats in the railroad car."

"You can't chain me forever."

"Here's the beauty part, kid," said Murray. "When you get to Fort Monroe, the deputy will turn you over to the Feds."

"Where's Fort Monroe?" asked Ontek.

"In Virginia," answered Grabowski.

"What's to keep me from taking off once I get there?"

"With the Feds in charge, it's a whole new ball game," chortled Murray. "It don't pay to get them mad."

"No camp'll keep me."

Murray replied, "It'll take you a year just to find a sign pointing to Pittsburgh." He grabbed a grinning Grabowski and headed for the door. Before leaving, Murray turned around and taunted Wynn. "Don't ever forget, I can always reach out and squash you, because that's what I like to do to piss ants."

Wynn shot him the finger as Murray slammed the heavy door shut.

"Think he was telling the truth?" asked Ontek.

"He's got all the cards."

"Then he has all those friends?"

"All the way from the county courthouse to the state capitol."

"What are you going to do?"

"Nothing until they unchain us at Fort Monroe."

"Then what?"

"My father's gone, and I've got no relatives. And sure as hell, I'm not welcome in Turtle Creek anymore."

"So how about giving the C's a chance, then?"

"Guess I've got no strings tied to me."

"Well, make up your mind."

"What the hell!" Wynn slowly answered. "Might as well make Judge Parsons proud of us."

Two days later, a deputy sheriff delivered Wynn and Ontek to Fort Monroe for processing in the CCC's, and the two young men embarked on their new careers.

CHAPTER FOUR

The sun had not risen when the first detachment of CCC men arrived at Bryomtown, a village crossroads five miles northwest of Marienville. A typical Western Pennsylvania spring day, four inches of slushy snow and a bone-chilling drizzle, greeted them.

The men had traveled overnight from Virginia in two dirty, unheated railroad cars. As the train slowly pulled onto the railroad siding, the men stood up and shuffled stiffly toward the exits.

Wynn Odum did not immediately leave his seat. Instead, he stretched his legs forward as far as possible, raised his arms high over his head, and yawned loudly. Then he wiped the condensation from the window. Peering out into the darkness, he said, "Jeez, I can't see a damn thing."

Wynn's comment awakened Ontek who had been sleeping. Rubbing his eyes with his fists, Ontek asked, "What did you say?"

Rising slowly, Wynn tapped Ontek on the shoulder before edging out into the aisle. "C'mon buddy, shake a leg."

Suddenly, three young men elbowed Wynn aside, pushing him onto Ontek's lap. "Out of my way," said a tall man, as he and his friends shoved their way to the front exit.

Fully awake now, Ontek slowly stood up. As his face turned red, he asked, "Who's them assholes?"

Wynn cautioned, "Easy pal!" Then he nudged his way into the crowded aisle again.

"They could have knocked you to the floor," complained Ontek.

Before Wynn could respond, he felt a sharp jab in his ribs. Turning around, he looked down on a skinny-faced kid, barely five feet tall. "You in a hurry?" Wynn asked.

17

"Yeah. Them's my buddies up there," the kid responded.

"What's their names?" asked Ontek.

"The big one's Harry O'Donnel."

Ontek's eyes narrowed as he tried to get a better look. "Don't I recognize him?"

The kid stood on his tiptoes so he could get a better look. "O'Donnel looks like Dick Tracy, don't he?"

"Who's the others?" asked Ontek.

"Lloyd Cartwright's the red-haired fella. The one wearing the green sweater's Buddy Selig. He coughs all the time."

"Should we be afraid of them, too?"

"Not like O'Donnel," the kid answered. "He's really mean!"

As Ontek moved out into the aisle, he asked, "And what's your name, shorty?"

"Albert Gray. But my friends call me Mousy."

Ontek laughed loudly, revealing his missing teeth. "Wynn, if this twerp had feathers, he'd be a fine looking bandy-legged rooster."

Mousy pointed to Ontek's mouth. "What happened? Did you run into someone's fist?"

"So you want to get to your buddies real quick-like?" asked Ontek. Then he grabbed Mousy around his midsection and heaved him above Wynn's head. "Take his feet," Ontek ordered. "And pass him along to his friends."

"Pass Mousy along," shouted Wynn.

Soon the cry, "Pass Mousy along," echoed throughout the car as the men accepted the squirming young man and hustled him forward like a case of beer zipping along a conveyer belt.

When they flipped a speechless Mousy into an upright position beside his pals, Ontek heard a loud cheer. He jumped up on the seat and yelled, "Happy now, Mousy?"

When O'Donnel shot Ontek the finger, Wynn said, "Looks like that O'Donnel fella is mad at you."

Ontek smiled and waved. His expression remained unchanged even when he reached the door where O'Donnel was waiting.

O'Donnel angrily poked his finger into Ontek's chest. "I don't like nobody messing with one of my boys."

"We got a real tough guy here," replied a still smiling Ontek.

When O'Donnel lunged at Ontek, Wynn and Cartwright jumped between them before either had a chance to throw a punch. While Wynn held Ontek's arms, Cartwright led O'Donnel toward the exit.

"If you get into a fight, they'll toss your can back into the klink at Philly," said Cartwright.

As O'Donnel stood at the door, he waved at Ontek. "That shit-eating grin will be the first thing to go." Then he jumped from the top step of the car into the swirling rain.

Cartwright and Selig quickly followed.

But before Mousy jumped, he turned to Ontek and, in a high pitched voice, said, "I told you not to get him mad."

Wynn watched the four young men disappear quickly. "Those guys sure got lost in a hurry," he said.

"Must have had lots of practice," said Ontek.

When Wynn stepped down, a cold rain pelted him in the face, causing him to hesitate.

"Move along," someone shouted.

Wynn turned toward his detractor and pumped his right arm defiantly toward the soggy heavens. He wiped the rain from his face and yelled, "Oh, shit!" Then he leaped toward a dry patch of ground. Landing upright, he turned easily toward Ontek. "You're next, wise guy."

Laughing at his friend, Ontek stood at the door. "You still ain't got it right, Wynn. It's shee...it!"

"Goddammit, get moving," someone from inside the car shouted.

Still another yelled, "Yeah, you're holding up the whole damn shooting match."

A sharp elbow in the back caused Ontek to leap before he was ready. He landed short of Wynn's position. The slush exploded high above Ontek's knees, soaking his trousers and filling his shoes with water. As he sloshed toward Wynn, Ontek groaned, "The Wilmerding jail was better than this."

Wynn and Ontek watched the remainder of the enrollees, stiff and cold, stumble out of the cars. The last young man, who had emerged from the car, took only a few steps before he slipped and fell. While the others roared derisively, Wynn ran over and helped the kid up. "Welcome to the CCC, buddy," said Wynn.

The young man looked at Wynn dumbly, while extending his hand. "Thanks. I'm George Higgleston. Even Erie, Pennsylvania, is nicer than this dump." Before Wynn could reply, the dazed young man wondered off quickly into the crowd.

As the enrollees swirled around him, Wynn felt strangely alone. His life in the Valley had been paved streets, noise, and constant motion. Nothing here was familiar. While gray sheets of rain enveloped everybody, Wynn became momentarily uncertain. He grabbed a young man who stood beside him and asked, "How in hell did we get ourselves into this mess?"

The man stared at Wynn and mumbled, "Do you have anything to eat?"

Someone else shouted, "When's the next train back to Pittsburgh?"

When a whistle temporarily diverted their attention, Wynn cupped his hand above his eyes to shield them from the rain. He saw a tall figure striding toward him.

The stranger blew his whistle in short, piercing blasts to get the men's attention. "Men, I'm Sergeant Michael Dougherty."

"And I'm tired and I want to go home," wailed a voice from the midst of the enrollees.

Dougherty, a veteran of the Muse-Argonne Offensive, looked in the direction of the critic. "Damned civilians! Helpless and hopeless." He blew the whistle again as if to emphasize the need for an exclamation point to his opinion.

Dougherty's whistle helped refocus Wynn's attention. No longer feeling sorry for himself, Wynn, instead, reacted instinctively, as if he were in the ring, fighting to stay on his feet. "Hey, Sarge, we're soaking wet and haven't eaten a decent meal since yesterday."

"Who said that?" demanded Dougherty.

Wynn picked his way through the huddled group. Elbowing a skinny kid out of the way, Wynn faced Dougherty and said, "I did."

"Who are you?"

"Wynn Odum, Sir."

Sergeant Dougherty, in his mid-forties, stood ramrod straight and towered a full four inches over Wynn. Dougherty thrust his nose downward into Wynn's face. "You're not afraid of me?"

"Should I be?"

"Not yet, Yardbird. Not yet." Then Dougherty fixed his gaze upon the men who huddled about him. "Here's the straight poop. It's almost four miles to camp, and we won't get there by pissing and moaning. So let's form a column of ducks, girls."

"What's a column of ducks?" someone asked.

Dougherty pointed to Ontek and Wynn. "Line up single file behind these birds." When a semblance of a line began to form, he roared, "Company...Tenshut!"

Most recognized this command, but when Dougherty yelled, "Left face," twenty men tripped over each other. Undismayed, he shouted, "Forward March," and unwittingly launched the CCC from the planning tables of Washington into the soggy reality of the field.

While the men struggled through the mud that the United States Forest Service called a road, the increasing number of stragglers caused Dougherty's column of ducks to disintegrate. Finally, he ordered, "Troops, route step."

"What the hell does he mean by that?" asked Ontek.

"Just keep going," said Wynn.

As the march continued, Ontek began to limp noticeably.

"What's wrong?" asked Wynn.

"My toe hurts like hell," answered Ontek. He walked in silence for another fifty yards before pulling Wynn from the line.

Wynn pointed to a huge rock and ordered, "Sit there."

"I'll get piles if I sit on that cold rock," complained Ontek.

Wynn disregarded Ontek's fear and forced him to sit down. Once seated, Ontek kicked off his left shoe. His sock was saturated because of a hole in the sole of his shoe. His big toe stuck through a gaping hole. "Jeez, it's turning purple!"

"The hole choked off the blood to your toe," said Wynn. He took out a pack of gum. "Black Jack chewing gum," he said. "My favorite. Here, have a stick."

"I don't need gum," wailed Ontek. "I got a hole in my shoe and my toe hurts something awful."

Wynn deliberately pealed the foil from another piece and

21

popped it into his mouth. He chewed slowly as if taking on the cares of the world. "What a sorry sight," he commented, as the weary men trudged by.

"The hope of tomorrow."

"Shows you listened to the bullshit they told us back at Fort Monroe."

"They didn't say nothing about the weather," grumbled Ontek.

As more men passed by, Wynn said, "Some of them's dressed like they're going to a picnic."

"Look. That guy there doesn't even have a sweater on."

"But we do have a couple of things in common, Ontek."

"What's that?"

"We're all poor..."

Ontek interrupted, "...and we're all soaking wet, too."

Listening to the men coughing, Wynn said, "Sounds like many of them belong in a hospital." Then he asked aloud, "How'd they ever pass the physical?"

"All you had to be was warm," remembered Ontek. "The doctor didn't even listen to my heart."

Standing up, Wynn said, "We'd better get moving."

"What about my foot?"

Wynn took the gum out of his mouth and with his thumb and forefinger flattened it into the size of a fifty cent piece. "Put that wad on the inside of the shoe over the hole. Then fold the tip of your sock over the top of your toe. That should help."

As Ontek was putting on his sock and shoe, Sergeant Dougherty thundered, "What's going on back there?"

"Sock repair, Sergeant," responded Wynn.

"Get back into formation," ordered Dougherty.

"Think you can make it?" asked Wynn.

Ontek got up and tested his weight upon his sore toe. Then he turned around rapidly two times before taking three giant steps forward. His face broke out into a wide smile. "Seems all right," he announced.

"Let's get moving," said Wynn who broke into a slow dog-trot toward the head of the column.

Ontek followed along, showing little of the lameness that had bothered him. He pulled his collar up around his ears and plodded ahead. When he caught up to Wynn, he said, "Thanks, buddy."

Reaching the top of the first hill, Wynn saw nothing but brush, scrub trees, and rocks. The view remained unchanged when they came over the second hill.

After another mile, Dougherty raced ahead of the column. He gestured excitedly toward a clearing one half mile away. "There she is, men. Your home. Ain't she beautiful?"

Wynn saw only six army tents rising from the middle of a muddy, open field. A row of scrub oak trees, still wearing last year's leaves, lined the compound on three sides.

"Where's the buildings?" someone asked.

"Won't be any until next winter," answered Dougherty.

"You mean we're going to live in tents?" asked Ontek.

"Did you expect the Ritz?" asked Dougherty.

"I could have froze to death easier back home," whined another young man.

Someone else asked, "Where's the street lights?"

The question was plaintive but foolish. So many derisive catcalls descended upon the innocent questioner that few heard Dougherty's command to halt. But they stopped anyway, because a huge mudhole obstructed their path.

"It don't look any better here than back at the railroad siding," said Ontek.

When a United States Army officer emerged from a tent, Wynn poked Ontek. "She...it! Do you see who I see?"

"Yeah," answered Ontek. "It's Grabowski."

"He looks like a movie usher."

Grabowski's uniform was impeccable. Above the left jacket pocket were two ribbons signifying a Good Conduct Medal and a Purple Heart. His shoes were flawlessly shined. And when he began to speak, his chest puffed out like a bird trying to shed water from its feathers. "I am Lieutenant Philip Grabowski, United States Army Reserve, your company commander."

Ontek nudged Wynn. "Is he for real?"

"Just another joke cooked up by the army," replied Wynn.

"Yeah, like the weather," groaned Ontek.

Grabowski cleared his throat and continued with his speech. "You are here because there is no work at home. I am here because I've got work for you to do. Eight hours a day, forty hours a week. As you can see, this camp is organized like the United States Army. You don't have to salute me, but you must call me 'Sir.'" Looking at Dougherty, Grabowski said, "And you are going to get plenty of old fashioned discipline. That means there will be plenty of inspections, too."

As Grabowski droned on, Wynn became interested in how Grabowski was going to get back into his tent without dirtying his shiny shoes. "There's no way he can do it without getting mud on them," Wynn muttered.

When Grabowski paused to catch his breath, Ontek began to chuckle. "Guess you can't see, but he's standing on a plank that goes back to his tent." As Grabowski rambled on, Ontek observed, "He's different now that his Uncle Murray ain't with him."

"Maybe he feels more at home here," said Wynn.

"You are an army with shovels," proclaimed Grabowski. "Armed with that noble tool, each man will go forth and stop the natural forces that are ravaging our land. History will be made here at Camp One. And you men are part of that history. Decades from now, you will remember the CCC experience as the highpoint of your lives."

With this pronouncement, Grabowski clicked his heals, did an about face, and slipped into the ankle-deep mud. But without losing his military decorum, he sloshed back into his tent.

Then Dougherty took over. "We got to have roll call. And the sooner we get it done, the sooner we eat."

When Dougherty got to Higgleston, Wynn interrupted. "Sarge, can't you read faster. We're drowning back here."

"Nothing hurries the military, Odum. Not snow, not sleet, rain, or high water."

"He must have been a mailman when he was a civilian," said Ontek.

When Dougherty reached the Z's, the cheers nearly drowned out Sammy Zambini's, "Yo, Sarge."

But Dougherty still had more to say. "After I dismiss you, go

24

to the mess tent, pick up your mess gear, and eat. After chow, report directly to the supply tent where Uncle Sam will give you clothes and shoes. Then at 1100 hours, that's eleven A.M. to you civilians, we'll meet back here for work assignments. Got it? Dismissed!"

CHAPTER FIVE

Red Dawson casually leaned against the supply tent's ridge pole while waiting for the men. He wore high-water pants, caulked boots, and a checkered shirt that hung loosely from his tall, thin frame. During his six year tenure in the Allegheny National Forest, Red had become the best forest fire foreman in the state. But during the eight months outside of the fire season, he was a Jack-of-All-Trades, doubling as a surveyor, a road builder, a bulldozer operator, and a tree planter. On this day, he was in charge of supply distribution.

When Ontek and Wynn ambled up to the tent, Ontek did an immediate double take. "Is he another joke or is that get-up for real?"

After everyone had arrived from breakfast, Red took command. Unlike Dougherty, who led by shouting, Red gave orders quickly and quietly, transforming a chaotic group into an organized body in less than ten minutes. Then he grabbed Wynn and Ontek and placed them at the head of the supply line.

"What'd we do?" asked Ontek.

"You guys are my guinea pigs." Red hopped up on a chair and cautioned them about the expected service. "Boys, none of us ever worked in clothing store. We're more at home with a pick or a shovel." Then he pointed to his assistants who stood behind mountains of World War I clothing. "Although we work for the Forest Service, you'll find us damned efficient." He jumped down and motioned to the ragged line. "Okay, boys, let's get this experiment moving."

Easing down the line, Ontek complained, "These clothes look like leftovers from the war."

"Which one?" muttered Wynn.

"I wonder if I'll get a gas mask?"

No one answered, but suddenly a bald-headed man, with a tape measure hanging from his shoulders, threw two pairs of size twenty-eight trousers and three size fifteen shirts at Ontek.

Red's aides worked efficiently, but their concern for a proper fit was not a primary importance. Instead, the whole process was similar to a game of chance. One man behind the counter sized up each enrollee and then relayed the pertinent information to a colleague who dealt out clothing.

As Wynn shuffled down the line, he accepted the clothes but worried about their fit. "The pants are too big and this hat falls down on my ears."

The allocation of the shoes was as haphazard. When Ontek tried on a pair, he wriggled his toes and immediately started to protest. "Hey, Mr. Dawson."

"My name's Red, kid. What's the matter now?"

"These shoes. They're too big."

"Wear two pair of socks!"

When Ontek tried on the regulation four-buckle boots over the ill-fitting shoes, his griping intensified. He stomped around the tent in the oversized boots before leaning against a table. "Whenever I take two steps forward, I slide back at least one."

Red winked at Ontek. "We call them sheep boots."

Immediately, Ontek began to laugh. He fastened the boots together and threw them over his shoulder. "I'm a country boy, Red. I know damn well what you mean." When nobody laughed, Ontek began to explain the joke.

"Don't tell them a thing," roared Red. "It's just a ba...aad joke!"

Ontek poked Wynn in the ribs. "I like this guy."

Becoming business-like again, Red ordered, "Cut the gab, gentlemen. Next stop is the overcoat department."

The coats hung on five clothing racks that blocked the rear entrance of the tent. When Wynn saw the coats, he exclaimed, "There's more coats here than in Gimbel's Department Store!" Accepting a forty-two long, he tried it on. The sleeves were a bit long but that did not bother him. He buttoned the coat and pulled the belt tightly around him. Then he paused and looked at Red.

"Where was this coat when I needed it?"

Ontek tried on two coats before selecting one. He nudged Wynn and said, "How do I look, buddy?"

Wynn saw that Ontek's coat nearly reached to the floor. But upon seeing Ontek's beaming face, Wynn said, "You look great, pal. Just great!"

Ontek walked proudly around the supply tent. He stopped and asked an enrollee, "Feel the material! Ain't it great?" Then he twirled around like a model on a runway before parading back to Wynn.

"Okay, fellas. That's the last stop," Red shouted. "Now put everything into your duffle bags."

"Do I have to take off this coat?" asked Ontek.

Red pointed outside. "Pull up a seat out there until everyone else suits up."

Wynn and Ontek stepped from the supply tent and carefully walked through the mud toward the edge of the compound. "At least with these new shoes, my feet ain't wet no more," said Ontek. He sat down on a log cut from a fallen tree. "Pull up a stump and take the weight off your dogs."

Wynn sat down while making sure that his duffle bag rested securely on his feet and not in the mud. "Got to make sure everything's high and dry," he said.

Ontek heaved his bag crossway on the log. While he cradled the back of his head with his hands, he stretched out on the log and draped his feet over the bag. He looked intently into the sky and watched a ray of sunlight reach down to the horizon. He sat up and pointed to it. "My mom always said that's a bad sign," he said.

"It only means that the sun is trying to come out," responded Wynn.

"She told me that was always a sign of death."

"If that Hitler guy keeps it up, it might be a bad sign for a lot of us," said Wynn.

"Naw, that sign's for someone here," said Ontek. " I just know it."

"C'mon," joked Wynn. "Who'd want to croak in such a nice place like this?"

"My mom has the gift of 'seeing.' She says that I got it, too.

That it runs in the family."

"Do you?" asked Wynn.

"I've 'seen' a couple of things over the past two years," said Ontek. "Nothing really big. But I'll tell you, the whole thing is sort of scary."

As a diversion, Wynn tossed his duffle bag on Ontek's feet and quickly straddled his body. Then he grabbed Ontek's head and began to give him a dutch-rub. "Say Uncle, or the next thing I'm going to do is to start tickling you," threatened Wynn.

"Uncle, uncle," pleaded Ontek.

When Wynn released his friend, Ontek got up and raced to the edge of the clearing. There he spied a large black ball in the top of a slender poplar tree. "Hey, Wynn. It's a porky. Come on over and see it." Since the tree was only twenty feet tall and was as slight as a reed, Ontek grabbed the tree and began to shake it vigorously.

When the animal continued to cling to its perch, Wynn said, "If that thing falls on you, "I'll be picking quills out of you for a month of Sundays."

Ontek soon lost interest. He shook the tree one more time before wandering back to his log seat. As he sat down, he asked, "Wynn?"

"What now?"

"I never owned nothing as elegant. Fact is, I never owned a overcoat before."

"I never had so many new clothes in my life," admitted Wynn.

The two young men sat there in silent agreement watching the other enrollees receive their supplies. Finally, Ontek said, "Maybe that judge did us a big favor?"

"What's your drift?"

"Last year, I couldn't get a job, and we had no coal to heat our house. My one little sister, Anna, died of whooping cough, and the littler one, Sara, almost starved because we had so little food."

"You're not alone." Wynn waved toward the supply tent. "I bet almost all of them were in the same boat."

"I thought of my folks when I stuffed myself at breakfast."

"It was a helluva spread," agreed Wynn."

"Where'd they get that good meat?"

"They were canned hams...Leftover from the Great War."

"No shit," said Ontek.

"That's she...it," said Wynn who watched Ontek begin to stare at the sky again. Playfully, Wynn nudged Ontek. "C'mon. We've been down that road already."

Ontek bent over and pulled up a yellowed piece of grass that grew at the base of the log. He positioned the grass between his thumbs and put it against his lips. Then he blew mightily but only succeeded in blowing the grass from his grip. He picked another piece and repeated the whole procedure. This time he created a long, screeching noise.

"Jeez," winced Wynn. "Sounds like a dying cow."

A big grin appeared on Ontek's face. "There was this guy back home who could play 'Yankee Doodle' on a blade of grass."

"No she...it."

"Of course that was in the summer when the grass was in better shape," said Ontek. Then he found a piece of timothy that had somehow survived the winter. He put its long spike into his mouth and began to chew it. "It's still sweet." He took it from his mouth and hurled it like a javelin toward the edge of the woods. "Mind that thirty dollars a month we get for being in the C's?"

"Twenty-five bucks of that goes straight home."

"My mom'll have enough to keep the house and eat, too."

"Don't forget, we still have five dollars that's all ours."

"What happens to your extra dough since you don't have no folks?"

"The army will hold it until I get out," explained Wynn.

"Phwey! That's going to be a pile of money."

"I'm going to use it to go to college."

"Why?"

"I've been doing a lot of figuring. A college education means a job. A damn good job!"

"Jeez," exclaimed Ontek, I never knew a college man before."

"No she...it."

"No she...it," responded Ontek who once again wore a big smile on his face.

When Red began shouting at them, they picked up their bags, slogged through the mud, and joined the men who waited for new orders.

"Go to the mess tent and change into your work clothes," ordered Red.

A voice from the rear asked Red. "Where'll we put our gear?"

"At the supply tent."

"What if someone steals it?" asked another enrollee.

Red stiffened at the suggestion of theft. His pale face colored with anger, but his voice remained calm. "Nobody," he said quietly, "and I mean nobody, steals in Camp One." Then he smiled and said, "Let's go to work."

The boys' first task was to build wooden platforms for the tents, their living quarters until the civilian crews completed the permanent barracks. Working with pre-cut lumber, the men more skilled in carpentry completed their platforms before sunset. That night they slept on cots set on a dry foundation.

Those enrollees unable to complete their floors before dusk learned a painful lesson. They spent their first night sleeping inches above the mud only to awake to find their clothes and their backsides soaked. The next morning, those men quickly built a buffer zone between them and the mire which grew steadily deeper.

By the evening of the second day, the CCC's presence had begun to alter the countryside. Neat gravel pathways, offering some relief from the omnipresent mud, outlined the camp. Four rows of army tents, each secure on a wooden platform, rose out of the clearing. Mud packed on each of the outside tent flaps kept the unfriendly chill from the living quarters, while tiny candle lights flickered from within the tents. The men had begun carving out an existence at this forlorn spot.

CHAPTER SIX

Inside Tent Number Eight, Ontek opened the door of a portable field stove and put in a few small pieces of wood. "These'll keep us warm."

The stove, a marvel of compactness, sat on four short legs that locked into position at each corner of the fire chamber. Its telescopic chimney extended precariously through the hole in the peak of the tent. Like the uniforms they had received, the stove, too, was an old but functional vestige of the Great War.

Satisfied that the stove was burning properly, Ontek walked over to his cot. "Good food and a dry place to sleep in. What a life!"

"And the work details aren't bad either," added Wynn, who was stretched out on his bed with his feet propped over his duffle bag.

Suddenly, Sergeant Dougherty yanked open the flap and shouted, "Ten...Shut!"

As the two young men rose, Lieutenant Grabowski briskly entered. He stamped his feet vigorously, allowing large chunks of mud to fall from his boots. "Got room for more yardbirds?" Without waiting for a reply, he yelled, "C'mon in, boys." Then he shouted to Wynn and Ontek, "I'd like you to meet the Schuylkill River Rats."

"She...it, Wynn! It's little Mousy and his tough-guy pals," groaned Ontek.

"You know them?" asked Grabowski.

"We sort of bumped in to each other," replied Wynn.

"I assigned them here, because like you and Adamchink..."

"Excuse me, Sir," interrupted Ontek. "It's Adamcheck. Ontek Adamcheck. They rhyme."

Grabowski's face turned beet-red as he shouted, "Don't ever interrupt me! Do you understand?" Then he stomped angrily around the tent and demanded, "Where's your bed, Adamchink?" When Ontek pointed to it, Grabowski pulled a fifty-cent piece from his pocket and flipped it onto the bed. When the coin did not bounce, a large smile appeared on his face. "You see that, Sergeant Dougherty?"

"Indeed I did, Sir"

"What does it mean, Sergeant?" asked Grabowski.

"The bed has not been made in a proper military fashion, Sir."

"That's correct, Sergeant." With that pronouncement, Grabowski reached down and ripped the bedclothes from the cot, throwing them on the mud-covered floor. "Consider you and your pal Odum on report."

"But Sir," Ontek responded, "Wynn didn't do nothing."

"You're the Gold Dust Twins!" yelled Grabowski. "Every time one of you screws up, the other will pay..."

Suddenly, Mark Selig began to cough, hard and rasping from deep within his chest. He pulled out a handkerchief and tried to cover his mouth, but he still sprayed his friends. Finally, he bent over, gasping for air.

"For God's sake, do something," ordered Grabowski.

Mousy said, "I don't know what to do."

"He's been that way for two days," offered Cartwright.

"Sounds like whooping cough to me," observed Ontek.

"Who died and made you doctor?" asked O'Donnel.

"Because that's what my sister had." Then Ontek added, "She died, you know."

While Selig continued to cough, Grabowski asked uneasily, "Sergeant Dougherty, When's the doctor coming on board?"

"Tomorrow, Sir."

O'Donnel reached over and smacked Selig on his back. The force of the blow was so hard that it knocked him against Wynn.

"You want to kill him?" asked Wynn, who continued to support Selig until he had stopped coughing. Then Wynn led the young man over to a unoccupied cot and sat him down.

As Selig sat on the cot with his head between his legs, Grabowski tried to encourage him. "Buck up, kid! One more good meal and you'll be able to work with the best of them." He turned from Selig and stalked through the tent. He glared first at the River

Rats and then at the Gold Dust Twins, while tapping the palm of his right hand with a riding crop. His jodhpurs and puttees made him look like a relic from the Indian campaigns. "You fellas have been sent to the CCC by the courts," he said.

"This a jail?" asked O'Donnel.

"Not on your tintype," offered Dougherty. "Except for the River Rats and the Gold Dust Twins, everybody else joined the C's willingly."

"I believe that anyone can redeem himself, especially if he works hard," announced Grabowski as he put his arm around O'Donnel. "I can even salvage you. I've watched you work, O'Donnel. You're a leader, and I can help you."

"What do I have to do?"

"Watch the Gold Dust Twins. If you do that, I'll be able to run the camp with a lot less trouble." Turning his attention to Mousy, Grabowski asked, "How tall are you?"

"Five-foot, five, Sir."

"Sergeant," said Grabowski.

"Sir?"

"Measure him."

Dougherty took out his tape measure and held it against Mousy who stood on his tip toes. Then Dougherty stuck his hand on top of Mousy's head and firmly pushed down. After completing the measurement, Dougherty exclaimed proudly, "Only an inch above five feet, Sir."

"What's the minimum height requirement for the C's, Sergeant?"

"Five-feet, six inches, Sir."

Grabowski scrutinized Mousy intently.

Mousy remained silent, barely breathing.

Finally, Grabowski broke the tension. "Sergeant, I believe you've made a mistake. I'd judge this fine lad to be five-foot, six inches tall." When Dougherty nodded in agreement, Grabowski continued. "Sergeant, see that this kid drinks a gallon of milk a day."

"Yes, Sir. But may I ask why, Sir?"

"Milk causes a person to grow." Grabowski softly patted Mousy's shoulder with the riding crop. "This boy's my Dog Robber."

"What's that?" asked a bewildered Mousy.

"You'll be my Boy Friday. You'll live in the administrative tent."

"But Sir, do I got to leave my friends?"

"Hell's Bells, son," shouted Dougherty. "You're moving less than two hundred feet away."

Grabowski pivoted quickly as he saw a large piece of mud beside Wynn's bed. "What's this? Another screw-up?" Grabowski grabbed Wynn's cot and heaved it against the tent wall. Then he stood on Wynn's bedclothes while berating the young man. "I'll drive your slacker-ass back to the bread lines in no time." When Wynn did not respond, Grabowski challenged him. "You want to hit me, don't you, boy? I can see it in your eyes!" Grabowski moved back two steps and put his right index finger to his jaw. "Go ahead, you little sonnavabitching crook. Give me your best shot." When the tirade failed to provoke Wynn, Grabowski kicked Wynn's sheets against the tent wall. "Goddamned little coward!" Then Grabowski dropped to his hands and knees and stuffed the bedclothes between the tent wall and the tent platform. When Grabowski got up, he was gasping, completely out of breath. After he had caught his breath, he wheezed, "Sergeant Dougherty. Assign every shitty detail to the Gold Dust Twins." Then he charged out of the tent with Dougherty and Mousy closely behind.

When things had quieted down, O'Donnel walked across the tent and threw his gear onto Wynn's overturned bed. "That was a helluva show, Odum. You and your buddy's in deep shit."

In one fluid motion, Wynn drop-kicked O'Donnel's duffle bag across the tent. "Get another bed, asshole!"

"Do I have to lick you, too?"

"Goddamned sure of yourself, aren't you?"

"O'Donnel!" said Ontek, "I got first dibs on you, don't you remember?"

Selig, who had momentarily stopped coughing, pointed to three vacant cots toward the rear of the tent. "C'mon, O'Donnel, over here. There's plenty of room."

When Wynn began to pick up his clothes, Ontek asked, "You all right?"

"Grabowski's not going to chase me out of here."

"No way!" agreed Ontek. Pointing to the River Rats, he said, "Besides, I'd miss the company of those hoity-toity neighbors."

Wynn picked up his cot and began to make his bed. When he spread his blanket over the bed, he saw more mud spots. "Grabowski has the manners of a goat."

"Maybe we can use our sheep boots on him."

Annoyed, Wynn replied, "So what?"

"You see, a lonely sheepherder puts the sheep's hind feet in the boots and they...Ah...You know!"

Wynn began to smile. "If Grabowski has his way, that's exactly what he's going to do to us."

"Only if we let him," said Ontek as he walked over to the stove and put more wood into it.

"That feels better," said Wynn who turned his backside to the stove and bent over, touching the palms of his hands onto the tent floor. "This position helps get the kinks out of my back."

When Wynn straightened up, Ontek began to laugh.

"What's so funny?"

"Whenever Grabowski's around, it's a good idea that you never bend over like that."

"You're an odd one," replied Wynn. "We're up to our chins in shit, and it don't worry you at all."

"Life's a big joke," Ontek explained. "Ain't none of us going to get out alive."

Uncomfortable with that thought, Wynn simply changed the subject. "The River Rats remind me of the Dagos down in the Valley."

"What do you mean?" asked Ontek.

"Sometimes when I'd come into a room, I'd hear them talking up a storm in English. But bingo! When they saw me, they'd switch to their lingo quicker than a hot knife cutting through butter."

"But the River Rats speak English," said Ontek.

"Yeah, they're whispering like they're hiding something."

"Looks like we can't trust nobody," said Ontek.

When the bugler signaled the end of the day, an uneasy truce had settled over Tent Number Eight. Each group had accepted its tent space, and whatever else needed to be finished could wait until another day. Minutes after the bugler's last note had faded away, snores replaced the angry threats.

O'Donnel was a wheezer who sounded like an old Ford on a cold morning. Ontek's snores, however, were straight-forward blasts and bleeps, more like factory sounds.

While their heavy snoring continued, Wynn stared into the darkness, unable to sleep. Finally, Wynn nudged Ontek and whispered, "Listen to you. Competing with O'Donnel even while you're sleeping."

CHAPTER SEVEN

At roll call, Ontek and Wynn hid deep into the fourth row, out of sight from Dougherty. Since Ontek still had not become accustomed to standing in ankle-deep mud, his attention span began to waver after the first five minutes. "How much longer do you think he's going to talk?"

"Probably all day," murmured Wynn.

"Who's that new kid in the first row?" whispered Ontek. "The one with the suitcase."

Softly, Wynn answered, "Iorio's his name. Came in during the middle of the night"

As Dougherty walked down the line, he pointed to the young man and said, "Men. I'd like you to meet our newest addition to Camp One." Then he stuck his nose in the young man's face and asked, "What's your name, soldier?"

The muscular, twenty-one year old answered, "Michael Angelo Ioiro."

"You weren't here last night. Who brought you here?"

Iorio looked around and pointed to Wynn. "That guy picked me up at Byromtown around midnight. Then I bunked with the cooks in their tent."

Dougherty shouted, "Odum! Front and center!" As Wynn picked his way through the formation, Dougherty asked, "And who gave you permission to leave the camp?"

Calmly, Wynn answered, "The Mess Sergeant cleared it with Grabowski late last evening."

"Oh," said Dougherty. Then he glared at Iorio. "What to you have in that suitcase? The family jewels?" When Iorio didn't respond, Dougherty shouted, "Well, open it up so me and Odum can take a look."

The young man knelt on the ground and carefully opened the suitcase. "These are my stone cutting tools," he said.

Wynn saw that the suitcase's interior was lined in a faded green velvet, reminiscent of the inside of a family silver chest that his father had once owned. But instead of silverwear, points and wedges fit neatly into the small flaps.

When Dougherty reached down and pulled out a four inch wedge, Iorio winced. "Careful," he warned, "that'll cut paper."

Returning the wedge to its proper place, Dougherty told the formation, "If all your foot lockers was this neat, I'd have to throw away my gig-pencil." As he began to move down the line again, Dougherty peered at the men in the front row, making sure each man wore the proper uniform and had washed and shaved. Then he wheeled around and returned to Iorio. "Kid, you have a lot of moxie. You say your name is..."

"Iorio, Sergeant. Michael Angelo Iorio."

"Hmm...Michael Angelo...Naw, we don't need any house painters up here."

"I cut stone, Sergeant."

"You got a nickname?"

"No, Sergeant I never had one."

"Well, that won't do." Dougherty pointed to the formation and said, " A lot of guys here have monikers like Ace, Cabbage, or Boots."

"Don't forget Peaches and the Dutchman," somebody shouted.

As Iorio began to fidget uneasily, he said, "My folks came from Italy."

"Can we call you Dago Red?" asked Dougherty.

When he saw Iorio's face begin to flush, Wynn reached out and touched the young man on his shoulder.

"No offense intended," said Dougherty. As a few giggles subsided, he slowly repeated Iorio's name aloud and then spelled it. After doing this two more times, Dougherty shouted, "By Jingo! I've got it! You're 10-R-10."

"10-R-10?" Wynn asked.

"Sure, it's that simple. His name spells out 10-R-10." Stepping

back, Dougherty announced, Boys, I'd like you to meet 10-R-10."
Waving Wynn back into the formation, Dougherty added, "And it
looks like we've got a helluva find because 10-R-10 is a stone cutter."

When Wynn walked back to the rear line, Ontek moaned, "I'm
hungry!"

"And I'm really ticked off! Dougherty made that kid feel like
two cents."

O'Donnel, who stood in front of Ontek, said, "At least, we
agree on something."

Immediately, Wynn complained, "Shut up! You're going to get
us hosed."

O'Donnel remained expressionless. "Screw you," he muttered.

Shielding O'Donnel from Dougherty was Clinton Hasselrig.
Mentally four degrees off plumb, Hasselrig constantly fingered
himself in his crotch. Then he poked his buddy, Izzy Rykowski, who
giggled.

Wynn nudged Ontek. "That kid's riding for a fall."

Hasselrig kept clearing his throat, stopping just short of
coughing out loud. Unfortunately, it always coincided with a major
point of Dougherty's announcement.

A purple flush spread rapidly above Dougherty's shirt to his
hair line. He stopped and wheeled to his left, where he eyeballed
Hasselrig. "Yardbird, you're a stupid-assed blivit."

Hasselrig, his eyes bulging, asked meekly, "What's that, Sir?"

"A blivit's ten pounds of shit rolled into a two pound
package."

A few giggles rippled through the first row, followed by some
large laughs. Then someone from the rear said, "Yowser, yowser!"

Ontek bit his lips, trying to contain his laughter.

Wynn whispered, "For God's sake, don't laugh,"

The warning was too late. Ontek's laughter became louder.
Soon, it spread through the formation.

Dougherty's glare killed the merriment.

"Sheee...it," muttered Wynn aloud. "Now we're in ankle-deep
blivits."

First, Dougherty ordered Hasselrig, "Front and center!"

The rookie obeyed quickly.

Dougherty stuck his nose into Hasselrig's face. "From now on, Mr. Blivit, you're in charge of the shit-cans in the latrine." After breathing heavily into Hasselrig's face, Dougherty bellowed, "All right, Mr. Blivit...Back in formation."

Dougherty then singled out Ontek. "You think Mr. Blivit's funny?"

"No, Sergeant."

"Why did you laugh, then?"

"No excuse, Sergeant."

"You're Mr. Blivit's assistant for the next week. And I'll personally check the cans to see they've been cleaned in the proper military manner."

"Yes, Sergeant."

"Civilians! Goddamned civilians!" complained Dougherty. Then he turned his wrath on the rest of the men. "Wise asses! Give me thirty pushups or no breakfast!"

The men hit the ground as requested. While Wynn breezed through them easily, he watched O'Donnel trying to cheat. "Hey, River Rat! Afraid to get your clothes dirty?"

This caught Dougherty's attention. He allowed O'Donnel to complete his pushups before placing his foot squarely on O'Donnel's behind. Then he applied enough pressure so that O'Donnel collapsed facedown in the mud. "Now do twenty-five more, while Odum counts."

Wynn led the way with the official count. The first ten pushups went easily, while O'Donnel's tempo slowed considerably for the next ten. The last five were painful and slow. When he stiffly got up, the cheers drowned out O'Donnel's obscenities.

"You got a little over an hour to chow down," Dougherty yelled. "Report back here for work at 0730."

"What's on tap, today?" asked Cartwright.

"Eight hours of damn hard work, that's what!" Then Dougherty shouted, "Everyone but Odum is dismissed."

"Now what?" muttered Wynn.

"Got your brother this morning, didn't I?" chortled Dougherty.

"He'll do okay."

41

"Just following my CO's orders."

"Yeah, I'm sure."

"I've got a choice job for you."

"What kind of job?"

Dougherty laughed aloud. "One for a strong back and a weak mind."

"Just right for me."

"Got this moving job at Kane."

"Where's that?"

"Twenty-five miles north of here."

"How am I going to get there?"

"Red Dawson will drive the truck."

"Who or what are we going to move?"

"Dr. Millet, the camp doctor, that's who! You're going to bring his medical stuff here." Then he snapped, "Go to the head of the chow line and eat. Dawson's waiting for you."

CHAPTER EIGHT

When Wynn came from the mess tent, Red laid on the horn. "C'mon, get your rear in gear." As the young man climbed into the truck, Red grabbed Wynn's hand and shook it. "We've already met, remember?"

"And I'm still waiting to grow into my shoes."

"The system ain't quite perfect, yet. But we're working on it." Red slowly eased the truck out of the compound, avoiding men who were returning from breakfast. Once clear, he floored the accelerator, double clutched the vehicle into second, and roared across the bridge and up the hill toward the main highway. "We're going to stop at the fire tower," he shouted over the engine's roar.

"What about Kane?"

"Got to get a faulty telephone first."

"You're the driver."

Red drove faster when he pulled out onto the highway, heading south toward Marienville. The state had paved the road as part of Governor Pinchot's campaign pledge to get the farmers out of the mud, and Red took full advantage of the promise. As he sped down the road, Red began humming "Old Man River." Then he launched into a vocal, "Pennies from Heaven." Halfway through a shaky "Blue Skies," he jammed on the brakes, throwing the truck into a severe skid. When it bounced to a stop, he rolled down the window disgustedly. "Cripes," he complained. "I did it again."

"Did what?"

"I missed the tower by a hundred yards." Red promptly jammed the truck into reverse, and this time, the truck roared backwards like a snake without a compass. When Red hit the brakes again, the truck stopped less than three feet from the tower's entrance.

Getting out of the truck, he pointed to the top of the tower. "We're going up there."

Wynn laughed aloud. "You don't say?"

"Do you know of any other way?" snapped Red.

"How about an airplane?"

"Not on my budget."

The tower had seven levels, each ten feet high. On every level, a flight of steps crisscrossed diagonally from one level back to another. Gradually tapered from the bottom to the top, the tower had a ten foot shack perched on its top.

"You sure <u>that</u> isn't going to fall off?"

"Never lost one yet," shouted Red as he raced up the first six levels. When Red looked back, he noticed Wynn's lagging behind. "Scared of heights?"

"Not really," said Wynn who soon joined Red.

"You're not even out of breath."

"Should I be?"

Red inhaled deeply. "Smell the air. Isn't it sweet?"

"Just like spring," said Wynn. After they had rested, he asked, "How are we going to get into the shack?"

"See that little trap door on the bottom," explained Red, "it opens right out into the steps. And we'll crawl right into it." When they reached the top level, he lowered the trap door and went in. Then he reached out and pulled Wynn into the shack.

Located in the middle of the shack was a large wooden circle, two feet in diameter, sitting on a post forty inches off the floor. The outside of the circle had degree markings from zero to three hundred and sixty. On its face was a forest map of the tower's viewing radius. An alidade, a sighting instrument for fire location, sat on a pivot post in the center of the circle.

Pointing to the circle, Wynn asked, "What's that?"

"The heart of fire fighting network. With this equipment, the tower operator locates the fires."

"This the only tower around?"

"We've got eight scattered throughout the forest."

Wynn opened a window, allowing a breeze to sweep through. While staring out over the Allegheny Plateau, he savored the fresh smell of a new season. "I can see forever!" he exclaimed.

"Thirty miles would be more accurate," said Red.

Wynn cupped his hand over his eyes and stared intently toward the horizon. "It's hard to tell where the land ends and exactly where the sky begins."

"The height's too much?"

"Naw. But if you don't laugh, I'll tell you how I really feel." When Red smiled, Wynn continued. "It's like I'm a giant in one of those old Greek stories." Wynn waved his arm in a sweeping gesture. "And all of this is mine," he proclaimed.

Red pushed a three-legged stool over toward Wynn. "Sit down, young man."

"What's up?"

"I heard about your run-in with Grabowski."

"It's nothing."

"The hell it isn't. Your ass is dead meat if you screw up." Red pulled up the remaining stool and looked out the window. "Up here a fella can see just how big the Allegheny is. Sort of makes a person seem insignificant. Thousands and thousands of acres of land stretching out as far as the eye can see." The wind began to blow harder, causing the guy wires on the tower to make a high-pitched wail. He reached over and closed the window, shutting out most of the sound. "There's something about this place that always makes me feel better." Red pulled the stool closer to Wynn "You're a natural leader," Red said, "and I want you on my Snap Fire Crew."

"What's that?"

"Our first line of defense against forest fires." Red went to the window and looked out. "If you look in any direction, you'll see burned-out land." He pointed toward the east. "Over there, the Bear Creek Fire in 1926 burned over forty thousand acres in less than six days."

"Why so many fires?"

"For the past fifty years, the logging and the sawmill companies took from this land and left nothing but stumps and tree tops. In some places, the underbrush is almost twenty feet high. And it is all ready to burn." Red looked out toward Marienville. "We never had the men to fight those fires like Bear Creek. But with the coming of the C's, we've got the manpower to stop the fires dead in their tracks." He twirled around quickly and sat down again. "And that's where you come in. I'll train you and the crew. And we'll keep the little fires from growing into the big ones." He tapped Wynn's knee. "You interested?"

"What about Ontek?"

"He's in, too. But here's the rub! Both you fellas have to lay low. Stay out of Grabowski's hair. Within a week, I'll have the crew organized."

"But don't Grabowski control everything?"

"The army runs the camp. The Forest Service runs <u>every</u> work project." He stood up and put his hand on Wynn's shoulder. "And I have the pick of the litter!" Red reached down and opened the trap door. "Let's head for Kane."

"Wait, Red. Don't forget the telephone."

"The telephone was an excuse for you to see <u>my</u> world from eighty feet."

When they reached the ground, Red handed Wynn the keys to the truck. "You drive?" he asked.

"Sure."

"Then, Jeeves, on to Kane!"

CHAPTER NINE

The highway to Kane cut north through the heart of the Allegheny National Forest. Giant hemlock trees, a hundred feet high, formed a dense canopy, causing Wynn to turn on the headlights. As the lights illuminated the thickets along the sides of the road, he saw small beech trees bravely rising from the forest floor.

"How can they grow?" Wynn asked. "There's hardly no sunlight."

"They're shade-tolerant trees," answered Red, "and require very little light to grow."

A few clearings occasionally broke through the forest barrier. In each one there was a cluster of houses, standing as if in defiance to the encroaching forest. The houses looked sad and neglected, little more than shacks. Some houses had porches that looked as if they were ready to collapse momentarily. Most buildings were sided with tar paper, while others had ugly looking furring strips that covered the cracks between the weather-bleached boards.

The children, who stood in their weed-infested yards, remained expressionless as the truck passed by. When Wynn waved at them, not one child acknowledged his friendly gesture.

Chagrined, Wynn said, "The kids look as pitiful as the houses they live in." Continuing northward, Wynn saw road signs pointing down narrow dirt roads that seemed to disappear into the forest. "You mean somebody lives back in those woods?" he asked.

"You'd be surprised at the number of hamlets scattered throughout the forest," replied Red.

"But who'd want to live in Pig's Ear?"

Smiling, Red asked, "Who'd want to live in Turtle Creek?"

"I get your point," said Wynn.

When they had passed a sign pointing toward Corduroy, Wynn asked, "Where do those people work?"

"An awful lot of them don't work anymore," answered Red. "The glass plants and the sawmills are all down." Then he added, "The gas leases still employ a few men."

When they entered another stand of hemlocks, Wynn said, "It's almost like driving into a tunnel." Flipping the lights on high, he said, "The forest looks different here than it did up in the tower."

"Forty years ago, this area was a frontier, like Dodge City."

"You're joking?"

"The logging and sawmill business attracted strong folks." Red paused as a deer ran across the road. "Only thing was that nobody wrote dime-store novels about what happened here."

Wynn smiled slightly, for he was not quite sure if Red were telling the truth. "You're not trying to kid a kidder, are you?" When the sunlight began to filter through the trees, Wynn turned off the truck lights. "This would be a helluva place to hide," he speculated.

"A lot of people did just that. Take the Sicilians for instance. When they came to the United States, they had their passage paid for by the Black Hand."

"We had those guys in the Valley, too."

"Once the Wops landed in New York, it didn't take them long to figure out that the organization had them over a barrel." Red pointed at a skunk that crossed in front of them. "The Hand charged those suckers two hundred percent interest for their passage."

"Good God! Even Murray didn't charge that kind of interest."

Red continued with his story. "Some skipped out. Headed west, often finding work around here in the wood camps. Figuring nobody would ever find them. But the Hand sent out goons to hunt them down. Then kill them. Usually by slitting their throats."

"I thought that only happened in the Valley."

"When I was a kid, I brought supplies to a wood camp. I had some time to kill, so I wandered off to pick blackberries. I jumped right into the bushes and tripped, smack-dab, over a naked, headless body."

"What did you do?"

"Puked up my breakfast, right off!"

48

"Who was it?"

"The sheriff looked at the remains and grunted, 'He ain't no American.' Back then, if a Wop killed another Wop, the law looked the other way." Red paused to warn Wynn. "Better slow down. Road gets pretty treacherous."

Wynn shifted to low gear as he guided the truck down a eight per cent grade containing a nasty S turn. When he got to the bottom, he asked, "A drunken snake lay out this road?"

"Probably some scared Wop running from his killer," answered Red.

"And I thought this was a nice place to live. With all the trees and such."

"Life has always been unforgiving."

"Sounds like a war," said Wynn."

"It is."

When Wynn finally saw a row of houses on each side of the road, he asked, "Are we here?"

"That's the outskirts of Kane, the Icebox of Pennsylvania." As they began to climb a small hill, Red pointed ahead. "Turn right at the second street."

Wynn turned onto Hemlock Avenue, a broad street lined with attractive frame houses, each two or three stories high. Tall maple trees rose above the homes, giving them a look of elegance. As Wynn drove down the street, he remarked, "Everything's so clean."

"No steel mills around here."

"What house are we looking for?"

"A three story brown house with a blue Packard parked in front of it."

Wynn pointed up the street and said, "There it is." When Wynn parked the truck, he saw an older man in an army uniform, standing on the front steps. "That must be the doctor," said Wynn, as he and Red got out of the truck.

CHAPTER TEN

Doctor Frank Millet quickly motioned for Red and Wynn to join him. Introducing himself, he said, "Gentlemen, I'm so happy that you're here. Have you eaten?"

Wynn said, "Not since breakfast, Sir."

"Come into my study. I'll scratch up something." He took them into a comfortable looking room and gestured for them to sit down. "I'll be right back," he said as he left the room.

Wynn sat in an easy chair that nearly swallowed him. "Phwey, this is first-class!" He looked around the elegantly appointed room. "Have you ever seen so many books?"

"Not since I visited the Carnegie Library in Pittsburgh," answered Red.

Wynn walked over to the fireplace. Hanging above the mantle were the doctor's medical diploma and his honorable discharge from the United States Army. After reading them, Wynn whispered, "He's a graduate of Harvard."

"And one helluva doctor, so I've heard."

Four books, each bound in a handsome red cover, sat on top of the mantle. Wynn ran his fingers over each cover as if he were caressing a fine piece of leather. Then he read the titles aloud: "MAINSTREET. MY ANTONIA. SPOON RIVER ANTHOLOGY. LADY CHATTERLY'S LOVER. Phewy, those are high-powered books!"

"Ever read any of them?"

"Two of them," answered Wynn. "MAINSTREET's about a guy who hated the small town he lived in. And the town hated him right back!" Then he added, "Something like me and Turtle Creek." He softly touched the cover of SPOON RIVER. "I wish I could meet a woman like Lucinda Matlock. She'd set anything straight."

"Who was she?" asked Red. "Somebody from the Valley?"

Wynn's face flushed a bit when he realized he was showing a very private feeling. "Naw," he said. "She lived a hundred years ago out in Illinois. And she was some kind of tough lady!"

"Lucinda Matlock is my kind of woman, too," said Frank as he stood at the doorway holding a tray of sandwiches. Two inches shorter than Wynn, Frank had deep lines etched into his face that made him look older than his fifty-five years. But his eyes, sharp and keen, belied his age.

Wynn immediately retreated from the mantle and sat down. "I've always liked to read."

As Frank handed each man a thick ham sandwich, he said to Wynn, "Seems as if I've discovered a kindred spirit." Then he added, "I'm sorry I don't have any milk, but my housekeeper has cleaned out my icebox."

"You going to close down the house?" asked Red.

"No. My housekeeper will stay here, and I'll come back now and then."

Pointing at the two walls lined with books, Wynn asked, "We're going to take all those books?"

"Only those boxes I have in the gym."

"A gym? Can we see it?"

"Certainly."

Wynn followed Red and Frank down the narrow hallway that led to a large airy room. When he saw the equipment, Wynn stopped and stared in awe. A speed punching bag hung in one corner. In the middle of the room, a heavy punching bag hung from the ceiling. He looked at Frank and then at the big bag. "Can I?"

"Sure, go ahead," said Frank.

Wynn danced over and punched the bag with a rapid one-two combination. Then he repeated it again. As the bag slowly stopped bouncing, Wynn said, "That really feels good."

Frank picked up a jumping rope and placed it in a small basket next to a rack that held small barbells. "You have good coordination, Wynn."

"Did you ever box?" asked Wynn.

51

"In college...A long time ago."

"Wynn's a boxer, too," said Red.

"How'd you know?" asked Wynn.

"I read your personnel file."

"How good are you?" asked Frank.

Wynn looked down at his shoes. "I quit boxing."

"Boxing is a fine character builder," said Frank.

Red looked at the packed boxes that lined the room. "I hate to break up this up, but we still have a job to do."

Frank nodded in agreement.

When they had finished loading the truck, Wynn asked, "Doc, where's your medical instruments?"

Frank patted his black bag. "Everything I need is in here."

"Wynn, you'll have to go back to camp with the Doc," shouted Red as he started the truck's engine.

"Why?"

"I've have to scout a site for a new camp down on the Kinzua Creek."

"Good," said Frank. "I'll have someone to talk with." He motioned for Wynn to get into the car. "I want to go back into the house and make sure that everything's all right."

Wynn climbed into the passenger's seat and stretched his legs as far as they would go before looking into the rear of the car. In addition to the huge rear seat that easily could hold four people, a jump seat extended from the rear of driver's seat. Then he leaned back in his plush seat as far as he could and closed his eyes. When Frank got into the car, Wynn awakened quickly.

"Sorry I startled you," said Frank who immediately started the engine. "Purrs like a kitten, doesn't she?" Then he shifted the car into low gear and edged out onto Hemlock Street. As Frank turned south, he said, "It's going to be an hour's trip. So let's talk. It's obvious you like to read. Have you attended college?"

"Yeah, I read a lot, and no, I never went to college."

"Are you uncomfortable, Wynn?"

"Naw. The car's great."

"I mean about our talking?"

Wynn listened to the engine hum steadily. Then he said, "I got

52

kicked out of school two months before graduation."

"For what reason?"

"I decked a teacher." Wynn looked at Frank, who remained silent. "It's something I'm not proud of," Wynn said.

"Because you hurt the teacher?"

"No. It's because I lost my chance to graduate."

"What caused the blow-up?"

"Mr. Zukowski claimed my fights were fixed."

"Was he right?"

"Yeah." But Wynn quickly added, "I didn't know about it until my last one."

"Well, it's done and over with, Wynn. And you have to move on. That's what's so great about the CCC. It's an opportunity for both of us."

"But you're a doctor."

"Yes, I am. But something nags at me. That tells me there's more to life than..."

Wynn interrupted. "No offense, Doc, but you sound like one of those New Dealers."

Then Frank started to laugh. "Perhaps I am, Wynn. But just think of it! We're part of Roosevelt's grand experiment."

"I saw Roosevelt, once."

"You did?"

"Last October, when he was running against Hoover. He came to Pittsburgh. Since I had nothing better to do, I went downtown to check him out. And I couldn't believe what I saw!"

"What was that?"

"A big limo stopped right in front of me on Grant Street. Two guys jumped out, lifted this man out of the car, and stood him up. I asked the fella next to me, 'Where's FDR?' And the guy answered, 'You ninny, that's him.' Then it hit me! Roosevelt was a cripple!"

"Roosevelt's legs are paralyzed. He had infantile paralysis."

"But he's not a cripple in the newsreels!"

"That's because the reporters won't invade his privacy."

"But that ain't right," protested Wynn. "I never saw a picture of him in a wheelchair. And the newspaper cartoons always show him as a football player leading Congress down the field or as a ship's captain standing on the helm shouting, 'Full steam ahead.'"

"Almost everyone knows of FDR's illness and that he's confined to a wheelchair," explained Frank. "The reporters grant him his privacy even though he carries ten pounds of braces on his legs. They don't want to show him as an invalid." Then Frank added, "And I don't really want to think of him as an invalid. To me Roosevelt's an inspiration. Because of him, I joined the CCC."

When Frank turned onto the Durhing Road, Wynn said, "Now comes the fun, Doc. Potholes and ruts until we get there." As Frank skillfully avoided the larger holes, Wynn noted the strength in Frank's upper arms. "You're pretty strong to tool this big car through roads like this."

"Sometimes, it's like driving a tank." Upon reaching the top of a hill overlooking the camp, Frank parked the car, got out, and took a careful look at his new practice. He took off his hat and hurled as if he were a discus thrower.

Wynn watched it clear the trees and then fall into the stream below. "What was that for?"

"This marks a whole new beginning for me." Then Frank climbed into his car, and he and Wynn headed for the camp.

As they pulled into camp, Wynn said, "The hospital tent's over by the stream."

"That's going to be a problem with mosquitoes."

"Haven't noticed any, yet."

Frank parked the Packard on a tiny island of solid land. Getting out of the car, he said, "Wynn, please come with me. I must report to the Company Commander."

When they approached the tent, Sergeant Dougherty came charging out as if his posterior were in flames. Recognizing the two silver bars on Frank's shoulders, Dougherty threw a snappy salute.

Frank returned the salute. "I'm the camp doctor and I would like to meet the Commanding Officer."

Dougherty opened the tent flaps, making sure that Frank entered first. "Lieutenant Grabowski's inspecting the men's progress. I'll go get him." Dougherty saluted again and rushed from the tent.

Facing the tent's entrance were a chair and a desk. The pencils and pens were in separate glass containers beside an empty "In and

Out" box. A spotless green desk pad helped outline the desk.

With precise military decorum, Grabowski strode into the tent, while Dougherty followed at a proper military distance. Grabowski acknowledged Frank with a wave and sat down behind the desk. Then he screamed at Wynn. "Odum, what in hell are you doing here?"

Frank said, "He's with me."

"Captain, if he belongs to you, please have him leave."

"As you wish, Lieutenant." Frank turned to Wynn. "Please wait outside."

As Wynn left, Grabowski asked, "Sergeant Dougherty, don't you have any work to do?"

"Yes, Sir. Indeed I do, Sir," said Dougherty, who saluted Grabowski and left.

Reaching into a desk drawer, Grabowski pulled out Frank's files. "I see that you were in the Big One, too. Well, I made it as far as Belgium before I fell into a trench and broke my leg." Tapping his left thigh above the knee, he said, "Infection set in, and before long, a damn Frog doctor wanted to take my leg, but I told him the only part of me I was going to leave in his God forsaken country was some of my seed!" He slapped his good leg and continued. "I fought that quack as much as anybody fought those miserable Huns!" He pointed to his left leg. "It tells me when the weather is going to change, but I'm still a whole man! The only thing that galls me is that I never saw any real action." He patted his stomach and said, "That always gives me a sunken feeling right here, like I was robbed of something." He rose from his chair and smoothed the wrinkles in his tunic. "I've been here for only a few days, and the men already have a poem about me. Do you want to hear it?" He did not wait for Frank to respond.

> Camp One's got a CO,
> Grabowski's his name.
> And he likes the baseball game!
> You play ball with me,
> Says he!
> And I'll play ball with you.
> Says who?
> Trouble is, say the men

We're always in the field.
'Cause he has all the balls!

"They think I haven't heard this. They're wrong. I like it! It shows I've made a solid impression. Maybe that man in the White House says my boys are civilians, but he's in Washington, and I'm here! And by damned, I'm going to run this camp just like the army."

Before Frank could comment, Sergeant Dougherty raised into the tent. "Sir! Sir!"

"Didn't I tell you to knock before entering?"

Dougherty looked at the tent flaps and then at Grabowski.

"What is it?"

"It's Selig, Sir. He's coughing real bad and spitting up blood."

"Doc, would you check the kid out?" asked Grabowski.

"Wynn, come in here," Frank shouted. "I want you to go with Sergeant Dougherty and bring Selig over to the hospital tent. I'll be waiting for you there."

CHAPTER ELEVEN

Wynn and Mark Wasko splashed into the hospital tent carrying Selig on a litter. Sergeant Dougherty, who had drafted Wasko for the detail, followed.

Pointing to the examination table, Frank ordered, "Put him up there."

Exhausted by his effort, Wasko began coughing so violently that he could not lift Selig.

Frank listened to Wasko's coughing and winced. "Go pick a bed! You're next!"

"Sir," said Dougherty. "I'm getting sick."

"My God, do you have pneumonia, too?"

"I can't stand to be around sick people. Can I leave, Sir?"

"Dismissed, Sergeant."

Without waiting for Frank to return his salute, Dougherty bolted from the tent.

Frank turned to Wynn and asked, "Son, can you help me?"

"I've never even been inside a hospital."

"I need somebody now."

"What can I do?"

Frank spit out orders similar to a machine gun's firing short bursts. "Get Wasko into bed. Make sure his feet are dry. Put a blanket over him. Then get back here."

Frank had just finished listening to Selig's chest when Wynn returned. "How's Wasko?" Frank asked.

"In bed, Sir."

Frank continued his examination while Wynn watched intently. "Dyspnea is marked."

"What's that?" asked Wynn.

"Breathing is difficult." When Frank took the thermometer from Selig's mouth, he looked at it and said, "It's pneumonia."

"My old man called it the 'old person's friend,' because the patient always died."

"Don't worry. There are several ways to treat this illness." Then Frank asked, "Will you be my orderly?"

"Only until you get a replacement."

"Why?"

"Red Dawson's offered me a spot on his fire fighting crew."

"Will you stay until I can find your replacement?"

"Yes, Sir."

"Good. We'll leave Selig here, and I'll examine Wasko at his bed."

"None of us slept last night because Selig was coughing so bad," Wynn said.

Frank listened to Wasko's chest. "There's fluid present." Then he checked Wasko's sputum. "It's like prune juice. Not a good sign." After taking the young man's temperature, Frank said, "Now, we've got two cases."

"Can I do anything else?" asked Wynn.

"Please go over to the mess tent and ask Cookie to make me some beef tea. It will help the patients."

Upon returning, Wynn heard a strange hollow tapping sound. "What the hell's that?" he muttered when he saw Frank vigorously striking Selig's upper body.

When Frank saw Wynn watching, he said, "I'm doing a type of massage. The percussion strokes cause a vibration in the chest cavity that loosens congestion And since I have elevated his stomach and chest, he should be able to cough the mucous out." As he continued working on Selig, Frank said, "Do you want to try it?"

"Ah, Er...Sure."

When Wynn began, Frank cautioned, "You must cup two to three blows per second. These are strong but not violent blows." He repositioned Wynn's hands and guided Wynn's blows by tracing the outline of Selig's lungs with an index finger. Then Frank said, "Two more times around each lung should do the trick."

When they had finished, Mess Sergeant Roy Garlicki barged

into the hospital tent, carrying two thermos bottles. "This one has beef tea while the other one has some strong, black coffee." Then he gave a large hoot of laughter. "If you need more, just give a holler."

Wynn looked the beef tea and made a face. "It looks awful."

"It's good for someone who can't take solid food," said Frank. While they sipped their coffee, Frank explained his philosophy. "To heal my patients, I use medicine and drugs, and sometimes, the knife. These are the accepted techniques. But I've discovered that massage heals, too." He stood up and stretched his arms high over his head before sitting down again. "The human body is a remarkable piece of work, Wynn. At times, I think healing is nothing more than tender loving care." Frank walked over to Selig and gently lifted him into a near sitting position. Putting a cup of tea to Selig's lips, Frank said, "Sip it slowly."

Wasko sat up when Wynn offered him soup. Without saying a word, Wasko took the cup and drank it quickly.

Then Frank said, "Sponge down Selig's chest and arms. Allow Wasko to wash himself. I'm going to make mustard plasters."

Fifteen minutes later, Frank returned pushing a cart that contained two towels covered by a golden gray colored paste. Carefully, he folded a towel over Wasko's chest. Then Frank applied the other to Selig. "A mustard plaster," explained Frank, "gives off an oil that causes an irritation on the chest."

"Doesn't it hurt?"

"The oil counteracts the pain and inflammation in the lungs." He picked up a corner of the towel and checked Selig's skin. "The trick is," he continued, "not to let it get too hot, because it can burn."

"How do you know when to take it off?"

Frank checked Wasko's plaster. "Easy enough. The patient's skin turns a bright red." After a few minutes, he examined Selig's chest again. "There. It's done." Glancing at Wynn, Frank asked, "What color is Wasko's skin?"

"Very red."

"Take off the plaster and wash his chest with hot water."

When Wynn had completed his task, George Higgleston pushed open the tent flaps. "Doc, I'm so damn sick!" he said before collapsing onto the floor.

Wynn picked Higgleston up and carried him to a bed. As he took off the young man's shoes and socks, Wynn said, "This kid can't weigh more than a hundred pounds."

"I suspect we've got some malnutrition cases, too." Before beginning Higgleston's examination, Frank said, "Check Wasko and Selig. Then take a break. You've earned one."

Wynn found Selig lying on his back. Lifting him into a sitting position, Wynn replaced the pillows under Selig's back and head. "Keep them like this, because it'll make you more comfortable." Then he checked Wasko, who was snoring loudly.

Satisfied, Wynn went outside and drew a deep breath of air. It cleared his mind, making him feel better. He searched the sky unsuccessfully for a star. "It's so dark," he said aloud. "Like someone turned out the lights all over the world."

"Talking to yourself?" asked Frank.

"In the city there's always a reflection in the sky, usually from the molten slag being dumped on the slag heaps," said Wynn.

"Night is the worst time for severely ill patients," said Frank.

Puzzled, Wynn asked, "Why?"

"They can lose all sense of reality."

"My old man always had trouble sleeping, especially toward the end," admitted Wynn. "He would choke when he slept. He woke me up a lot of times, just gasping for air. Got so that he'd sleep in a chair and then with one eye open. Like he was scared of something."

"Darkness and death are a team, Wynn."

"I never think of death," said Wynn.

"That's why old men send out young men to fight in our wars."

"Were you in the war, Doc?"

"I was a surgeon in a field hospital," answered Frank. "On nights like this, we'd have death visit us frequently. The men were sick and frightened, their young bodies broken by bullets or explosions. Most had never been more than ten miles away from home. Now they were in France, thousands of miles from home, dying alone." As Frank peered out into the darkness, he continued. "After trying to reduce their pain, I spent as much time as I could doing little things for those kids. Holding their hands or wiping the perspiration from their brows or just talking to them. Anything to show them they were not alone. Anything that would restore some dignity to their battered bodies. Anything at all to make it easier for them to let go." He stopped talking and gripped the infirmary's railing that separated him from the darkness of the Allegheny night. When he spoke, he finally spoke to that darkness. "If I learned anything during those awful years, it was that the worst thing that could happen to a person was to die alone."

"My old man died by himself," Wynn said quietly.

"Where were you, Wynn?"

"Knocked out by the men who killed him."

"Sounds as if you tried to help him."

"A lot of help I was," whispered Wynn.

"At least my father died at home in his own bed, cared for by two priests and four nuns." Frank sighed before continuing. "For the longest time we didn't get along. His big dream was for me to practice with him. But I didn't want to live under his shadow. So I did everything under the sun to avoid it. After completing medical school, I literally ran away, spending almost seven years in France before the war started. Then in 1915, a friend wrote me that father had cancer. I began writing to him...With some reluctance, I might add. By the time America entered the war, we had reconciled. I even had assured him that I would maintain his practice after the war."

"But I met you in Kane."

"Father lived in St. Marys, thirty miles east of Kane. I went back in 1919, but I couldn't stay there. Everything there reminded me of him. That's why I eventually established a practice in Kane."

"Doc, are you afraid to die?"

Without pausing, Frank said, "There's a long Christian tradition dating back to the apostle Paul where death is seen as the enemy, that is, someone who brings punishment to man for the sins of Adam and Eve. I just can't accept that. While studying Eastern thought, I learned that those people viewed death as a natural part of the eternal cycle. Life and death...Two opposites, yet integral parts that made up the universal whole. For life to continue there must be death. And from death comes renewal."

"You've not answered my question, Doc."

61

"I'm not afraid to die, Wynn. And I haven't been for over twenty years." Frank put his arm around Wynn's shoulder. Then he said, "To live a good life is the very best preparation for death."

Confused, Wynn said, "But Doc, your job is to heal people. Not let them die."

"As a doctor, I win a lot of small battles. I help many of my patients to recover. That way, I cheat death. At least for a little while." When footsteps on the gravel path interrupted him, Frank asked, "May I help you?"

"Tell Odum he's got a work formation at 0530," snapped Lieutenant Grabowski.

Frank struck a match and looked at his watch. "That's less than four hours from now."

Its flicker illuminated Grabowski's face, giving form to an angry voice. "Between 0530 and 1700, he's mine, Doctor. After that you can have that little bugger."

"Then get me an orderly." When Grabowski failed to answer that request, Frank asked, ""Are you interested in the well-being of the boys I have in the hospital?"

"That's what the army's paying you for, Captain!" said Grabowski who turned and stormed across the darkened compound.

After Grabowski had left, Wynn said, "You've got me until a replacement shows up."

"It means double shifts, Wynn."

"Grabowski's not going to chase me out of the C's."

"Then use one of the hospital beds and get some sleep."

Wynn kicked off his boots and crawled into a bed. His mind was whirling. Wynn could not dismiss what he had heard. He resolved to continue thinking about it, for no adult had ever shared his innermost thoughts with him. He felt good about himself, and he felt a kinship with Frank. When Higgleston began to thrash about, Wynn opened his eyes and watched Frank sit down beside Higgleston. "Can I be of some help, Doc?" asked Wynn.

"Get some sleep. And that's an order!" said Frank.

The last things Wynn remembered before falling asleep were Frank's talking quietly to Higgleston and holding the young man's hand.

CHAPTER TWELVE

At roll call that morning, Wynn and Onteck stood at the rear of the formation. "How you holding up, buddy?" asked Wynn.

"Maybe I'll learn a trade yet."

Wynn sniffed the air. "As least you don't smell of shit."

"Where were you last night?"

"I got drafted as an hospital orderly."

"Remind me not to get sick," kidded Ontek.

Just as Wynn began to tell Ontek about the pneumonia cases, Sergeant Dougherty blew his whistle sharply. They stopped talking as Dougherty began to take roll.

On that chilly morning, Camp One had its full complement, two hundred men. Most were street-wise young men from Pittsburgh, Philadelphia, or Scranton. A handful came from the South, mostly Georgia and Alabama.

After roll call, Dougherty shouted, "We need ten truck drivers." When twenty-six men raised their hands immediately, he smiled broadly. "Report down at the gravel pit right after breakfast. Each man will get a truck."

Chickie Peters, a skinny kid from Scranton, raised his hand. "Begging the Sergeant's pardon, but there ain't no trucks there, only wheelbarrows."

"I know, Rookie, I know. Those are the trucks I'm talking about! Next time, don't be so damned anxious to volunteer!" A smile spread over his face as he made the next announcement. "After chow, everyone's to report to the Medical Tent."

"What for, Sergeant?"

"Maybe, for a short arm inspection," chortled Dougherty. Then he said, "All right, men. Let's get back to business. I need three people for KP." When no one raised his hand, he said, "Looks like I'll have to select some warm bodies myself." His eyes darted up and down the company. Suddenly, he stopped and glared at an anxious recruit.

"He sure likes tormenting people," whispered Wynn.

"I wonder if he had a mother?" offered Ontek.

Wynn shook his head. "Naw, he was hatched on a fence post."

Dougherty singled out Peaches Oskowski and Dutch Osterman. Then he barked, "Odum, lead the detail to the kitchen, pronto!" Sarcastically, Dougherty added, "I send only the best to the kitchen."

When Wynn headed for the kitchen, Dutch was close behind with Peaches bringing up the rear. As Wynn and Dutch carefully walked around the large puddles, Peaches ran through them in effort to keep up. Whenever he caught up, Peaches constantly tugged at Wynn's sleeve and kept asking, "Sir?"

Even though Dutch finally slowed down, Wynn continued ahead.

Peaches trotted past Dutch and finally caught up to Wynn. This time he pulled at Wynn's sleeve more forcefully. "Sir?" Peaches cried.

Wynn twirled around, causing Peaches to bump into him. Brushing the mud from his trousers, Wynn growled, "Do you see any stripes on my arm or bars on my shoulders?" His voice softened when he recognized that he had frightened the youngster. "How old are you?"

"Seventeen last month."

"Bullshit on the parade! I doubt if you're fifteen."

With a heavy German accent, Dutch Osterman blurted, "He is too seventeen!" Dutch peered through his thick glasses, first at Peaches and then at Wynn. "Please, don't turn him in."

"Hell no!" said Wynn. "The CCC is like the French Foreign Legion."

"There's a desert around here?" interrupted Peaches.

"Naw. In the C's, your past is nobody's business."

"Thanks, Sir."

"Kid, my name's Wynn. Wynn Odum."

Dutch smiled and touched Peaches' arm lightly. "Now you got

two friends, little buddy."

"You see Sir...Wynn...Sir, everybody makes fun of Dutch because of his thick glasses and his funny talk."

"And the other guys ride Peaches because he's so young," said Dutch.

"So that's why me and Dutch are such good friends," said Peaches.

When they reached the mess tent, Cookie was waiting for them. Pointing at Dutch, he shouted, "Get those potato bags and start peeling" Then he grabbed Peaches and steered him to the serving line. "I want you to ladle out food as the men pass through." When he saw Wynn, Cookie asked. "What the hell are you doing here?"

"Grabowski figures a lot of sixteen hour days will drive me out of the C's."

"Is it going to work?"

"No way, Sergeant."

Cookie slapped Wynn on his shoulder. "Way to go!" Then he pointed at the cook stove, a black cast-iron monster, covered with soot and grime. "I want the stove polished so well that I'll be able to see myself in it."

Peaches Oskowski served the food routinely. Having a short attention span, he did not pay attention to his job. When Salvatore DePalma walked through the serving line, Peaches absent-mindedly dumped scrambled eggs atop De Palma's oatmeal and then allowed a spoonful of fried potatoes to drop into his coffee.

DePalma screamed Italian epithets and threw his tray at the ceiling. Then he leaped over the counter, knocked Peaches to the floor, and began pummeling him.

Wynn had just taken a break when he heard the commotion. As he rushed to the serving line, he saw DePalma punching poor, defenseless Peaches. Quickly, Wynn pulled DePalma away and then knocked DePalma out with a slick right jab.

While the men roared their approval, Peaches stood up, clutched his serving spoon, and resumed his position behind the serving line.

After breakfast, Cookie inspected the stove, scrutinizing every inch of it. Finally, he said, "Wynn, that was a real ball-buster. I've never seen that stove looking better."

"Thanks, Cookie. Got anything else you want done?"

Cookie pointed at Clyde McGowen, his chief cook. "Help him cut up the chicken for tomorrow."

McGowen, suffering from a hangover, chopped at a chicken carcass that bounced from the table and landed between his feet. He tried to spear the bird, but instead, impaled his left shoe. Finally, he retrieved the chicken and placed it on the table. Striking it repeatedly, he succeeded only in bruising it. Then he threw the carving knife into the air. As the knife bounced harmlessly on the floor, he asked Wynn, "Cut them up for me, will you?"

Wynn felt the knives. "These are so damned dull I could slide on them all the way to New York City on my bare ass without even breaking my skin. I bet Red Dawson can help us. He's got lots of tools over in the shed." Within an hour, Wynn returned with the sharpened knives. He cut the chicken easily, and had enough time to help Peaches set up the serving line.

Pleased with the new KPs' efficiency, Cookie said, "Boys, take a break and eat. You deserve it."

Wynn watched Peaches pile his tray with scrambled eggs, bacon, sausage, fried potatoes, and three helpings of toast. "When was the last time you ate?"

"I'm hungry," mumbled Peaches as he shoveled food into his mouth.

"His family nearly starved to death last winter," whispered Dutch, who had sat down beside Wynn.

"How many kids in your family?" asked Wynn.

"Ten," said Peaches.

Cookie brought over a bowl of fried potatoes and placed it beside Peaches, who sucked up the potatoes. As Cookie turned to get more potatoes, he said, "With that kid around, food just won't stand a chance."

Peaches smiled innocently. "I wish my mother was here."

"Why? asked Cookie.

"Because there's so much food here."

"Since you like food so much," said Cookie, "I'll put you on the serving line for lunch and supper."

A smile filled Peaches' face. "Thank you, Sir." Then he reached for more toast.

After the DePalma fight, Wynn adopted a fraternal attitude toward Peaches. His age made him stand out, even in a crowd. And since Peaches weighed less than a hundred pounds soaking-wet, Wynn keenly sensed the kid's vulnerability. Wynn had never felt this need to protect someone before, but he freely accepted this responsibility.

Peaches had an uncanny ability to screw-up. He always had his nose buried in a Buddy Lane novel about the old west. Even while peeling potatoes, Peaches would straddle a potato bag, pretending it was a horse, bouncing up and down as if it had broken out into a gallop. Sometimes, to slow his imaginary mount, Peaches would dig his knees into the potato sack with such a force that the bag would tip over, tossing the neophyte cowboy to the floor.

Peaches had begun throwing an old clothes rope, his trusty lariat, at Dutch Osterman, who was his willing target. This was a trade-off for Peaches' teaching the Dutchman how to speak English without a German accent. Peaches would read a paragraph from a Buddy Lane novel and then ask Dutch to read it aloud. Then Peaches would correct Dutch. This was an ongoing lesson whenever they worked together.

Wynn gave it little thought when he saw a copy of the GOLDEN DAWN fall from Peaches' apron pocket. As Wynn stooped down to get the book, he asked, "How many of those do you read a week?"

"At least two."

"Where do you get them?"

"From the camp library."

During their conversation, Peaches was putting wieners into the giant steam kettle, while jogging up and down as if he were riding his favorite mount. As he opened another bag of wieners, Peaches said, "You should read this one, Wynn!"

"I don't have time!" His quick answer made Peaches cringe. Immediately recognizing Peaches' reaction, Wynn said, "Go ahead, kid. Give me the lowdown."

Beaming, Peaches began, "This woman named Josie is pledged to one man but she loves another."

"That sounds like all his other books."

"Buddy Lane <u>would</u> never repeat himself." Peaches took a deep breath and continued the synopsis. "You see, this man, Billy Bob Hackett, was rescued out in the desert by the Mormons who were fighting Utah's worst cattle rustler, Black Bart, but both of them was in love with this beautiful half breed, Josie. Then Billy Bob has to go deep into the desert to bring Josie back as his own...But Billy Bob found out that the rustlers had kidnapped his beloved Josie and took her deep into the Dry Gultch Territory...You know the Indians was even scared to go in there...That's as far as I got. Ain't that an exciting tale? Do you think Billy Bob and Josie will get together, Wynn?"

"Hell, kid, I don't know. Maybe they'll find an oasis and start up a little business."

"Gee, Wynn, you already read this book?"

"Read it yourself and tell me what happens. In the meantime, don't let that steam boiler overheat. Those valves aren't reliable." As he showed Peaches how to regulate them, Wynn said, "I'm going to be gone for about ten minutes. Grabowski wants to see me and Cookie." When he left the kitchen, Wynn saw Peaches pull up a bag of potatoes and begin to read.

As Wynn and Cookie walked across the compound, they saw Grabowski waiting impatiently for them. "Looks like the Old Man is pissed," said Cookie.

"Yeah," agreed Wynn. "At me!"

"Just be quiet," cautioned Cookie. "Let me do the talking."

Upon seeing the two men approaching him, Grabowski yelled, "Sergeant, you're late!" Scowling at Wynn, Grabowski asked, "Is it because of your inferior help?" Then he motioned for Cookie and Wynn to enter the tent.

Stiffly, Grabowski sat down and tapped the top of his desk with his fingers. While continuing to glare at Wynn, Grabowski motioned for Cookie to sit down. Finally, Grabowski said, "Having trouble with this wiseacre?"

"He's the best KP I've had so far, Sir," answered Cookie. "He's a lifesaver, too."

"Stick him in the kitchen," said Grabowski. "This way, I'll be able to watch him better."

"What about his work as an orderly?"

"He can still do that, too." Interrupted by an explosion, Grabowski shouted, "What the hell was that?"

"Sounds like it came from the kitchen," said Cookie.

"I just hope that crazy kid hasn't blown himself up along with the Dutchman," said Wynn.

"What the hell are you talking about?" fumed Grabowski.

"Sir, let's get over there and see what's left," answered Cookie.

When the three men entered the kitchen, they saw Dutch holding a fire extinguisher. He had sprayed water on everything, including Peaches who sat cross-legged on the floor. Chunks of wieners, shreds of sauerkraut, and white foam covered the soaked pages of the GOLDEN DAWN that lay between his legs.

"What happened?" screamed Grabowski.

"Your horse throw you, pal?" asked Wynn as he helped Peaches to his feet.

"It just went Varroom!" sputtered Dutch.

Suddenly, Peaches began to cry. "The book's ruined. I'll never be able to take out another book. What am I going to do?" As he faced this terrible truth, larger tears rolled down his face.

Grabowski asked, "Who's responsible?"

Between sobs, Peaches blubbered, "I am, Sir."

"No, I am," said Dutch.

Grabowski raged at both men. "Because of your incompetence, you've recklessly endangered the whole camp!"

As he listened to Grabowski's harangue, Wynn realized that Grabowski was about ready to kick Peaches and Dutch out of the C's. Wynn caught the attention of Cookie and mouthed, "Let me..."

Cookie shook his head vigorously. Skillfully, he interrupted Grabowski. "Begging your pardon, Sir, but I feel that I'm partially at fault."

Grabowski stopped and stared at Cookie.

"I didn't give these young men enough time to learn the fine points of the steam kettle. It's a damn complicated machine."

Grabowski said, "Go on."

"I was derelict in my duty by going over to your office."

"But I had ordered you and Odum to meet with me."

"That's right, Sir. But it's not your fault, either. And since I'm the Mess Sergeant, it's part my fault, so I think I should discipline the lads. That is, if it meets with your approval."

Grabowski cleared his throat. "Very well, Sergeant, I accept your proposal. Make the penalty fit the crime and pass it on for my approval."

"I've got it right now."

"What is it?"

"Scratch Odum as permanent KP." Cookie pointed at Peaches and Dutch. "Replace Odum with these two jokers. That way if they foul up again, I'll nail their asses to the flag pole!"

"An outstanding idea. I'll put Odum on tree planting detail." Grabowski pivoted perfectly, and strode from the kitchen before a glob of sauerkraut fell silently from the ceiling, narrowly missing him.

When Grabowski had disappeared, Dutch and Peaches warmly shook Cookie's hand. "I promise to do better, next time, Sir," said Peaches, while Dutch said something in German.

"Let's clean the joint up," said Cookie. Then he turned to Wynn. "You'd better take off. The Doc's going to need you, and tree planting don't sound like a whole helluva lot of fun."

CHAPTER THIRTEEN

When Wynn returned to the infirmary, he was surprised to find that the number of patients had increased to seven. "Where'd they come from?" he asked.

Frank poured Wynn a cup of coffee before responding. "I ran a screening today and found four more pneumonia cases. Now comes the toughest part of the fight." Then Frank said, "You did a helluva fine job, yesterday. Finish your coffee and let's make rounds."

Their first patient was Selig, who had become incoherent. Frank took his temperature and felt his pulse. "I would judge that he had been sick at least four days. The next forty-eight hours will tell the tale." He took a damp wash cloth and rubbed the perspiration from Selig's face and neck, holding it a bit longer on the boy's forehead, as if trying to drain away the fever. He placed the palm of his hand on Selig's sternum and kept it there for two minutes. "Touch is comforting, and it improves the body's healing processes while reducing pain." When he heard a commotion outside, Frank said, "Wynn, please see what all the fuss is about."

Wynn pulled open the tent flaps and saw Harry O'Donnel, Lloyd Cartwright, and Mousy Gray standing there.

O'Donnel was the spokesman. "We want to see Selig."

"I'm sorry, O'Donnel. You can't."

"Why not?"

"He's sick."

"Who says so?"

"Doctor Millet wants him isolated."

"Bull!"

"It's for his own good."

"Ain't the doctor afraid that you might give him something?"

While Cartwright pushed forward, O'Donnel made a sucking sound with his mouth.

"Get out of my way before I send the Doc another patient," threatened O'Donnel.

As Frank walked over to the entrance, O'Donnel tried an end-run. In one fluid motion, Wynn grabbed O'Donnel's arm, twirled him around, and guided him outside.

"Bravo," said Frank. "I haven't seen a move that slick since the last Fred Astaire movie." Turning to O'Donnel, Frank asked, "Just what is your problem?"

"It's our friend, Doc."

"I ordered no visitors."

"We just want to know how he's doing," piped up Mousy.

O'Donnel took off his hat and folded it in his hands. "Is there anything we can do to help our pal?"

"The well-being of every sick boy interests me. Not just your friend. Selig is resting comfortably. If you come around tomorrow, I'll have my orderly give you an update. Come on Wynn, we've got more work to do." As Frank turned to leave, he said, "Remind Sergeant Dougherty that I need an orderly. Tell him I'm disappointed that he hasn't come through for me."

The young men walked down the gravel path muttering to themselves. "Tell the Sergeant that...Never!" said O'Donnel.

Cartwright agreed. "An orderly. Sheeit! That's a broad's job."

Putting the confrontation behind them, Frank and Wynn continued their rounds. Howard Petrosky and Casimer Villic were next. Frank checked their pulses and listened to their chests, while Wynn took their temperatures. Since Petrosky had been coughing and was uncomfortable, Frank motioned for Wynn to begin postural drainage on the young man.

"Do you want him cupped, too?"

Frank nodded his head as he began sponging down Villic's chest and arms. After Wynn had finished cupping Petrosky, Frank called Wynn over to Jimmy Feeney's bed. "Next to Selig, this is our most serious case. His temperature has shot up two degrees since this morning." While Wynn changed the young man's bed and gave him a dry pillow, Frank gave the young man a sponge bath.

Just as they had finished, Joey Flaherty, the camp carpenter, stuck his head in the tent. He had brought the table that Frank had requested earlier. "The plans were perfect. The materials were just laying around, and all I had to do was to measure, cut, and nail. I made a slight change to your design. I put wheels on the one end. That way, it moves easier."

The table was six feet long and three and a half feet high. It had two handles on one end that stuck out like wheelbarrow handles. Six sturdy legs supported it.

"This is even better than I thought," Frank exclaimed. He acted like a child who had just received an early Christmas gift. "Flaherty didn't miss a trick! He even covered the edges of the facial cut-out with a soft cloth. Now, when we put someone in a postural drainage position, his hips will be comfortably elevated." Frank picked up the table and wheeled it over to Higgleston's bed. "Let's give him the honor of breaking it in." Turning toward Wynn, Frank asked, "Would you fetch me the brown box that's over beside my desk?" When Wynn returned with it, Frank opened it and counted out ten small bottles, each containing different colored liquids. "These are aromatherapy essences that come from various plants and flowers." He opened a bottle and put it under Wynn's nose.

Inhaling deeply, Wynn responded emphatically. "Phewy! That sure cleans the head fast." Then he added, "I should have had that for my last fight."

"That's eucalyptus. It's good for colds and bronchitis. The other bottles hold cardamon, lavender, thyme, and rosemary. There's usually a long and interesting history with each herb. For example, back in England hundreds of years ago, people rubbed rosemary on a robber's feet to cure him of stealing."

"Did it work?"

"A pleasant fairy tale, that's all." Frank pulled the cork from another bottle and smelled it. "Thyme is a strong disinfectant and used for a mouthwash" Allowing Wynn to smell it, Frank said, "Notice its strong lemony smell. Ancient Greek men made themselves elegant by rubbing their bodies with thyme." As a wry grin slowly spread on Wynn's face, Frank asked, "What's so funny?"

"It's all those Greeks rubbing lemon juice on each other. That's enough to pucker my lips."

Frank put two drops of eucalyptus essence and a cupful of soya oil into a glass. He added a pinch of wheat germ into the solution. Then he shook the concoction vigorously. "That will keep it from turning sour."

Removing Higgleston from his bed, they put him on the new table. When Frank poured the solution into his palm, a pungent eucalyptus smell spread rapidly through the tent. As he worked the liquid into Higgleston's back, Frank remarked, "That should relieve much of his congestion." Then he started the cupping procedure. After that, he moved into the final stage of the treatment. Slowly and delicately, with his fingertips barely brushing his patient's back, he began the lightest of brushing strokes, drawing his hands toward himself. As he finished the procedure, he said, "Feathering is ideal for saying good-bye to that part of the body I have just worked on."

When they put Higgleston back to bed, Wynn noticed that the young man's breathing seemed to be better. "That stuff really works," he said. But he finally had to leave the tent, because the eucalyptus smell was overpowering.

Outside, Wynn inhaled the fresh, cold air and watched the stars twinkle in the sky. While a slight wind whistled through the pin-oak trees, he tried vainly to locate a lonely owl hooting in the dark. Wynn was strangely relieved when he heard its mate respond from the opposite hill.

Transfixed, he stared into the star-filled sky and realized that Turtle Creek, boxing, bread lines, and even Murray were far away, in another world and another time. As he stood there on that late April evening, Wynn could only ponder on how deep was the forest's sky.

CHAPTER FOURTEEN

It was 0545 as Wynn Odum stood in formation waiting for Sergeant Dougherty to call the company to order. "Seems to me that all we do is stand around waiting for him to make a decision."

"Don't complain," said Ontek. "Dougherty took me off the shit detail."

"I thought he stuck you with it for a week?"

"A new guy dropped the flag at Retreat and right in front of Dougherty, too."

"I guess that chump will be on the Blivit Detail forever."

"Not quite. Dougherty gave him eight days."

"Company, tenshut!" commanded Dougherty. When he was satisfied that the men stood like a regular army unit, he shouted, "At ease." After he had taken roll, he told the men, "Today, I've got a brand new job assignment. The lucky folks whose last names begin with A through O will be on the tree planting detail. The rest of you bums will be carrying rocks for a truck trail."

After Dougherty dismissed them, Ontek poked Wynn. "Well, here we are, together again."

"Sounds like a song."

"Anything beats taking shit from Hasselrig."

After breakfast, six trucks rolled out from Camp One and took the men to a steep hillside. Their task was formidable: to replant huge sections of the forest destroyed by man.

When Wynn got out of the truck, he looked up the hill. Some scrub poplar trees clung to the hill, while a sea of brown briars covered the dead tree tops left there by a logging company. Dismayed, he asked, "Are we going to work on that?" Then he saw a line of yellow directional flags that disappeared into the weeds. To

75

his right he saw long rows of red flags that vanished into the trees. "I can't see the end of those either," he said. Cupping his hand over his eyes so that he might see better, he asked, "Do those flags go on forever?"

Tom Divine, the planting foreman, said, "Those yellow flags mark the eastern and the western boundaries of the plantation." Then he pointed toward the red flags. "They're laid out in a north and south direction and run parallel to the road. And we are going to plant on the red ones."

"How much are we planting?" asked Wynn.

"A thousand acres," replied Devine.

"Today?" asked Ontek.

"It'll take at least six weeks," answered Devine. "And I've got to warn you, it's a lot harder than it looks."

Bobby Roggo and Tate Kline, Junior Foresters from West Virginia, took over. They divided the crew into teams of two men each. One man received a mattock, while the other got a canvas apron, containing a pouch large enough to hold fifty seedlings. After that, they demonstrated the correct planting technique. First, Roggo scraped the debris from the ground with his mattock, followed by well-aimed blows that opened a six inch wide hole, ten inches deep. Two steps behind his partner, Kline dropped an upright seedling into the hole, stooped down and covered soil around its roots with his hands, and then stood up while imbedding the tiny tree into the hole with his heel.

Just before they moved into the brambles, Ontek asked, "Is there rattlesnakes out there, Mr. Devine?"

"They really are quite shy and will do everything to avoid a human. With so many men tramping over the hill today, I don't believe snakes will be a problem."

Ontek asked, "What happens if one bites me?"

"Don't panic," was Divine's simple retort. "I have four snake bite kits."

"You're going to cut me?"

Newt Blaustine, recently arrived from Santee, Georgia, yelled, "I never heard of anyone dying from a little old snake bite."

"You've been bitten by a rattler?" asked Ontek.

Newt pulled up his pant leg, letting everyone admire two pinpricks on the calf of his left leg. "I was good as new in a couple of days," he said proudly.

Instantly, Newt became a celebrity.

"Did you have a snake bite kit when it bit you" asked Ontek.

"Holy dog pecker! First, I killed the snake. Then my daddy took out his pocket knife, made two little cuts over the fang marks, and sucked the snake juice out."

Devine pointed up the hill. "All right, men, the seedlings are drying up. Start planting on the red flags. After that, plant one tree every six feet, staying parallel to the yellow flags. You fellows with the mattocks, watch the guys to your left. Make sure that the line is straight."

Before the line of men surged from the red flags, Harry O'Donnel yelled to the foreman, "How many of these little buggers do I got to plant today?"

Devine looked at the men who stood poised ready to go. "Maybe two or three hundred."

"I ought to have that done by noon!"

"We'll see how you feel about that eight hours from now," chuckled Devine.

Wynn gave Ontek a push. "Get going. I can't plant trees until you dig the hole."

Ontek had to remove dead tree tops before he could see where to dig the hole. Frequently, he allowed branches to whip back and hit Wynn, who filled the air with obscenities. As the morning went on, the difficulty of the work increased. From the underbrush, Ontek complained, "This here's stoop labor. Are we the new breed of Chinks?"

Devine's response was simple and to the point. "Keep the line straight."

At 1130, Jack Kulack, the lead truck driver, returned to the work site carrying lunch. He started a fire and placed a ten gallon can filled with water and coffee over it. As the coffee brewed, he walked back to the truck and blew the horn, signaling the lunch hour.

Ontek and Wynn were the first ones to reach the truck. They watched a subdued group appear from the brambles and brush heaps.

Kulack looked up from the serving line. "It's a lot harder than it looks, ain't it?"

"Tough on the back," said Wynn.

"Would you help me pass out the lunches?"

Every person received three peanut butter and jelly sandwiches, a piece of cheese, and a large red apple. There were the usual complaints, but nobody refused his lunch. Each man took his canteen cup, filled it with boiled coffee, and retreated to a spot where only a few weeds grew. As the food began to take effect, everyone became more animated.

Harry O'Donnel tossed an apple core toward Kulack. "How in hell did you get such a cushy job?"

"Looks, I guess."

"Bullshit," shouted Cartwright. "Must have been somebody you knew. Let me know when there's an opening in the motor pool. Sure beats the hell out of this job."

Ontek had begun to warm his hands over the fire. Without any warning, the wind changed, blowing the smoke into his face. Coughing violently, he tripped over two men as he retreated from the fire.

O'Donnel yelled, "Smoke follows beauty, Adamchunk!"

Ontek responded with a one finger salute before finding a patch of dry moss to sit on. Then he asked a question that still nagged him. "Newt, did you say your old man saved your life by sucking the poison out of your leg?"

"Sure did, and I'm here to tell y'all about it."

A tall, strapping man, with a ready smile, Newt was an example of the CCC's ability to affect dramatically a person's life. Out of work for three years, he and his friends had agreed to a radical solution to their desperate problem: to rob the local bank. On the morning of the planned robbery, he had enlisted in the CCC. The recruiter whisked him off to the processing station without allowing him to go home. The robbery, however, went off on schedule, and the police apprehended his friends, each of whom received thirty year prison terms.

"I got a big question," said Ontek.

"What is it?" asked Newt.

"Let's say that I have to take a leak," said Ontek, "and I pull it out and let go." As a few snickers came from the men, Ontek continued. "Then Wango! A snake gets me right here." He pointed to his crotch. "Who's going to help me?"

A few limbs from the fire dropped into the red coals, making the blaze explode. The showering embers briefly caught the attention of the men, but clearly, their focus was on, Ontek, the hypothetical victim, and Newt, the wizard of first aid.

"Yeah," shouted Wynn. "What would you do?"

Newt walked over to Ontek and put his left arm around the Ontek's shoulders. Very softly, he uttered, "If that ever happens, y'all get to find out real quick who your true friends are!"

"Damned if I'll ever take a leak in the woods again no matter what!" Ontek wailed.

While everyone howled at Ontek's plight, Newt said, "I'd like to ask y'all an important question." As the men leaned forward, he asked, "What's the meanest animal in the whole world?"

This question got an enthusiastic response, and, for a minute, it sounded like the Tower of Babel revisited. Finally, Newt restored order by insisting that each person speak one at a time.

O'Donnel offered that the grizzly bear could rip open a man with one powerful blow. Getting back into the fray, Ontek volunteered the skunk because of its aim and awful spray. The crew hooted his response down. In quick succession, everyone rejected a mountain lion, a thirty foot python, and a wolverine.

"Well, what is it?" asked Ontek.

"The rhinoceros," Newt proclaimed. "Five years ago, I visited the Atlanta Zoo where I saw this fierce looking animal. It had an awful looking horn right in the middle of its head. Folks watching it paid no attention to the sign, 'Beware of spray,' posted beside the creature's cage. When I got closer, I saw all that hate stored up inside that animal. Then, without any warning, it let go, pissing. Now this devil just wasn't a regular pisser, from between his front legs like an ordinary animal. No sir! That sucker shot a brown stream sideways! It even got off a backward shot, too! Hit my brother square in the face. Puked for days he did!"

"She...it Reb, you ain't heard anything," said Wynn.

"All right, Odum," said Newt. "It's your turn. But I can't help but notice that a lot of y'all dumped out your brown coffee. Is there something wrong with it?"

Wynn walked toward the smoldering fire and threw in a piece of wood. Then he turned around and faced the group. "Ever hear of the crockagator?" Since no one had, Wynn continued. "On one end, this creature has a head of a crocodile." He paused slightly before adding, "And on the other end, there's this terrible looking head of an alligator!"

Cartwright piped up, "Your story is a crock of shit. What would make the crockagator the meanest animal in the whole world?"

A broad smile spread over Wynn's face. Then he walked toward Cartwright and asked, "If you couldn't shit, wouldn't you be awful mean, too?"

Tom Divine called a halt to the stories and made the men resume their planting duties. They continued planting on this site until they had completed the first CCC tree plantation in the country. Even though the work was hard, stoop labor, it was a significant start toward binding the wounds of the forest.

CHAPTER FIFTEEN

After Wynn had returned from tree planting duties, he washed up and ate. Then he hurried to the infirmary. As he entered the tent, he saw a tired-looking Frank sponging down Higgleston. "Get any sleep?"

"No, but I'm glad you're here. You can help me with the rest of the patients."

"How long has it been since you slept?"

"Three...four days."

"Let me finish doing Higgleston while you grab some shut-eye."

"Sounds like a good idea," said Frank as he began to look for an empty bed.

Wynn immediately began cupping the young man. When he had finished, he heard someone walking up the gravel path. He assumed it was Cookie, bringing some coffee. It jolted him when he heard a woman's voice.

"Captain, may I see you please?" Her voice rose at least one more decibel when she repeated her request.

"Can I help you ma'am?" asked Wynn.

"My name is Mary Feeney, Jimmy's mother," she said, stepping into the tent. When she saw that Wynn was not a doctor, she demanded, "Where's the doctor?"

"He's sleeping."

"I want to see the doctor," she insisted.

"He's been on his feet for the past three days."

A tall, rawboned woman, Mary Feeney was determined to help her son. "A CCC driver came to Ridgway yesterday afternoon for supplies. He told me that my son was very ill."

Mrs. Feeney's confrontation with Wynn had awakened Frank,

who slowly got out of bed and looked in her direction. "Hello, there," he said sleepily. "Won't you sit down."

"I came here to nurse my son." When she sat down, she asked, "What's his condition?"

"Serious."

"I'm a nurse. I'm familiar with pneumonia."

"Mrs. Feeney, this is a government hospital. There are regulations."

Dutch Osterman interrupted them when he walked into the tent. "Doctor, excuse me. Cookie has your supper ready. He wants you to come over to the mess hall."

Mrs. Feeney ignored Dutch. Instead she continued to press Frank for a positive answer. "Jimmy's all I've got."

"I believe you know that it is unwise to treat someone who is so close to you?"

"Sick people are treated all the time at home."

"That's true, Mrs. Feeney."

"You've been here less than a week so most of your patients haven't reached the crisis stage. You'll need all the help you can get."

"We don't have any accommodations," argued Frank.

"I have a friend who lives at Pigeon."

"Mrs. Mary Feeney, you've stated your position logically. And your points are correct."

"Don't be condescending!"

"I'm sorry, Mrs. Feeney. I meant no offense." Frank shrugged his shoulders and surrendered. "Make a mustard plaster for your son while I eat my supper. Wynn will show you where we keep the supplies."

Mrs. Feeney brought the mustard plaster to her son who was still half asleep. Then she pulled the covers down to his waist and applied it.

"Mom...What are you doing here?"

"Hush, I'm here to take care of you."

"Are you going to take me home?"

"No, Jimmy. We'll do everything here."

As he closed his eyes, Jimmy said, "I'm glad you're here."

After removing the mustard plaster, she loosened the sheet at the foot of the bed, so his feet had room to move.

Wynn continued working, thankful that he was not alone. He brought beef tea over to Mrs. Feeney. "This will help."

"Thank you. I'll give it to him when he awakens."

Then Wynn gave tea to the other patients. Wasko wolfed his down without a word, while Villic drank his without having a coughing spasm. After taking the first sip, George Higgleston choked badly. Wynn reached for the basin that lay beside the bed.

"Why am I doing this?" Higgleston moaned. Between spasms, he complained, "There's six chips in this basin, and it's rusty!"

When Wasko began to throw up, Selig yelled, "Make him stop it."

Mrs. Feeney was too late to reach Wasko, who vomited beef tea on his sheets. She gave a basin to Selig just before he began to vomit.

When Frank returned, he motioned for Wynn to begin cupping Higgleston. Wynn wheeled the table over to Higgleston's bed, and he and Mrs. Feeney rolled the young man onto it. Then Wynn poured eucalyptus oil on his hands and began massaging Higgleston.

While Frank worked on Villic, he said to Mrs. Feeney, "Check the patients' mouths. Have them gargle in salt water if they can. Otherwise use the atomizer."

Efficiently, the three of them had met the immediate needs of the patients. When they had finished, Frank waved to Mrs. Feeney, smiled, and said, "Thank you."

Before he had time to sit down, Frank heard an ominous noise coming from Selig. His bed was actually shaking. Frank listened to the young man's chest, while Mrs. Feeney took his temperature. His breathing was shallow, almost as if he were panting.

"He's reached crisis, Mrs. Feeney. Would you and Wynn watch the rest of the patients while I stay with him?"

At the same time, Jimmy Feeney began to scream. "The moose! The moose! It's going to get me!"

Frank had removed the sheets from Selig, leaving only a towel draped over his waist. As Selig continued to shake, Frank sponged the young man's body with alcohol in an effort to reduce the kid's temperature.

"I want water," Jimmy cried. "I'm burning up!" When his mother gave him ice flakes, Jimmy sucked on them, as if he were in a desert. "If I don't get more water, I'm going to die." While his mother bathed him, he wailed, "The moose, don't let him get me! Mrs. Barkus, the moose is going to get your dog."

Wynn saw Mrs. Feeney's color drain from her face. "Who's Mrs. Barkus?"

"A widow who had been our neighbor back before the war. She owned a little dog, Trixie. Unfortunately, Trixie always did her business on Joe Slavoda's front yard. One day, Mrs. Barkus was in the yard with Trixie and Jimmy when Mr. Slavoda showed up carrying a shotgun. He pointed the gun directly at the dog and threatened to kill it."

"Where's Mrs. Barkus?" Jimmy screamed. "Slavoda's going to kill poor Trixie."

"A week later, Jimmy was playing in the back yard. He found the dead dog stuffed in a bag under the back porch. Mrs. Barkus went into mourning, while Mr. Slavoda boasted about the bitter pill he had given to the dog." Mrs. Feeney stopped long enough fluff her son's pillow. "The next day, Jimmy took food over to Mrs. Barkus. He found her dead. She had killed herself by drinking lye."

As Wynn gave Mrs. Feeney the eucalyptus oil, he said, "Now I know this place is no different than the Valley."

Mrs. Feeney shook her head. "It's a hard world no matter where you live."

Wynn went over to Selig's bed. "How is he?"

"His breathing has slowed down, and he has stopped shaking." replied Frank. He took out his thermometer and placed it under the young man's tongue. Frank waited three minutes before checking it. "Its going down!" He stood up, stretched, and walked over to Jimmy. After listening the boy's chest, he said, "I don't know what medicine you used, Mrs. Feeney, but his chest is less congested. I'd let him sleep." Frank touched Mrs. Feeney's arm and said, "Go to your friend's house and get some sleep. Come back tomorrow. Wynn and I will watch the store." He turned to Wynn and said, "Please take Mrs. Feeney to her car."

As she was about to leave, she turned to Frank and said, "With

84

your approval, I'd like to help until everyone is well."

"I would appreciate that," he said. After she had left, Frank said, "There goes one good nurse." Then he sat down on an empty bed, stretched out, and closed his eyes.

Grabowski's noisy entrance into the infirmary, wakened Frank. Opening his eyes, he said, "Yes, Lieutenant, can I help you?"

"What's a woman doing at my camp?"

"Mrs. Feeney is a registered nurse. She's taking care of her son, who is critically ill."

"I don't care if she's Whistler's Mother. Get her out of here."

"If you feel so strongly about her presence, then give me additional money for a trained nurse."

"You know damn well that I don't have any extra money." Then he added, "And don't give me a bill for her services."

"She's donating her services, and she has agreed to return until the last pneumonia patient leaves the hospital."

"Well, if you say she's not costing me a penny..." After a brief pause, Grabowski said, "Doctor, regarding yesterday's screening...The paper work is inadequate."

"Lieutenant Grabowski, there are seven cases of pneumonia in here. I diagnosed four cases from my screening. All the other men in camp are fine." As Grabowski tapped his foot impatiently on the floor, Frank added, "When I have time, the United States Army will have a complete report to file away in some obscure office."

"Doctor, you're on report to your district commander."

"Fine. Give Porky my regards. He's an old Harvard chum!"

Grabowski spun on his heels and charged outside, nearly knocking Wynn over.

"I heard everything, Doc. Aren't you worried?"

"I've had a great day, Wynn. Everyone is resting comfortably. As for Grabowski...There'll be no report! He won't want to have anyone in command thinking that he's got any problems."

CHAPTER SIXTEEN

The mud had begun to dry and a slight, warm breeze, a forerunner of improved weather, had replaced the damp chill. The men reacted to it and stood taller in formation. Even Dougherty was more efficient. He ran through the roll call quickly and then turned to Red Dawson.

Red called the names of eight men, including Wynn Odum and Harry O'Donnel. They were all to become members of the Snap Fire Crew.

"Are we setting them or putting them out?" asked O'Donnel.

"Sonny, if you don't want to do it," snapped Red, "I'll pick someone else."

O'Donnel threw up his hands in mock surrender. "Okay, Pop, don't blow a cork."

"You guys will meet me over at the maintenance shed right after breakfast." Then Red gave the company back to Dougherty.

"Listen up, men!" said Dougherty. "For those who ain't on the planting crew, I got a soft job that'll last until the end of October."

"What's that," asked Timmy Nedshe hesitatingly.

"Ever build a road, Rookie?"

Timmy shook his head, while never once looking at Dougherty.

Dougherty held up a long handled hammer. "This is a United States government regulation knapping hammer and it weighs four pounds two ounces." He wheeled around and stuck his nose into Nedshe's face. "What's it used for, dummy?"

"To pound something?"

"Not your meat, that's for damn sure!" Dougherty backed away from the trembling young man. "With that hammer, your only job will be to make big rocks into little ones."

About to dismiss the company, Dougherty realized that he had forgotten something. He put one hand on his hip and in a sing-song voice said, "One more thing, guys. The doctor needs an orderly. Any takers?" Then, returning to his normal voice, he singled out Wynn. "Anybody that's got a question ask Odum. He's good at emptying bed pans and giving baths."

Immediately, Ontek grabbed Wynn's arm and whispered, "Don't let him get your goat."

There were a few snickers, but Dougherty smiled and waited. "No takers on this girl's job? Going, going, gone!" Then he shouted, "Dismissed!"

Red Dawson waited in the maintenance shed for the men. His specialty was fighting forest fires. He had participated in all the big fires, including the Bear Creek Fire of 1926 where he had saved four men.

Wynn, Ontek, and Danny Witkowski came into the shed together followed by Dante Marconi and Sammy Zambini. Lefty Malone came alone. Finally, Lloyd Cartwright and Harry O'Donnel sauntered in.

After Red had finished the head count, he picked up a common garden rake and held it up. "This here rake will be your first line of attack against fires. Your best buddy by the time the fire season's over."

"You going to teach us how to use that?" asked O'Donnel.

"What's those other tools?" asked Danny Witkowski.

When Red picked up a Pulaski tool, Ontek said, "Looks like an axe to me,"

"One side is a single bit axe," said Red, "but the other side is shaped just like a hoe. I've cut and dug with this sucker on many a fire line." Then Red reached down and picked up an Indian tank sprayer. "This little beauty weighs over fifty pounds when it's filled."

"We got to carry all that into a fire?" asked Ontek.

"To be a fire fighter, you've got to have the endurance of a long distance runner, the strength of a plow horse, and the brains of a mule."

Sammy Zambini raised his hand. "Can we smoke, Red?"

"No, you can't."

"How come you picked us?" blurted Danny Witkowski.

"You have leadership ability." As O'Donnel and Cartwright began to smile, Red said, "But don't get fat heads. If there's screwing around, you're gone." Moving toward the door, he said, "Gentlemen, I've got a treat. Let's go for a little walk through the woods." He held the door open as they jogged out into the compound. Then Red moved ahead, leading the way.

As the crew passed Ivan Ruttman, he leaned on his shovel and yelled wistfully, "Hey, when you get back, tell me what it's like out there."

The men passed quickly through the camp entrance and across a small bridge. "Where we heading?" shouted Wynn.

"Pigeon," responded Red.

"There ain't no place that's got a name like that," yelled O'Donnel.

"Save your breath," advised Red.

The first mile was easy. The second mile was uphill. As the second mile neared completion, Sammy Zambini rasped, "A little walk in the woods. This here's a damned death march!"

Red chugged to the front and then dropped back to the rear where he encouraged Dante Marconi. From there, Red shouted to Cartwright, "Just like running from the Philly cops?" Then Red sprinted to the front where he caught up to Wynn. "You're in pretty good shape, kid."

"I'm good for another ten miles."

Red matched him stride-for-stride. "You really want this job, don't you?"

"No one's going to get in my way."

"You remind me of somebody I knew a long time ago."

"Anybody I know?

"Someday, I'll tell you," said Red as he fell back to the middle of the column. From there, he shouted encouragement to the crew. "You're here to keep the little fires from becoming the big ones! And you'll eat so much sonnavabitching smoke that you'll never light up a cigarette again."

When Red called a halt after the third mile, everyone except

Wynn collapsed. Red taunted Sammy Zambini, who was on all fours, throwing up. "Lard Ass," Red said, "you're going to have to lose your baby fat real fast." He turned to O'Donnel, who lay on the ground, gasping for breath. "To put out a fire, you've got to get to it first." Red moved from the men and jumped up on a rock. "Fires kill when you least expect it! And don't ever forget that!" He jumped from the rock and began running back to the camp. Turning around, he shouted, "Let's head for the maintenance shed. That's where we'll have our next session."

Ontek smiled weakly before nudging Wynn. "Cripes! You mean we got to run back? I thought they'd have a truck waiting for us."

"Getting back is a snap. It's all downhill," said Wynn.

Going back was easier. The men ran more smoothly, and their faces were no longer contorted. As they made the final turn into camp, Red called out, "You're looking better." Then he sprinted toward the maintenance shed, nearly two hundred yards away.

Wynn immediately accepted the challenge. Within fifteen strides, he closed the gap between them. Then he pulled even. The last fifty yards was a dead heat, and when they reached the shed, neither man could claim victory. Wynn leaned against the shed while he regained his breath. "You're pretty fast for an old coot," rasped Wynn.

Still breathing deeply, Red growled, "Let's see how fast you are with a water sprayer on your back."

Red regarded fire fighting as a war between himself and the fire. His philosophy came from Nathan Bedford Forrest, a Confederate general, whose motto was, "Git thar fust with the most." This was the concept behind the snap fire crew, too.

After a break, Red asked, "Does anybody know how to read a compass?"

Four men, Ontek, Witkowski, Malone, and Zambini, raised their hands. Red gave them compasses and then looked at the crew. "You guys have lined up according to friendships, and I don't like it at all. Here's the new team pairings: Wynn with Malone; Ontek with O'Donnel; Zambini, you go with Marconi; Cartwright you're with Witkowski." When O'Donnel groaned and Ontek ground his teeth, Red

89

said, "If some of you don't like each other, tough shit!"

O'Donnel and Ontek sat warily next to each other. O'Donnel looked toward Cartwright who had moved reluctantly next to Witkowski. Everyone else seemed comfortable with the pairings.

"If you haven't noticed, each team has a member who can read a compass. When we go out to the field this afternoon, that person will teach compass reading to his buddy. After lunch we'll go into our next training phase."

Red was sitting in the rear of the Ford truck when the men returned from lunch. A surprised Red asked, "Back so soon?" Then he motioned for the crew to join him. "Our next lesson will be up here," he said.

"How about me giving some lessons to a couple of babes from Marienville," shouted Lefty Malone, a tall, bean-pole of a kid.

"Don't you wish?" snorted Red.

As O'Donnel climbed into the bed of the truck, he muttered, "The back end of a truck! First class, all the way."

"Look, kid!" said Red. "They don't make a better truck than a Ford, and don't you ever forget that."

The Ford truck was only one year old, but the many dents and scratches attested to its rugged use. With the motor pool modifications, it had become a fast attack vehicle against fires. In addition to replacing the standard front and rear bumpers with reinforced six inch iron pipes, the mechanics had also attached a mechanical winch directly in the center of the new front bumper. The bed of the truck had a large tool box containing mattocks, shovels, saws and water pumps, all necessary fire fighting weapons. There was a bench on each side of the bed for the crew. The truck had become a utilitarian means of carrying out General Forrest's philosophy.

Red sat on the tool box, facing his students. "And now for a little paper learning." Handing each man a packet, he explained, "These are topographical maps, but the pros call them topos or quads! Take a few minutes. Study the map's key. That'll tell you everything you need to know."

"Hey, this ain't an ordinary map!" exclaimed Zambini.

"Right you are, kid," agreed Red. "A topo map is to a fire

fighter as to what a Bible is to a preacher." Red held the topo map up in the air. "If you can read this and a compass, no forest, no matter how big, will stop you."

"What's these tiny black blocks, Red?"

"They're buildings, most likely houses, Wynn."

Red moved down the line, answering the questions as they arose. Then he moved on to a key point. "Look at your fingers."

The men did so obediently.

"Notice the little whorls on the fingertips," said Red.

"What's a whorl," asked Ontek.

"Those patterns on your fingers."

"You mean fingerprints?" asked Ontek.

"That's right," said Red. "Now look at the quads. Those lines that look like finger prints are called contour lines. The distance between each line is ten feet."

"Yeah, but sometimes the lines are far apart and then other times they're bunched together. What does that mean?" asked Marconi.

"The closer together, the steeper the land," said Red.

"And if they are far apart, then the land's flat?" asked Wynn.

"You've got it," said Red.

"Jeez," marveled Marconi, "look how fast the land drops to the Clarion River near Hallton!"

"But yet at the Owls Nest, there's a half mile between the lines," added Wynn.

"Will you need climbing shoes or hip boots?" asked Red.

"Hip boots, I guess because there's a big pond of water located there," answered Wynn.

"Red, what's those little numbers in the middle of the swirls?"

"Elevation markers, Ontek. That's the highest point in that zone." Red stood up and jabbed at Wynn. "With a good eye and a lot of practice, anyone can recognize cliffs, swamps, rock outcroppings, dead end ravines, and drainage systems." Somberly, Red added, "Also escape routes from a fire." He jumped up on the tool box and announced, "Put away the maps. I've got a little assignment."

"Not another 'walk in the woods?'" moaned Zambini.

"Something better than that," replied Red.

As the boys began to do battle with the large maps, Red grew impatient. "Don't roll them, damn it! That's like a Russian carrying a ladder through the woods sideways!" Then he showed them the correct way to fold a map. "Put the map on the ground, face up with the north at the top and the part with the key closest to your body. Take the right edge and fold it over to the left side. Make sure it's even! Then fold the left side back to the right, keeping it even again." He held the map in the air so all could see it. "Now you've got a strip of paper six inches by twenty-eight inches. Fold this strip in half and repeat it one more time." As he put the folded map into his pocket, he said, "What's left will fit like a glove in your hip pocket." After the boys had mastered the technique, he gave them their assignments.

Looking at his assignment, Wynn whistled softly. "That's going to be a helluva walk, Red."

Red ignored him. Instead, he directed his attention to the rest of the crew. "Gentlemen," he said, "let a compass and the topo map be your guides."

"But I don't know how to read a compass," moaned Marconi.

"Your buddy Zambini does," said Red.

"But what if we get lost?"

"We'll sent out the Girl Scouts, Marconi." After the snickering had died down, Red said, "After you've finished, walk back to the road and wait for me. I'll pick you up between 1800 and 1900. Let's just hope that your corns aren't hurting."

"What about eating?" asked Ontek.

"Cookie will save you food. So quit worrying." Red motioned for the men to get in the truck. Then he hopped into the cab. When the last man got aboard, Red started the engine, ground transmission, and double-clutched the Ford down the road in a cloud of dust.

CHAPTER SEVENTEEN

As the fire season approached, Red intensified the crew's training. His daily walk in the woods became a ritual. He worked them twelve hours a day, requiring long hours of hacking fire lines, carrying heavy equipment, and climbing hills, ridges, and draws. Whenever someone griped, his stock reply was, "It only hurts until the pain goes away!"

For the crew's final test, Red decided to start a controlled burn a mile south from the camp where Spring Creek intersected the road to Four Corners. Then he went into the plot and started a fire. Upon returning, he sat down and ate lunch.

While Wynn nervously watched the smoke rise, he asked, "What did you do that for?"

"Practice."

"What if it runs away?"

Closing his dinner-pail, Red got up, looked at the fire, and announced, "I'm depending on my Snap Fire Crew to make sure that it doesn't." Calling his crew around him, he said, "Up until now, we've been playing. Now comes your first test." He pointed to the rising smoke. "There's the real McCoy!" After appointing Wynn fire boss, he climbed a tall beech tree.

"What the hell is he doing that for?" asked Marconi.

"He's leaving us all alone to put this thing out?" complained Zambini.

"Quit your blubbering," said Wynn. "Up there, he'll have a better view."

By this time, Red was sixty feet from the ground, his feet dangling from a large limb that reached out over the boys. Then he shouted, "Go to it, boys!"

Wynn realized that the fire was contained on three sides. As a result he had some time for planning. Checking his topo map, he saw that the road made a rapid bend toward the creek. "We'll make the fire line between the road and the stream," he said. Calling Zambini to his side, he said, "Walk up the stream and see how far this sucker is burning. And scout out some good lines of defense, too."

As they approached the fire, Wynn saw that it was moving slowly. He signaled to Cartwright, Marconi, and O'Donnel. "You guys stay here and make the line wider. The rest of you start wedging the fire toward the stream by using your spray pumps."

Wynn knew this was a textbook fire, the kind you talked about in the safety of the maintenance shed. He began to feel comfortable until Ontek started screaming.

Ontek stumbled out from the smoke. "Everything blowed up in my face," he gasped. "I thought I was a goner."

Wynn checked his friend's clothes for any fire. Then he looked for burns. Upon looking at Ontek's face again, Wynn began to laugh.

Sheepishly, Ontek asked, "What's wrong?"

"You don't have any eyebrows."

"That explosion singed them off?"

"Yep."

"Guess I ain't fireproof, am I?"

Wynn pointed to the origin of the explosion.

"That's just a pine log burning," said Ontek.

"Here's your trouble, Ontek. The gas inside the pine must have blown up."

When Zambini reported back to Wynn, the crew gradually wedged the fire toward the creek. Within another hour, they had stopped the fire's advance. After that, it was only matter of putting out the remaining hot spots.

When the fire was out, Red climbed down from the tree and called them together. The still-smoking land behind him was his classroom, and Red began to teach. Using an axe handle as a pointer, he pointed first at one student and then another, highlighting each of boy's work, whether it was good or bad.

"This one was a cakewalk, boys! Don't kid yourselves." He singled out Wynn. "I saw you use your topo map. Good job! Did you make any provisions for an escape route?"

"We didn't need any since the fire was hemmed in on three sides."

"Never assume anything, Odum. Your first duty is to identify escape routes."

Next he criticized Cartwright and O'Donnel. "I noticed when everyone moved into the fire perimeter, the Philly boys stopped working." Pointing an the axe handle at O'Donnel, he said, "In fact, I saw you sitting down!"

"I had a helluva big stone in my shoe," O'Donnel whined.

Red ignored O'Donnel's excuse and turned to Lefty Malone. "I've just promoted you to fire boss. You're on an unfamiliar ridge. How can you find escape routes?"

O'Donnel laughed loudly, while Cartwright said, "Malone as fire boss. That's a joke!"

"I'd look for game trails, because deer and other big animals take the easiest routes." When Red nodded his approval, Malone glared in triumph at the River Rats.

"Wynn, why did you move within the fire perimeter and attack the fire?"

"The fire wasn't moving fast. We pinched it toward the creek by attacking its flank."

Then Red fired a question at Marconi, who was having trouble staying awake. "Marconi, what other natural barriers should you use to wedge a fire?"

Surprising everyone, he answered, "Green timber or a road, I s'pose."

"Don't suppose nothing. Remember four things: high winds, low humidity, steep terrain, and burnable materials on the forest floor. When those conditions exist, stay away from ridges. You could have a chimney effect."

"Can't you outrun the fire?" asked Malone.

"Fires can run as fast as sixty miles an hour. At Bear Creek it raced up over the hill faster than that old Dodge truck I was driving."

During Red's lesson, O'Donnel picked his nose and shot boogers at Malone.

95

Finally, Red asked, "O'Donnel, you got a problem?"

"I'm just sitting at your feet, soaking everything up."

"If that's the case, wisenheimer, give me an example of a poor defensive position in a fire."

"Don't start one in the first place."

Red turned to Zambini. "Help that idiot out!"

"Lots of trees on the ground that might blaze up."

"How about one more, Ontek?"

"Backed up against a cliff with no place to run."

Red nodded in agreement. "That's the worst one, because about all a guy can do is bend over, put his head between his legs, and kiss his ass good-bye."

When O'Donnel had finished picking a scab on his left arm, he stood up, and said, "Quit trying to scare us."

Still holding the axe handle in his hand, Red moved a step closer to O'Donnel. "You know kid, you've got a helluva attitude problem."

Towering over Red, O'Donnel said, "We don't believe them horror stories you've been telling us. You make fires sound like a war."

"Kid, someday a fire's going to singe your ass..."

"Shut up, old man! Me and Cartwright had enough of your shit!"

Red waved off Wynn who had moved beside him. "This is my problem," said Red.

"I'm taking over this crew," hissed O'Donnel.

"Bullshit!" responded Red.

"You ain't nothing but an old windbag," screamed O'Donnel as he picked up a shovel and charged at Red.

Red adeptly dodged O'Donnel's charge and doubled him up with an axe handle blow to the midsection. Its force made him expel a noisy whoosh through his gaping mouth. Quickly, Red moved behind O'Donnel and smacked his hamstrings, knocking the young man to the ground as if he were pole-axed.

Looking straight at Cartwright, Red said, "Anyone else want to fight?" When no one responded, he pointed to Cartwright. "Help O'Donnel!" Then he asked the crew, "What do you want to do with these two?" When everyone remained quiet, Red went nose-to-nose with Wynn. "I'm putting you in for Sergeant. A Sergeant's got to make decisions. You've got the rank. Now make this decision!"

Wynn looked at Cartwright, who held a recovering O'Donnel upright. "Both you guys have dogged it from the start. Your attitude is piss-poor, always a smart remark about anything. Isn't that so?" As Cartwright looked at the ground, Wynn repeated the question.

"I guess so," mumbled Cartwright.

"That attitude will cost us a life." While the crew muttered its assent, Wynn said, "The CCC has given me a new start." He pointed to Cartwright and O'Donnel. "And them, too. Then in the spirit of the C's, they should get one more chance." He looked at the crew. "Any objections?"

Red moved beside Wynn. "What happened here will stay here, tucked away in the back of your mind." Then he added, "We've got a lot more work ahead, because I smell a big fire out there, waiting to test us." Red turned from the crew and began to walk toward the camp. "Let's go back to the barn."

When the crew returned to the camp, they cleaned up and headed for the mess hall. No one talked while eating.

Trying to get a rise out of anyone, Cookie asked, "How'd you like tonight's road kill?"

They kept on eating.

"O'Donnel, you look a little green around the gills. Fall down on the job?"

Marconi and Ontek laughed out loud.

"Christ, you guys are dead. Reminds me of the night I took this broad from Ridgway out for a little action. I paid her five bucks, and after I was finished, she gave me back four dollars in change!" As the boys continued to eat, Cookie walked behind Wynn and put his hands on the young man's shoulders. "Where's Red? Maybe I can get a rise out of him."

Wynn said, "He's over in Grabowski's office."

"Go tell him that his grub's getting cold."

Wynn left the mess hall and walked over to Grabowski's office. When he knocked on the tent's ridge pole, Wynn heard Grabowski's loud voice.

"What the hell are you trying to do, Dawson? Burn my camp down? You set an unauthorized fire and used my boys as guinea pigs." Then he angrily acknowledged Wynn's knocking. "Come in." When he saw Wynn, Grabowski bellowed, "Odum, you're derelict in your duty!"

"How, Sir?"

"You've stopped working at the hospital."

"Mrs. Feeney's filling in for me, Sir."

"Odum's covered," snapped Red. "He's on priority duty for me."

"By whose authority?"

"I have the green light from the Forest Service to establish a Snap Fire Crew. And I also <u>have</u> the authority to select the men for the crew."

"I am unaware of this order," said Grabowski.

"You haven't read the fine print in your manual." As Grabowski sat down at his desk, Red continued, "By the way, I've promoted Odum to Sergeant. And <u>that's</u> within my power, too!"

Grabowski made a complete circle in his swivel chair. He glared at Wynn, who was smiling. "Somewhere, sometime, I'll get you, Odum," he sputtered.

"Your uncle Murray once told me never to make threats unless you could back them up," said Wynn.

Grabowski stomped to the tent's entrance and looked out toward the mess hall. Without turning around, he said, "If you get those kids killed, it's your ass, Dawson, not mine." Then he spun around and confronted Red. "I'm calling your boss and demanding your head."

"Says who?" exploded Red.

Going nose-to-nose with Red, Grabowski said, "Lieutenant Philip Grabowski, that's who!"

"Bullshit!"

"That's insubordination, Dawson!"

"You've got one small problem. I'm not in the army. I work for the Forest Service, and the last time I looked at my paycheck, your name wasn't on it."

Grabowski stomped around the tent again. First he looked at

Wynn and then at Red. But he remained silent.

"Lieutenant, some time ago, I wrote in my work sheet about the need for a controlled burn. But I had to wait until conditions were favorable."

"What if the fire had run away?"

"We've got two hundred men here," explained Red. "Any fifty of them could've pissed the flames out!"

"I don't see any humor in a fire you deliberately set."

"Whoever reported this fire did not see my safeguards. We had the fire bounded on three sides by a creek, a road, and a ten foot fire line."

"When Mousy Gray told me there was a fire, I got upset. No one's going to burn my camp down."

"Soon, I'm going to have to lead my boys into a fire, and I guarantee you, they'll be properly trained."

"Dawson, I just don't want my boys hurt."

"Neither do I, but fire fighting is a war. And people get hurt and sometimes killed. As a military man, you know good training reduces casualties."

"Damn it Dawson, I was in the trenches."

"And I've been in the middle of a dozen forest fires."

"I'm putting a letter about this incident in your personnel jacket." Without waiting for a response, Grabowski pushed open the tent flaps, stepped outside, and walked toward his quarters.

After Grabowski had gone, Wynn said, "C'mon, Red. Cookie's waiting, and it's my treat."

CHAPTER EIGHTEEN

Wynn Odum's booming voice temporarily broke the quiet surrounding the infirmary. "Hey, Doc! Come on out see the deck chairs supply sent you."

Frank stumbled out into the mid-morning light, wearily rubbing his eyes. "So soon? I thought supply had promised them in three days!"

Wynn's laugher filled the compound. "They're on time. Where've you been?"

Placing his hand to his chin, Frank discovered a multi-day's growth of stubble. As he began to awaken, Frank said, "Put the chairs at the edge of the tent."

When Mrs. Feeney came out, Wynn asked, "How's Jimmy?"

"He's spent another restful night."

Frank acknowledged her comment with a broad smile. "Nurse Feeney, have you ever practiced heliotherapy?" When she shook her head, he continued. "I read about a French doctor's treatment of tuberculosis patients. He'd bundle them up warmly and expose them to the sun." Frank turned toward the sun and recited a litany to its healing powers. "It is the arrows of Apollo that everywhere quicken life and foster it toward ripeness. Through them, a new life springs all around, and the jubilant voice is heard that awakens the human soul."

Wynn turned to Mrs. Feeney. "Things are really picking up around here, aren't they?"

"Everyone's going to make it," she said.

Frank went into the hospital tent and reappeared with Selig. He helped the young man over to a deck chair. After tucking in a blanket around him, Frank said, "Wynn, get Wasko. He needs some color in his cheeks, too."

100

When Wynn returned, he helped Wasko sit down in the remaining deck chair. While Mary pulled a wool hat around Selig's ears, Frank placed a heavy scarf around Wasko's neck. "Take deep breaths," Frank said. "The deeper, the better."

As Cookie approached, Frank shouted in an affected French accent. "Ze best table for these young men." Acting as if he were reading a menu, he ordered for the two recovering young men. "These gentlemen would like hot tea with lemon and honey, <u>Monsieur</u>. Then from our finest hens, two poached eggs, ever so soft."

Mrs. Feeney began to chuckle, while the boys looked on in amazement.

Frank's accent began to get thicker. "Ze next course will be a piece of toast delicately browned. Make sure, <u>garcon</u>, that ze toast is dripping with butter. Later, ze <u>piece de resistance</u>, a thick, rich egg nog."

Cookie bowed in an elegant continental manner. "<u>Oui, mon Capitain</u>. Only ze best for our guests."

Selig grumbled, "Are they drunk?"

Wasko replied, "I just want to eat."

Frank motioned to Wynn. "Help them out while I take Mrs. Feeney to her car."

When Frank returned, he saw Grabowski and Dougherty standing beside the hospital tent. Loudly, Grabowski asked, "I thought these men had pneumonia. What are they doing out here?"

"I'm employing the heliotherapeutic technique."

"When are you freeing up these boys? I need them for planting season."

"Everyone will be here for two weeks minimum except Feeney and Selig. They'll be here for an additional week."

While Frank was talking, Grabowski's nose began to twitch like a rabbit's. When he walked into the tent, he took a deep breath. He stomped around the ward, constantly hitting the palm of his left hand with a riding crop, as if he were trying to make a point. Then he exploded. "This place smells like a cheap French whorehouse!"

Quietly, Frank said, "Beats the smell of death."

As some of the patients giggled, Sergeant Dougherty blurted, "As Procurement Officer, I'd like to know why you've ordered so many oranges?"

"That fruit is necessary for the men's recovery," responded Frank. "If you want to question my medical judgement any further, put it in writing and send it to my superior."

"That is not the real purpose of our visit," intervened Grabowski. Then he put his arm around Frank's shoulders. "It's come to our attention that you have a problem here."

Withdrawing from Grabowski's grasp, Frank replied, "With seven cases of pneumonia, I would have to agree with you."

"Oh, it's not that," Grabowski quickly answered. "It's your aide, Odum."

"Yes, Doctor Millet," Dougherty chimed in. "They say he's a homo."

"You mean Homo sapiens?"

"No, I mean homo as in queer!" said Grabowski.

Frank looked at Wynn, who had become visibly angry. "Let me answer this absurd charge, Wynn." Scowling, Frank said, "Lieutenant Grabowski?"

"Yes."

"Did you suffer injuries due to the War?"

"A broken leg, that's all."

"Oh, I thought the poison gas had affected your mind!" As Wynn began to laugh, Frank said, "May I remind you that we owe Wynn a great debt. Everything he did was under my direct orders." Frank used his index finger as an exclamation point, jabbing it closely to Grabowski's chin. "And what he did was akin to Dougherty's taking a civilian off the streets, giving him a gun, and then having that person perform brilliantly in combat!" As Dougherty and Grabowski retreated from the tent, Frank followed them. "This is a dastardly attack. If I hear anything more on this matter, I'll report you to Robert Fechner, who runs the whole CCC."

Wynn watched Frank pursue them down the gravel path. No longer able to hear Frank, Wynn knew that Dougherty and Grabowski were in full retreat. Then Wynn glanced at Selig and Wasko, who had heard the whole exchange.

They had smiles on their faces.

When Frank had returned, his face was still flushed. "I'm so sorry, Wynn. I'm still mad as a hornet. Those two men are a disgrace to their uniform!" As Frank walked around the tent, the redness in his face began to recede. Finally, he said, "Wynn, there's a bag of oranges sitting next to the examination table. Share it with your friends inside."

When Wynn entered the tent, Jimmy Feeney said, "Grabowski's full of shit!"

"And that's in spades, too!" said Higgleston. Pointing to the bag, he asked, "Going to give us any?"

"My mother put oranges and Brazil nuts in my Christmas stocking," said Jimmy Feeney.

Villic piped up, "Hey, Feeney, youse vas lucky. De only ting in my sock I git vas big hole!"

"But the best part always was reaching way down in the toe and finding a couple of pennies," said Feeney.

Bobby Fuller leaned on his elbow and said, "I got a piece of coal in my sock once."

Feeney began to laugh.

"What's so damn funny?"

"That's all you Scranton guys got. Lot's of hard coal."

"Get to hell out of here, Feeney," said Fuller.

The last remark signaled the start of a pillow war. Fuller and Higgleston scored direct hits on Feeney, who promptly unloaded his on Fuller. Villic heaved a pillow at Fuller, who ducked. It wrapped around Wynn's head. Everyone stopped while waiting for Wynn to react. Wynn looked at the pillow and then at Fuller. Then Wynn raised the pillow over his head and scored a direct hit on Fuller. Immediately, the war resumed its intensity.

When Frank walked inside, he ducked just in time, avoiding a direct hit from a US Army regulation pillow. "Gentlemen, you're supposed to be sick," he exclaimed as he turned tail and left the tent.

Over the next two weeks, the number of patients began to dwindle. One by one, Frank signed each man back to duty. Finally, Jimmy Feeney received the good news. Frank released him to Sergeant Dougherty.

CHAPTER NINETEEN

It was Wynn's turn to "borrow" Cookie's Ford Roadster. While Ontek pushed the car from the compound, Wynn steered. Once they reached the road, Wynn started the car and drove it slowly until they were out of earshot.

Their destination was Lindy's, a roadhouse north of Bradford, Pennsylvania, near the New York State line. Lindy's had good food, cheap booze, and women galore. It was a speakeasy and a whorehouse and a good one on both counts.

Miss Betty Kincade, an amply proportioned woman, ran the establishment with class and efficiency. Probably sixty-five, she looked considerably younger and was still an attractive woman. She always wore her blond hair at shoulder's length and her clothes were fashionable but never flashy.

When Wynn and Ontek entered the building, Miss Betty announced cheerfully, "Well, boys! What will it be? Food? Drinks? Or the works?" She winked knowingly as she approached Wynn. A broad smile spread over her face when Wynn told her how he had won enough money in poker games to stake Ontek and himself for a night's fun. In a big, friendly way, Miss Betty said, "No greater love..." Her voice tailed off as she moved closer to Wynn, her breasts almost touching him. "Why him? Looks like he needs a dose of vitamins!"

"Ontek's my best friend."

Miss Betty gently touched Wynn's arm. "That's three bucks each," she said in a business-like manner. Then she led them into the parlor and said, "Sit down and make yourselves at home."

While they waited, Wynn cleared his throat. "This your first time?" When Ontek nodded, Wynn said, "I don't believe it."

"It's the first time I've ever paid for it," Ontek said quickly. After a slight pause, he asked, "What about you?"

"There were always girls, especially after I started fighting. They'd feel my muscles, but what really turned them on was the violence of the fight game. Right after a fight, I'd be so hot and they'd rub up against me like a cat in heat." He stopped and smiled before adding, "Anyway, they were all freebies. I couldn't afford that classy house in Braddock. It was too expensive."

He was interrupted when two girls approached them.

"Hi, soldiers. I'm Miss Rose."

"And I'm Miss Ginny," whispered the other one.

"And I'm dead and gone to heaven," said Ontek as he looked at the long legs of Miss Rose. "They go on and on forever," he said.

Miss Rose tugged at Ontek's belt and beckoned him toward an open door.

"See you latter, buddy," said Ontek as Miss Rose closed the door behind him.

Miss Ginny, who had shiny, black hair, sat on Wynn's lap. "Can I be of service?" she teased as she put her arms around his neck and playfully nipped his left ear lobe. Then she took the hairpins from her hair and allowed it to tumble down around him. As she wriggled her bottom on Wynn's lap, she cooed, "I think something's coming up."

Ginny took Wynn down a dimly-lighted hallway that had four rooms on each side. She opened the door into the second room, switched on a floor lamp, and walked over to a single bed. Opposite the bed was a small cabinet containing a wash bowl and a few towels. Ginny sat down and took off her shoes. She stared at Wynn who had remained standing. "What's wrong, Sonny? Your first time."

"Naw."

"What's your business?"

"I'm in the C's."

"I heard them cooks put saltpeter in the food."

Wynn looked down at his trousers that sported a pronounced bulge. "If they did, it ain't working."

"Well then, c'mon to me baby."

When Wynn walked over to Ginny, she asked him to take off

her stockings. After that, she put his hand on a silken sash wrapped around her gown. As he held on to it, she slowly eased into bed. The loosened gown opened, revealing her breasts.

He inhaled deeply.

"What's the matter?" she asked.

"Everything is fine, except they're so small."

She cupped her breasts with her hands. "Don't you like them?"

Wynn realized that he had insulted her. To make amends, he bent down and brushed the nipples lightly with his fingertips. Then he kissed each one.

Ginny giggled. "That's nice."

"Why did you say that?"

"Most guys would be humping me by now."

He traced his hand from her breasts to her navel and then back to her breasts again. Then he held them with his hands. "Do you mind?"

"It's your money." She lifted her feet from the floor, placing them in a tuck position while pulling off her panties. Then she lay on the bed, revealing herself. Suddenly, she grabbed Wynn's necktie, using it to pull herself up. Slowly, she unbuttoned his fly and then unloosened his belt buckle. When she pulled down his pants, Ginny saw a manliness whose size interested even her. She patted the pillow suggestively. When he sat down, she loosened his tie and tossed it on the floor. As she unbuttoned his shirt, her fingers brushed against the hair on his chest. She helped him wriggle out of his shirt, and the two were in bed, naked and side by side.

Her hands moved downward until they enveloped something that had become nearly vertical. She caressed his manliness until it became moist. Then she sprung astride him, skillfully guiding it into her.

Wynn pulled her body down toward him and lifted his head so that he could nuzzle one nipple and then the other. As their bodies came together, he reveled in their erotic sounds and savored her musk-like smell. His intensity rose while he watched her breasts move in concert with his hips.

Just before a great shiver shot through him, she withdrew and took his manliness into her hands. As he unleashed one involuntary stream after another, she held it until its convulsive movements stopped. She towered over him while resting on her knees and touched her fingers to his lips and whispered, "Let me do everything."

Wynn had had sex with many young women, but those encounters were more of a push-pull click-click nature. His women were always pliant. To Wynn, sex was like boxing, a means of releasing tension. Feelings never entered into the act.

But Ginny was different. She controlled the rhythm and the flow of the movement. She lifted her body up and down, sometimes allowing him to enter her fully and other times permitting him to touch her ever so lightly. She used her long, black hair as a sexual tool, allowing it to flow over him while shrouding her total control. At other times, her tresses became hundreds of tiny switches, giving him a blissful hint of pain. Repeatedly, she delicately traced her hair slowly over his nipples and then down to his navel. She did not stop until he came with more force than the first time.

When she asked him to enter her in the missionary position, Wynn obeyed eagerly. He put his hands under her buttocks and lifted her against him, while driving deeper. As he threw his long arms around her, Wynn felt something unusual on her back. He quickly forgot about it when she wrapped her legs around him, creating a welter of arms and legs and sensual odors.

When he came again, she looked at the clock and whispered, "Time's up!" She rolled out from under him, stood up, and wrapped the gown around herself.

Wynn was surprised at her detachment. When he began to dress, he became surly. "Business is business, isn't it?"

"Just part of a night's work."

He rose from the bed, his penis now limp. Then he remembered her back. "Take off your gown! I want to see your back."

She dodged his lunge the first time. "Don't you think you ought to put your pants on? Besides, you look mighty silly with 'buster' bouncing around?"

His second attempt was successful. He pulled off her gown while twirling her around in a complete circle. When he saw her back, he exclaimed, "My God, girl! Who did that?"

She turned around and covered her breasts with her hands. "My stepdaddy. He had a awful hold over me." She closed her eyes and rubbed her hands against her body, her breasts pulsating with her sensuous movements. "Sometimes he made me feel so good! But then, he'd go and spoil it all. He'd start to boozing and then to beating me something awful. After each beating, he'd cry and cry and ask for forgiveness. Then he'd make me wear a church dress and parade around in front of him. After that, he'd beat me again."

"Why didn't you run away?"

"At first I liked it," she admitted. "But he wanted me to do all those unnatural things."

"Like what?"

"Nothing like we just did, I'll tell you that," she said. "So six months after my Mama died, I told him I was expecting. He beat me something awful. And then he <u>really</u> got drunk. That's when I busted a window, crawled out on a tin roof and shinnied down a tree. He followed me. But he was so pie-eyed that he slipped off the roof and fell kerplunk to the ground. I knew he was dead, so I ran. But the Wellsville police said I killed him. And the judge and the jury agreed." Shuddering, she explained, "Jail was worse than my stepdaddy. Some of those women were pigs! And the guards were no better. But there was one guard who protected me. For a price, I might add. He got it regularly, and I got what I wanted. Out of there! One day he just looked the other way, and I walked away from the joint." Giving a little laugh, she said, "Yeah, I escaped. But to what? Freight trains from New York to Chicago and then back again. I rode them all."

"I hung around the railroad yards a lot in Pitcairn, and I never saw girls down there."

"My first trip I was gang-banged all the way to Toledo by twenty pawing sonsabitches. They were ready to cut me real bad when a railroad dick saved me." She paused before saying, "For himself." She smiled a crooked little smile revealing stained brown teeth. Pointing to her mouth, she said, "But his dick ain't as big any more. That's when I decided that I'd better dress like a fella."

"What about your long hair?"

"I cut it off," she said sadly. Then her whole disposition changed. "Hey, kid," she squealed. "You still don't have no pants on."

Wynn looked down at his nakedness. Then he reached for his shoes and trousers. Buttoning up his pants, Wynn asked uneasily, "How did you get into this business?"

"When I hit Chicago the second time, it was either whore or starve."

"That's an awful strong word."

"Which one? Whore? Or starve?"

"I mean whore."

"That's what I am!" At least you guys don't have to sell your bodies. The CCC took you off the street and gave you a job. The government didn't do a damn thing for girls."

Puzzled, Wynn sat her down on the bed. He felt something for her, but he could not express it.

As he reached for her, she said, "Hey, wait a minute, bub. You already got your money's worth."

"No, it's not that."

"I ain't never met a guy like you before."

"Why don't you get out of this business?"

"I'm damn good at it."

Wynn remembered stories about the beatings that had occurred in the whorehouse at Braddock. And he knew there was no difference between the people up here and those who lived in the Valley. "But you might get hurt," he said.

"I can take care of myself."

"But some guys like to hurt whores."

"Miss Betty don't allow that!"

"Don't you understand what I want?"

"Sure I do. You got some good tail and you want more. Come and see me. Become a regular client. Wouldn't you like that?"

"That's not it."

She picked up a pillow, placing it between them. "You don't like me?"

"Yes, I do. But I'm afraid for you." Then he blurted, "Sleep with me and not anyone else."

She slapped Wynn on his face. "You're no different than

109

the other men I screw. Nobody twisted your arm to come here tonight." She took a deep breath, moved over to the water basin, and casually wet a wash cloth. She lifted her left leg onto the chair and began to wash between her legs. "You come sniffing around wanting action. And afterwards, you want to change me." She paused before sitting down beside him. "Want to braid my hair?" she asked in a child-like voice.

"I don't know how."

"Then I'll have to do it." As she braided it, she began to tease Wynn. "And where you going to get the dough to support me, John D.?"

"From card playing."

She started to laugh.

"And I'll have a nest egg when I get out of the C's."

"I make more in one week what you do in a month."

Wynn got up from the bed. "I'm sorry. I had no right to ask that." He walked toward the door and stopped. "Can I come up and see you? Maybe we could talk."

"You sure are one goofy guy." She twisted the wash cloth nervously as Wynn opened the door. Then she asked hesitantly, "If you saw me in Kane...That is...Would you buy me a coffee and talk to me even though everybody knew what I am?"

"Yes, Ginny. Yes, I would."

Wynn closed the door and walked into the hallway nearly bumping into another young lady and her client. He walked through the parlor and into the restaurant and joined Ontek who was eating a ham sandwich.

CHAPTER TWENTY

Staff Sergeant Cookie Garlicki presided over the Camp One mess hall. His thirty years of army field experience eminently qualified him to supply and to supervise a mess operation that arose from the mud.

Since everyone passed through the mess hall at least twice daily, it rapidly became the unofficial communications hub. Cookie and his assistants always knew what was happening. It wasn't because they were gossips. It was just that they listened carefully and then passed along the news.

Mousy Gray, a Dog Robber for Grabowski, worked the mess hall, too. With his omnipresent glass of milk in hand, Mousy oiled and greased his way from one table to another, constantly alert for news valuable to Grabowski. That's how Mousy helped expose the "inside agitator," who had encouraged enrollees to desert.

Ontek and Wynn had just begun eating their breakfast, chipped beef and gravy on toast, more commonly called shit on a shingle. Ontek looked puzzled, as if he had a problem. Gravely, Ontek asked, "How many Marx Brothers are there?"

"Five, I think." Wynn closed his eyes so he could count them. "Let's see, there's Harpo, he's the guy that can't talk. Then there's Chico, and of course, Groucho." When he opened his eyes, he put his hand to his chin, as if in deep thought. Then he remembered the others. "Gummo and Zeppo! Whenever they show up, everyone stops laughing."

"Are you sure there ain't one more?" asked Ontek.

"I've seen all their movies. I don't remember any more."

"There's got to be another one." Ontek closed his eyes and stuck his tongue through the gap in his teeth. Then after some more

111

thought, he exploded, "Karl, that's the other one! Karl Marx!"

"He started Communism," said Wynn.

"He's not in the movies?"

"No, he's not," said Wynn. "Who wants to know, anyway?"

"Last night over at the latrine, I was sitting on the throne, minding my own business. All of a sudden, Clarence O'Banion comes in and starts preaching about this Marx guy. O'Banion bitched about how the rich people use us poor folks to get more power. Is that true, Wynn?"

"We've got a job, we're eating three square meals a day, and your mom has enough money to keep the wolf away from her door," said Wynn. "All that comes from Roosevelt, not from some damn Communist."

"Before I left my seat, O'Banion had quite a crowd. He wants us to demand our rights."

During their conversation, Wynn had watched Mousy trying to eavesdrop. Finally, Wynn winked at Ontek. "Lookie at old Mousy. He dropped his knife and fork on the floor so's he could hear us better."

"On all fours, too. He looks natural, don't he?"

Wynn asked in a loud voice, "What was O'Banion yammering about?"

When Wynn winked again, Ontek said loudly, "That we should stop tree planting and road building, and all that sort of stuff."

"We're regular tools of the rich."

"How'd you know that, Wynn?"

"In high school, I did a report on the Russian Revolution." Astonished, Wynn said, "I never thought something I learned there would have any use in the real world."

Mousy craned his neck in an effort to hear them. Then he got up and joined them.

Neither Wynn nor Ontek liked Mousy. And since he had become so cozy with Grabowski, they had an additional reason to distrust him.

"Who asked him to sit down with us?" grunted Ontek.

"Can't a fella sit down?" asked Mousy. "Besides, my dogs hurt."

"Come on, Wynn. Let's eat at another table. I don't like mouse finks."

"Wait a minute!" Wynn responded. "Don't be in a rush." He put his hand on Ontek's arm. "Mousy has every right to know about the sixth Marx brother."

"The sixth Marx brother?" burbled Mousy. "Tell me! Tell me! Please."

"Jeez, Ontek, maybe good old Mousy is right."

"Yeah, tell me more about this Marx guy," begged Mousy.

While Ontek told the story, Wynn watched Mousy, who hung on Ontek's every word. Frequently, Mousy interrupted Ontek. At one point, Wynn asked, "Need some paper and a pencil? After all, you want to get this right for Grabowski."

Ignoring Wynn's comments, Mousy asked, "What's O'Banion's next move?"

"He's talked three fellas into taking off," Ontek answered. "After lights out, they're meeting at the bridge, and they're going to walk out to the highway."

"That'll make fifteen desertions in two weeks," said Mousy.

"From there, a car's waiting to take them to Pittsburgh."

"Ain't that something?" marveled Mousy, who suddenly excused himself, claiming that he had diarrhea.

Wynn looked out the window and watched Mousy run toward Grabowski's office. "That little bugger has diarrhea, all right. Diarrhea of the mouth!" Wynn poured two cups of coffee and brought them to Ontek's table. When Wynn looked out the window again, he saw Grabowski and Dougherty steam into the compound. Mousy was behind them, barely able to keep up. When the condensation from the steam kettles clouded the windows, Wynn used his handkerchief to wipe them clean. Then he saw Grabowski and Dougherty enter O'Banion's tent. Satisfied, Wynn said quietly, "Good-bye and good riddance, you red sonnavabitch."

Ontek asked, "What did you say?"

"Oh, I just said that Red's going to work us like sonnavabitches today." Wynn put down his empty cup. "Come on pal. We've had a busy breakfast. Let's go to work."

"Wait a minute, Wynn."

"What's wrong, buddy? You still got a problem?"

"Well...Yes."

"What is it?"

"I'm afraid to say for fear you might laugh."

"Try me."

"Fighting fires is dangerous, ain't it?" Ontek kept his eyes fixed in his coffee cup. Groping for words, Ontek said, "If I die...In a fire, I want...You to have this ring. It was my father's." He held the ring in his palm so Wynn could see it.

"If you what?"

"You heard me."

"What the hell are you talking about?"

"I've got an awful feeling."

Wynn closed Ontek's fingers over the ring. "Come off it! Nothing's going to happen."

Ontek persisted. "In case something does, I want you to have it."

"As long as I'm around, nothing will happen to you."

Ontek playfully punched Wynn's shoulder. "Promise?"

"A promise." Wynn put his arm around Ontek's shoulders and said, "Now put that smile back on your face, and let's go to work, pal."

Work never stopped in the mess hall, for it was a full-time operation. Either Cookie or Dutch, whom Grabowski had recently promoted to First Cook, was always in the mess hall. Soon everyone realized that the guys behind the serving lines were good listeners.

As significantly, Cookie frequently offered advice.

On a late spring morning, Wynn came over for a cup of coffee. He looked depressed. While he drank his coffee, Cookie sat down beside him. Wynn continued sipping the coffee, while staring straight ahead.

Putting his arm around Wynn's shoulder, Cookie tried to console the young man. "Need someone to talk to?"

Wynn pushed the coffee cup away as if it had burned his lips. "It's this girl."

"You mean at Lindy's?"

"How'd you know?"

"I saw you there three or four times. You was just sitting there like you wanted to see someone real bad."

"She's still screwing everybody."

"Ginny's like a democratic drawbridge," said Cookie. "She goes down for everyone."

"I just want to have her as a friend."

"If you want friendship, buy a dog."

"I want to talk to her, Cookie."

"You're thinking with your dingus."

"What of it?"

"Wynn, your bad for business. Sam, that big nigger who works for Miss Betty, is going to beat the shit out of you if you don't stop bothering them."

"Who said so?"

"Miss Betty asked me to talk to you like a Dutch Uncle, because the customers think you're checking up on them."

"I must see Ginny again."

"You're staying three steps ahead of Grabowski. Red promoted you to Sergeant, and the Doc's real high on you. But here you are, acting like a sick cow."

"Why won't she talk?"

"She don't get paid to talk! Besides why in God's name are you interested in her?"

"Maybe, she reminds me of myself. Both of us grew up on the run."

"Jesus, Wynn. If you throw a bag over Ginny's head and turn her upside down, she'll look like every other dame in the world."

Not willing to listen to Cookie's logic, Wynn got up from the table. "I want her on my terms."

"Wynn, you're riding for a fall."

Wynn stalked out of the building, not hearing Cookie's warning. As Wynn went down the steps, he accidentally stumbled into O'Donnel, who reacted by pushing Wynn against a railing.

After apologizing, O'Donnel whispered, "I screwed your old lady on Saturday night. That twat gave me the best blow job I ever had."

Fortunately, Red Dawson had followed O'Donnel up the steps. When Wynn lunged at O'Donnel, Red darted between them. "We got bigger problems than your personal differences, gentlemen. The first big fire of the year just blew up on the Clarion River near Hallton. Now we're going to put your training to the big test."

CHAPTER TWENTY-ONE

The Clarion River fire was not one fire, but a series of smaller fires ignited by thunderstorms that had moved quickly through the area. Spreading from tall hemlock trees, the fires flashed through the thick underbrush, and like fingers on a hand, they climbed steadily up the steep ridges. Burning embers spewed into the air and fell a quarter of a mile ahead, creating smaller fires. Eventually, the spot fires merged into one great fire, advancing up the mountain and feeding on itself.

Wynn drove the Ford truck as fast as good sense would allow. Red rode shotgun and never looked up from his topo maps. The remainder of the crew sat in the cramped rear of the truck. When they reached Hallton, Wynn saw people outside looking anxiously at the smoke.

Upon seeing the CCC truck, a man yelled, "This isn't going to be another Bear Creek fire, is it?"

"Not if we can help it," Red yelled through the open window.

Wynn drove upstream from Hallton another three miles before the road turned sharply up hill. When he saw wisps of smoke ahead, he stopped the truck and looked at the steep climb. "Are we going to make that?"

"It's only an eight per cent grade," said Red.

"What if the fire's crossed the road?"

Red looked skyward. "It hasn't yet, but let's not lollygag down here."

Halfway up the grade, Red pointed out Wynn's window. "If the fire jumps the road into that ravine, it could run unchecked for miles!"

Wynn looked into the gorge. "Must be a thirty degree slope straight down two hundred feet."

"That's nothing but trouble down there," said Red. "If you go in there, you'd be climbing from tree top to tree top." When the truck reached the top of the hill, he patted Wynn's arm and said, "I just wanted to keep your mind at ease."

"Red, I always liked your chin music." Wynn relaxed when the road ahead descended gently. He drove another mile before stopping at Buehler's Corners, located at the intersection of the Owls Nest and the Arroya roads.

As the men scrambled from the truck, Red announced, "This will be our command post." Then he looked toward the river where the smoke billowed into the sky. "The fire's too big for us to knock down. We've got to scout this one and then get some help." As he flattened a topo map on the hood of the truck, he called, "Witkowski! Cartwright."

"Yes, Sir," both men replied.

"Go due west for four miles." He tapped the map and said, "That'll bring you out at the gas fields, right here. Then blaze a trail back to our position."

"How long will that take?" asked Cartwright.

"Report to me at 1400." He winked at the two young men. "Just act like it's one of my little walks." Next he gave an assignment to O'Donnel and Malone. "From here, walk back one mile on the road to Hallton."

"You mean the road we just was on?" asked O'Donnel.

"Yes," answered Red. "Then turn due south and hike another mile until you come to a ridge that overlooks the river. Eyeball the fire from there. Give me a report by 1200." As they left, Red checked his maps for defensive positions to stop the fire.

"Why not use the Arroya road as a fire break?" asked Wynn.

Red agreed. "Good point. That goes straight down to the river." As he began to fold the map, he said, "Cartwright and Witkowski have got to come through. My ulcer tells me we will win or lose the battle on their line."

"What's for us?" complained Zambini.

"Nothing glamorous," Red replied. "Wynn and I will hightail it back to Hallton where I'll contact Grabowski." He pointed to the others. "Set up the Bell tent as the command post. Then build a fire

118

line within the perimeter of the clearing. I don't want this place under danger."

After the men had unloaded the truck, he and Wynn drove back to Hallton where Red found a telephone. He counted the rings impatiently.

When Mousy Gray finally answered the phone, Red said, "I want to talk to Lieutenant Grabowski."

"He ain't here."

"Where is he?"

"Over at his quarters."

"Get him!"

Finally, Grabowski came to the phone. "How bad is it?"

"I need a hundred-fifty boys down here, pronto! And tell Doctor Millet to come also. I'll have an aide station set up for him."

"I ordered more transportation when I heard how big the fire was."

"Good idea, Lieutenant! By the way, the safest way here will be to Four Corners, then over to Owls Nest. Our command post's at the intersection of those roads."

"What's wrong with the road through Hallton?" asked Grabowski.

"The fire will probably close it down."

"I'll be there by early tomorrow morning."

"Good! I'll have the attack plans drawn up by then."

Heavy smoke made their drive back to the command post more difficult. When they started up the hill, Red saw flying embers shooting across the road. "Don't slow down, kid, or we're going to get our asses scorched!"

Wynn down-shifted, and the truck lurched ahead. He clutched the steering wheel tightly as the high-pitch whine of the transmission became louder. "I hope this baby's good for one more mile," he yelled over the engine noise.

"I lost a truck at the Bear Creek fire," confessed Red. "As I was trying to outrun a fire, this damn Dodge truck died. And because of it, me and Jim Simpson almost died, too."

Wynn did not hear any of Red's confession, because an explosion averted Wynn's attention. Through the mirror he saw a fireball roll across the road, disappearing below them. "What the hell was that?"

"A blow up!" said Red. "It's headed toward the gas fields. If they blow, the whole damn county will get a hot-foot." When the truck reached the summit, Red patted the dashboard. "You can always count on a Ford when you really need it."

Upon reaching the command post, Red jumped out and signaled Ontek to join them. "I got to find out how big this sucker is. So I want you and Wynn to hike down to the river and locate the fire. I need information. What direction is it moving? What's on the forest floor? How fast is it running? And be back here at 1600."

"Want us to take our fire rakes?" asked Wynn.

"You might have to use them." Then he hit them on their butts and shouted, "Watch it boys. It's dangerous out there."

The first mile was all down hill, but when Wynn and Ontek reached the river, the walking became tougher. They crawled over, through, or around hemlock tops fifteen feet high. As they moved closer to the fire, they heard a high-pitched, wavering sound.

"What's that?" asked Ontek.

"Hemlock sap singing. It's being boiled out of the hemlock."

When they reached the fire's edge, they could not look directly into it. Coughing badly, Wynn muttered, "It's like looking into a smoke-filled tunnel."

"There's no way we're going to get Red any information."

"Then we have to go downstream. I won't go back empty-handed."

As they continued picking their way through the debris, Ontek slipped from a rotting log. Through a maze of dead tree tops, he yelled, "Maybe we ought to try swimming down the river."

Watching Ontek crawl through ground clutter, Wynn shouted, "Mind you don't eyeball no rattlers!"

"Hey, thanks a lot, pal." After that, Ontek whipped everything with his fire rake.

Suddenly, hemlock trees, a hundred yards from them, exploded, shooting embers skyward.

Awestruck, they stood there watching nature's fireworks.

"The green needles just went up into flame!" marveled Wynn.

"Like Roman Candles."

The intense heat forced them to retreat. When Wynn looked again, he made a frightening discovery. "The fire's jumped the river."

"You're kidding," said Ontek. "It's nearly two hundred feet wide."

Wynn pointed to the other side. "Then what's causing the smoke?" Knowing exactly what had to be done, Wynn said, "Ontek?" As Ontek looked quizzically at him, Wynn asked, "You know how to swim?"

"Sure, but ain't the river awful wide?"

When Ontek seemed hesitant, Wynn shouted, "Damn it, let's go!" Holding his fire rake above his head, Wynn waded into the river. He looked back at Ontek who stood on the river bank. "Come on," Wynn said. "Make Judge Parsons proud of you."

Suddenly, Ontek shouted, "Shee...it," and jumped into the river.

The water was warm and the current was not swift. They swam nearly a hundred feet before finally touching bottom. Then, half-swimming and half-crawling, they reached the other side.

Turning their attention to the spot fires, Wynn and Ontek began to put them out. One old stump had a particularly stubborn fire at its edges. Wynn successfully extinguished it by scraping fresh soil over it. Within one hour, they had put out three more.

As they waited for more spot fires, Wynn began to feel nervous. "It's awful quiet over here."

"Not a leaf's moving" said Ontek.

Wynn looked over to the other side of the river. "The fire's so hot that it's making its own wind."

"Look," said Ontek. "It's being sucked right up over the ridge toward the gas fields."

"Let's cross back and report to Red."

While fighting the spot fires, they had traveled three hundred yards downstream. When they reentered the river, the bottom suddenly dropped off.

"The current's swift," warned Wynn, who swam easily ahead. When he glanced back, he saw Ontek thrashing about. "What's wrong?"

"I can't straighten my leg out."

Wynn thrust his fire rake toward Ontek, who grabbed the handle so forcibly that it twisted them into the current. Swept quickly downstream, they spun out of control. Both went under and then resurfaced thirty feet downstream. Coughing badly, Wynn grabbed an edge of a large boulder that protruded from the water. He watched helplessly as Ontek smashed against the rock before bobbing downstream. Wynn released his grip on the rake and pushed off the rock, using the current to his advantage. With short, powerful strokes, he reached his companion as the current's force temporarily pinned them against another boulder. Wynn renewed his grip on Ontek just as the fire rake popped out of the water. He caught it with his other hand.

They clung to the rock until Ontek, whose head was bleeding, regained consciousness. "Thanks, pal," he gasped.

"We're not out of the soup yet," said Wynn. "Can you make it?"

"I'll follow when I get my second wind."

"No way, pal! We're doing this together."

"I'm done for, Wynn."

"If anything happens to you," said Wynn, "Red's going to be pissed."

"Tell him it was my fault," gasped Ontek.

"If you die, Red's going to kill me first and then you."

Ontek held his head upright and spit water from his mouth. "Yeah, he might really do that." Suddenly, a frightened Ontek screamed, "I can't feel my legs!"

Wynn responded like a teacher instructing a pupil. "We're going to let go of this rock, and I'll help you. Don't let go of the rake, understand?" He looked into Ontek's eyes. They were glassy. That frightened Wynn more than the water raging around them. "On the count of three, we'll shove off and head for shore." As Ontek began to slip under the water again, Wynn counted, "One, two, and three!" His momentum dragged Ontek with him.

Immediately, Ontek went under, but Wynn pulled him to the surface. They spun dizzily downstream until Wynn regained control. Then he swam diagonally toward the current's edge. As he struggled with an exhausted Ontek, Wynn felt the current weakening until he finally touched bottom. When he reached the river bank, Wynn gave the rake handle a sharp tug and heaved Ontek to solid ground.

Both men lay on the ground face down.

When Wynn stopped coughing, he began to laugh. "Red never trained us for this!" he said.

"Shows he ain't perfect."

When Wynn saw blood trickling down Ontek's face, he asked, "How you doing?"

Ontek turned over on his back. "I wish the sky would stop spinning."

"We got a tough climb back," said Wynn. "Let's stay here for an hour."

"I'll drink to that." As he closed his eyes, Ontek said, "Hey, Wynn."

"Now what?"

"I bet Red has already shit two bricks wondering what's become of us."

CHAPTER TWENTY-TWO

When Wynn and Ontek limped back to the compound, they were amazed at the changes that had occurred. Three large tents had been erected, while a team of men unloaded supplies.

When Wynn spotted the hospital tent, he said, "Look, Doc's here. You better go see him, buddy."

"Naw, I ain't that bad." As Ontek took a deep breath, he said, "Cookie and Dutch's here, too."

"How'd you know?"

"I can smell food a mile away."

"That bump didn't affect your nose, did it?"

"I still got ringing in my ears, though."

"That's better than bats in your belfry."

Ontek held his hands up as if he were surrendering. "Don't make me laugh. My head still hurts." As they walked through the compound, he said, "This here place looks like a war scene."

"It is a war," growled Red, who had walked up behind them. "And where in hell have you two been? You're four hours late."

"For a walk in the woods," said Ontek.

"Come off it, wiseacre." Then Red saw Ontek's injury. "What hit you?" he asked.

"A rock."

"And the rock won," said Wynn.

Red turned Ontek around and pointed him toward the hospital. "Doc's got to look at you."

"But Red."

"No goddamned buts! You're finished." Red turned to Wynn. "Let's take him to Doc."

"What about the fire?" asked Wynn.

"It'll be there when we get back."

As they entered the hospital, they saw Frank treating a young man. When Frank had finished, Red said, "Here's another one, Doc."

Frank motioned to Ontek. "Get up on the table."

"Can Wynn and I talk to the other patients while you work on him?" asked Red. When Frank agreed, Red walked over to the young man whom Frank had just treated. "What happened, son?"

"Sparks set my shirt on fire, but the Doc says I'll be good as new in a couple of days."

"How was it out there?" asked Red.

"I was scared as hell."

"Who was in charge?"

"That Witkowski kid. He had nerves of steel. When the fire closed in on us, he led us right out of there. He always had that map in his hands, like it was guiding him."

Red patted the young man on his arm. "Thanks, kid. Get some rest."

Wynn walked over to another man whose face was swollen badly. "Who hit you?"

Through puffy lips, the young man answered, "A son of a B of a bee bit me."

"Fires always stir up bees and hornets," explained Red. "Back on the Bear Creek fire...I knew of a guy who swallowed two hornets when he was drinking coffee."

When Wynn noticed that the young man had his shoes off, he asked, "Something wrong with your feet?"

"My socks ran down in my shoes. While I was fighting the fire, I could feel the blisters forming. By the time I came off the line, I could hardly walk."

Noticing that Frank had finished with Ontek, Wynn asked, "How is he, Doc?"

"He had a concussion, but his responses are good." Then Frank asked, "Wynn, after he was hit on the head, did you notice anything strange about his behavior?"

"He was pretty weak when we climbed out of the river. And it took an hour before I could get him to start walking. Even then, we had to take it real slow."

"He told me that you saved his life."

"I just gave him a swimming lesson, that's all."

Red patted Wynn on his back. "You're one helluva piece of work, Odum."

"When will he be able to work?" asked Wynn.

"I'm holding him for observation. If everything's normal, I'll discharge him tomorrow."

"Thanks, Doc," said Wynn.

Then Red turned to Frank. "What kind of injuries are coming in?"

"Nothing serious," said Frank. "Mostly blisters, some burns, and a few cuts. He pointed to the young man with the swollen face. "The wasps have caused the most trouble."

"Yeah," said Red. "They're always a problem."

"Five men have been stung. Fortunately, he's the only multiple sting victim."

"Can I talk to Ontek?" asked Wynn.

"Certainly."

Wynn walked over to Ontek, who was snoring loudly. Smiling at his sleeping friend, Wynn said, "He sounds normal to me."

Red touched Wynn's arm. "C'mon kid, we've got work to do."

Wynn tentatively touched Ontek's bed. "Doc, tell him...The ring's still his."

Wynn and Red walked from the hospital over to the command post. Before they went inside, Wynn stopped.

"What's wrong?" asked Red.

"I just want to say thanks, Red."

"For what?"

"Your training saved our asses."

When they entered the tent, their suppers were waiting. While they ate, Wynn told Red of their close call.

The food and the report revitalized Red. He slapped Wynn on the shoulders and pointed to a cot. "Get some sleep. The humidity will keep the fire down until morning. Then we'll jump on it."

Wynn took his shoes off and loosened his belt. When he collapsed on the cot, he heard Red humming "Old Man River."

CHAPTER TWENTY-THREE

The sun had not risen when Red's crew stumbled into the command post. When they sat down, Red began to brief them. "Lets get down to the basics," he said. "First off, I'm going to hold O'Donnel and Witkowski's crews in reserve."

"What about Malone's squad?" asked Zambini.

"They're out in the field." Everybody else except Wynn will take a crew and build a fire line to the gas fields." ·

"How'd we know what direction to go?" asked Zambini.

"Cartwright blazed the trail. He'll go with the lead team. Make sure you have your maps, because you're going to need them."

At daybreak, Peaches Oskowski brought Wynn and Red their breakfast. When they had begun to eat, Peaches said, "Three busses just pulled into the compound, Sir." Then he said, "There's two guys walking over here."

"Who are they?"

"I dunno, Sir."

"It's Grabowski and Jim Simpson."

"Who's Jim Simpson?" asked Wynn.

"The Fire Control Chief." When Wynn looked at Red dumbly, Red said, "Remember? He's the guy who was with me back on Bear Creek."

All business, Simpson wanted an immediate briefing. After Red had completed that, Simpson asked, "What about the inexperienced men out there?"

"A member of my crew is in charge of each squad. Right now they're building fire lines," answered Red as he showed Simpson the boundaries of the fire.

As he looked at the map, Simpson said, "I've got an idea."

"You're the boss," replied Red.

"Let's extend the fire line south from the gas wells down to the river. That way, we'll have the fire boxed in."

"That's dangerous terrain," replied Red.

"You vouch for your leaders?" asked Simpson. When Red nodded in agreement, Simpson said, "Then let's do it."

Red turned to Wynn, who had been listening. "Pick ten men and hook up with Malone's crew. Start at the gas wells and lay down a line toward the river."

Wynn left the command post immediately and selected men from the reserve pool. They gathered around him, as he spread out the map, glimpsing for the first time the extent of their job.

"We got to dig that far?" asked Timmy Nedshe.

"We got to walk to it?" asked Bobby Fuller.

"Know a better way?" asked Wynn. Then he retraced their route again. Before he dismissed them to the mess tent, he warned, "Eat a big meal. We're going to be there for a long time."

Within twenty minutes, the men had returned. As Wynn checked their equipment, he cautioned them. "Blouse your pants and make sure your shoes are tied tight and your socks are pulled up."

"Why?" asked Ivan Ruttman.

"Snakes and blisters!" he said.

As he led the men into the woods, Wynn decided not to match Red's standard pace. He felt it was unrealistic for inexperienced men.

Initially, the trip was all down hill. They walked, skidded, and slid until reaching the bottom of the ridge. As they took a short break, Timmy Nedshe looked up the steep incline and asked, "We got to climb up there?"

"The fire line Lefty Malone's crew dug will make it easier," said Wynn. His assessment was correct. They made it to the top in less than thirty minutes. When they got there, Malone's crew was waiting.

During the next three miles, their pace slowed significantly. Wynn ran from the front to the rear of the column, encouraging and helping his crew. He pulled Timmy Nedshe from the line and adjusted his shoulder pack. When Fuller and Ruttman slipped and rolled down the hill, Wynn helped them up. He even took Ruttman's Indian sprayer and carried it to the ridge top.

When they reached the gas fields, they began to build a fire line. "How many miles do we have to do?" yelled Ruttman.

"If I told you, it'll break your heart," said Wynn.

As the men dug the line, Wynn moved ahead, taking compass readings and adjusting the direction. Meanwhile, Malone made sure the men had dug the line properly.

When Bobby Fuller started to scream, Wynn ran over to him. "What's the matter?"

"I killed a snake."

"Where is it?"

"It must have got away."

"We've got to find it and kill it." Wynn took his rake and scraped underneath a large rock. When he heard the tell-tale rattling sound, he shined his flashlight under the stone. In one deft movement, Wynn jammed the rake against the creature, cutting it in half. When he pulled it out, the crew surrounded him.

"How long is it?"

"About five feet."

"What's the bulge in it?"

"Most likely ate a squirrel." Then Wynn severed the snake's head with his shovel. "Never leave a rattler's head on. Maybe three days from now, Fuller comes along and steps on it. The fangs still contain poison. Shortly after that, his mom gets a letter from Grabowski telling her what a good boy she had." Wynn dug a hole two feet deep. He placed the head into the hole and covered it with fresh brown dirt. Then he tamped it with his shovel. "If you want, I can save the body and give it to Cookie. Rattlesnake meat is as sweet as chicken."

Fuller made an ugly face. "I'd rather starve."

"I'd rather get back to work," responded Wynn.

"Beats the hell out of eating snake," offered Fuller.

The line had not progressed more than another hundred yards when two more men began screaming. When Wynn reached them, Timmy Nedshe had chopped a rattlesnake into small pieces. He kept striking it again and again until Wynn grabbed his arm.

"You can only kill it once, Timmy!"

"But the snake's dangerous."

Other crew members murmured in agreement.

Wynn jumped up on a large rock and spoke confidently. "The snakes are moving. They sense the fire, but that's no reason to kill them. Make sure your pants are tucked into your boots. That'll give you plenty of protection, because they can't reach above your knees." He turned to Timmy and ordered, "Bury the snake's head. The rest of you, back to the line. Your enemy's the fire not the snakes."

Once the line had begun moving again, Malone said, "Your speech saved the day."

"The snakes' movement bothers me," admitted Wynn. "Do you s'pose they can tell the fire's getting close?"

Malone shrugged his shoulders. "If it's getting closer to them, then it must be closer to us, too!"

As the crew moved down the ridge, Wynn noticed the smoke thickening. He called a halt to the digging, and motioned for Malone to join him. As they talked, Wynn saw sparks falling below him. "Stay behind the fire line," ordered Wynn.

Suddenly, there was a terrific roar as the fire blew up the ridge.

Fascinated, Wynn said, "It sounds like a freight train."

"It's coming straight for us," yelled Malone.

"Keep your wits about you!" shouted Wynn.

As the fire gained momentum, it created its own draft. Trees burned from the ground upwards to twenty feet, while the underbrush generated an intense heat.

The crew huddled behind the tenuous safety of a fire line while the fire devoured part of the ridge less than two hundred yards away.

"Doggies," said Newt Blaustine. "That fire's just gobbling up everything."

Then Eddie Lipchack screamed, "It's behind us." Before anyone could react, he bolted down the hill.

Wynn leaped over the line and raced after Lipchack, knocking him down with a flying tackle. They rolled to a stop in a small run that cut through the valley. Wynn held the struggling lad firmly with a leg-lock. As Wynn looked up, he saw a flame-front roaring toward them.

"Quit trying to drown me," screamed Lipchack.

When Lipchack tried to get up, Wynn punched him, knocking the frightened young man into the water. Shoving the kid toward the high side of the stream bank, Wynn said, "This water's not deep enough to drown in. Let's hope we don't get boiled alive in it!"

Lying face down, Wynn heard the flames hiss over him, and he still saw the reflection of the flames dancing over and around them. Then he felt his clothes getting warmer, almost to the point of discomfort. He became frightened when the water appeared to be boiling around him. Everything within his body urged him to jump out of there and start running. Fortunately, he quickly realized the "bubbles" were caused by tiny particles of debris dropping into the stream. As his fright subsided and his reason began to prevail, an ominous quiet descended. Now he couldn't see anything as a heavy cloud of smoke enveloped them like a deadly shroud. He could feel the unconscious Lipchack breathing, but Wynn could not hear anything else but his own rapid heartbeat. Agonizing minutes passed before he dared move. Finally, he poked his head above the stream bank.

When he stood up, Wynn heard the crew shouting, "He's alive! He's alive!"

Newt and Malone raced down the hill toward them. Newt jumped into the creek and gave Wynn a big bear hug, while Malone shouted, "They're all right."

Dazed, Lipchack asked, "What happened?"

"Y'all don't remember?" asked Newt.

Then Lipchack said, "You hit me, Wynn."

"You dumb galoot," laughed Malone. "This guy saved your life."

Wynn looked around at the smoldering forest floor. Everything was charred. "It's good to be alive."

As they left the run, Wynn said to Newt, "I'll need a head count."

"Sure, no problem." Newt hurried ahead and took a quick count. When Wynn arrived, Newt said, "Everyone present."

In The Shadow Of The Trees

As they looked down on the charred and smoldering area, Newt Blaustine said, "This reminds me of the Sunday a couple of years ago when my daddy took me to the Holy Lightness Church. We watched a few men pass rattlesnakes and copperheads back and forth like they were Christmas presents. The preacher told them they would be safe as long as they were true believers. He even quoted The Book of Matthew. But one man must have got careless because a big old copperhead bit him right on the juggler vein. He heaved the snake against the wall and fell over holding his neck. No one went near him as he twitched and kicked. Then he just laid there real silent. The preacher said he was dead, but even worse, he pronounced the dead man as a sinner, someone who was burning in Hell right that minute. That got the preacher to preach a long a sermon. He told us about the fire, brimstone, the smoke, and what's it like for a soul to have to live in the bowels of Hell for all eternity." Newt looked at Wynn and then up to the sky before adding, "Well now, I can go home and look that preacher straight into his eye and tell him he ain't the only one who's looked into the flaming pit. There was one right here, today. And I lived to tell about it!"

Wynn felt old, so much older than the young men who surrounded him. He remembered Frank's talking about all the young men who had died in France. At one time, Wynn thought that death was an old man's fear. But the day's events made him recognize his mortality. It was a sobering feeling. Now he understood why Red always said that fighting fire was a war. And in every war, there were losses. Today, Wynn knew that fate had favored them.

Quickly, he snapped out of his reflective mood. "Malone, you're in charge. I want your crew to continue digging the line toward the river. Blaustine...Take my squad and widen the line around the gas fields."

Malone asked, "What are you going to do?"

"Go back to the command post, and get backfire equipment.

"How long will it take?"

"I'll use Red's pace."

"Yeah, I know," said Malone. "One mile per fifteen minutes."

"If I hurry, it'll take me an hour."

132

CHAPTER TWENTY-FOUR

When Wynn walked into the command post, Red was sitting at an engineer's table, studying a map. Without looking up, he asked "Got any news about the explosion near Odum's crew?"

"Are you going to send out a search party for me?" asked Wynn as he touched Red's shoulder.

Upon hearing Wynn's voice, Red nearly jumped out of his chair. He pumped Wynn's hand and shouted, "You're a sight for sore eyes!" After he had determined that Wynn had not been injured, Red asked, "What the hell are you doing back here?"

"I came back to get your approval for a backfire."

"But you left your crew."

"It's in good hands. Malone's men are digging toward the river, and Newt Blaustine's taking my crew to the gas fields."

"Who's Blaustine?"

"The best man I have out there."

What about the backfire?" asked Red.

"If you approve it, we can go out there and lay it down before midnight."

Red began to pace around the tent. Then he leaned against the tent's ridge pole. "I've always fought fires by my gut feelings." He pointed at his belly and said, "Just like you did when you were in the ring. Fire fighting is just out-guessing the enemy." Red tapped the map with his pointer. "We've got it contained on two sides, and we know which way it's running." He studied the map again and said, "A backfire will work. What's the status of your crew?"

"Great, Red! They worked like troopers, today."

Peaches interrupted them. "Cookie sent me over with some food, Sir."

When they began to eat, Wynn asked, "Ontek been released from the hospital yet?"

"This afternoon."

"Where is he?"

"Walking the Arroya road."

"What about O'Donnel?"

"I sent him out an hour ago."

"Where?"

"He was supposed to cover a sector of your line."

As Red finished eating, Jim Simpson walked into the command post. "How are things?" he asked.

Red used the pointer to show Simpson the location of each crew. Then Red said, "Wynn wants to backfire."

As Simpson studied the map, he said, "That's quite a recommendation for someone on his first big fire."

"I've got no problems with it," said Red.

"It'll work, Sir."

"There's a heavy dew on the ground," said Simpson.

Red looked up from his map. "Let's go out there, hook up with the main body of the crew, and start a backfire. Any objection?" When Simpson remained quiet, Red said, "I'll go to the supply tent and get the fusees." Pointing to Wynn, Red said, "Go to the mess tent and get enough food for the crew. I'll meet you back here in thirty minutes."

Wynn was inside the tent waiting when Red returned. They put the food in the larger pack and the fusees in two smaller shoulder packs. After putting on a pack with the food, Wynn reached for a shoulder pack. "I'll carry this," he said.

"Brawn before brains," Red said.

With Red in the lead, they left the road and plunged into the darkness. When they lost sight of the camp lights, Wynn said, "I don't think I'll ever get used to this awful darkness."

"You ought to try it when it's foggy," said Red. As they jogged down the first ravine, Red asked, "One mile per fifteen minutes?"

"You bet."

"Think you'll keep up?"

134

"She...it!" responded Wynn.

As they moved through the first burnt-out area, Red stopped to check the fire damage. After a short deliberation, he observed, "Still some hot-spots, but the mop-up crew can put them out."

When they started to climb from the valley, Red began to see men standing on hemlock stumps. "What the hell's going on?" he asked.

"It's the snakes, Sir."

"What snakes?"

"Rattlesnakes, Sir. The men's up there because they're scared stiff of being bit."

"Who's your crew leader?"

"O'Donnel, Sir."

"What's your name, son?"

"Jefferson Post, Sir."

"Scared of snakes?"

"Hell no! I'm a Georgia boy. I killed two under my porch last summer."

"Good," said Red. "You're crew leader now. I want somebody walking the line all night to make sure the fire doesn't jump the line. Got any problems with that?"

The young man shook his head. "No, Sir," he said.

Then Red's voice echoed throughout the valley. "O'Donnel, where in hell are you?"

Finally, O'Donnel stumbled from the darkness. "What's the problem, Red?"

"Plenty," said Red. "Post's in charge of your crew."

"But..."

"Take Wynn's extra pack," Red ordered. We've got a lot of work ahead.

Immediately, Red started climbing the steep ridge while O'Donnel accepted the pack from Wynn and quickly followed. Halfway up the ridge, Red stopped. "I've got some more news for you, Wynn."

"If it's bad I don't want to hear it."

"It's the weather report."

"Let's hear it."

"Thunderstorms are moving in," he said while leaning against a tree. When O'Donnel had caught up with them, Red moved out quickly. "The only problem is that high winds may accompany the storms."

"That could spell trouble for the backfire."

Red entertained no notion of a failure of the backfire as he explained the maneuver to the crew. "The basic idea is simple," he said. "You start a fire to end a fire."

"Ain't that dangerous?" asked Timmy Nedshe.

"Not if it's done right,"replied Red.

Wynn took out the fusees. Each was about fifteen inches long and looked like a stick of dynamite. "Handle these babies with care," he said.

"Don't railroads use them?" asked Timmy Nedshe.

Red nodded his head.

"When we was kids, me and my brother stole them from the railroad shack to play with them."

Wynn looked at Nedshe in disbelief. "And you're afraid of rattlesnakes?"

Red handed Nedshe a fusee. "Since you know all about them, you've got a job."

All smiles, Nedshe said, "Gee, thanks Red."

"Always set backfires after dark," Red told the crew. "That way, the humidity is higher. And always start them between the fire line and the approaching fire." He wet his finger and held it in the air. "The wind is blowing toward the fire. Tomorrow, the main fire should suck the backfire toward it at a pretty good clip. When they collide, there'll be an explosion. Then both fires will go out."

After Red had distributed the fusees, he stood inside the line ready to help. Nedshe held the lead position and moved along easily. O'Donnel followed behind by twenty feet.

Red watched O'Donnel setting fire to everything. "Hey, Wynn," said Red pointing to O'Donnel. "Doesn't he look like one of those aborigines pictured in NATIONAL GEOGRAPHIC." Laughing, Red added, "Especially the way he's dancing around that fire."

The smoke rolled back to Wynn when he began his run. He only went a few footsteps when he fell and skidded thirty feet before

136

hitting a stump. He dropped his fusee, but Red tossed him another one. Going up the ridge was easier, because Nedshe and O'Donnel had slowed down. When Wynn reached the top, he saw a solid line of fire slowly burning toward the main fire.

"Good work, men," shouted Red. "Now let's grab the rakes and widen the line." After the crew had doubled the line, Red called a halt. They had worked into the early morning hours. "Gather around," he shouted. "You guys have done a fine job," he said.

Timmy Nedshe interrupted Red. "When are we going to eat?"

"We brought along sandwiches," replied Red. "Eat and then get some sleep. I'll stand the first watch. Nedshe and O'Donnel will take over in two hours. Wynn, you take the final watch. It'll be getting daylight by that time."

As Red and Wynn passed out the food, the men wolfed it down and looked for a comfortable place to sleep. When they found it, they used their ponchos for ground cover and were soon asleep.

By the next morning, Red sent a crew under Newt Blaustine to patrol the gas fields to the river. Then Red ordered everyone else to head back to the command post.

Climbing over the first ridge, they heard an explosion.

"What was that?" asked Wynn.

"The backfire meeting the main fire," answered Red.

As they climbed the second ridge, the wind began to blow, causing the clouds to move in rapidly. "What we need," said Red, "is a good old fashioned Allegheny downpour."

"The wind is blowing pretty strong," said Wynn. "But so far, I don't see it spreading any sparks."

As the rain began to fall, it stuck the hot spots causing puffs of steam to rise. While Wynn walked through it, he said, "It looks like we're in some type of a ghost movie."

Wynn began to walk faster when he saw men in the distance. Watching them come closer, he broke into a large smile. "Hey, Ontek," he yelled. "It's about time that you stopped goofing off."

When the two young men reached each other, Ontek picked up Wynn and whirled him around as if he were a polka dancer who had lost his sense of direction. "You old bugger," Ontek exclaimed, "I thought you was lost."

"Hell no," said Wynn. "I knew where I was all the time."

Red walked up between them, placing his arms around their shoulders. "You two guys did one helluva job on this fire."

Simpson joined Red and his two brightest students. "Gentlemen, if it hadn't been for you, this fire would still be burning. Then he turned to the crew. "You CCC boys have made a believer out of me." He stopped and looked at the blackened ridge. "For the first time, I believe we have the upper hand."

Then another voice prevailed. "Red, when are we going back to camp?"

"Stop worrying," said Red, "Open house is still two days away."

"It'll take me two days just to get cleaned up," moaned Nedshe.

Newt asked, "They'll be plenty of girls there?"

"Looks like nearly everybody from Marienville is coming," said Red. Turning toward the trail, he said, "Let's head for the barn. I certainly don't want to be a party to holding up your love-life."

CHAPTER TWENTY-FIVE

On official duty, Wynn sat at the camp entrance and had counted nearly four hundred people who had accepted Grabowski's Open House invitation. By mid-morning, Wynn believed that the entire town had come.

His broad smile and his bright yellow lapel flower matched the festive mood. When a large school bus rumbled by, Wynn whistled and waved at the girls, who giggled and waved back. He ran after the bus until it had disappeared around the curve. Returning to his station, he saw Peaches coming toward him. "What's going on, little buddy?"

"I can't find Dutch."

"Maybe he's got a girl."

"Oh, I hope not! Since Dutch's found women, Grabowski don't allow him to leave the camp."

"The Dutchman's still engaged to two women?"

Peaches thought for a minute before saying, "There's three now."

"Three! She...it! He can't keep his pants buttoned, can he?"

Peaches nervously wrung his hands. "Grabowski told me it's my fault if Dutch asks one more girl to marry him. Please help me."

Wynn put his hands on Peaches' shoulders. "Let's see what we can do."

"Don't you have to stay here?"

"Grabowski stuck me here until 1000." Wynn looked at his pocket watch. "I've already put in ten minutes overtime."

"Where should we start?"

"Down by the stream."

"Why?"

"We have to start somewhere."

When they reached the creek, Wynn saw Dougherty setting up three picnic tables. "What's going on, Sarge?"

"I got to get things ready a watermelon eating contest."

Peaches began to drool. As he wiped his mouth with his sleeve, he asked, "A watermelon eating contest?"

"That's what I said, Yardbird!"

Peaches tugged at Wynn's sleeve. "Would you mind if I stayed and helped? Would you, huh? Would you?"

Wynn took Peaches aside. "I thought you were afraid of him?"

"Not when there's food around."

Wynn poked Peaches in the ribs. "Stay and help. I'll find the Dutchman."

Peaches turned toward Dougherty. "What can I do, Sir?"

"Do you see any bars on my shoulders?"

"No, Sir."

Dougherty threw his arms in the air. "Civilians!" Then he pointed to a truck parked next to the creek. "Start unloading the watermelons. There's got to be a ton of them."

As Peaches rushed to the truck, Wynn began his search. He walked throughout the camp, but Dutch was nowhere to be found. Then Wynn sat down and watched the children dig in a sandpile for pennies. When a woman took her screaming kid from the sand, Wynn remembered his original mission. "Where would I go if I wanted some action?" He rubbed his chin and closed his eyes. "What better place," he remembered, "but Pebble Dell?"

Pebble Dell, a twenty minute walk from camp, was a small, green meadow, surrounded by evergreen trees. Two picnic tables sat near a clear trout stream that flowed through the field. This out-of-the-way spot had become the place for men to meet their female companions.

When he got there, Wynn saw and heard no one. Then he jumped up on a picnic table. After careful scrutiny, he muttered, "Damn! I thought I'd be able to find him from here." While still standing atop the table, he watched the huge dust clouds raised by the incoming traffic. Then he listened to the cheerful sounds coming from camp. He sat down and thought about Dutch. "Three engagements. In less than three months. It's all my fault," he muttered. In frustration, he pounded his open hand with his fist. "That fireman's dance was his undoing," he said aloud.

Wynn remembered when Dutch first came to camp. He was a shy person who spoke with a heavy German accent. Since everybody but Peaches and Wynn made fun of him, Dutch never left the camp.

Toward the end of May, Wynn dragged an unwilling Dutch to a dance. Within minutes, Wynn had acquired a dance partner. After the fourth dance, he noticed Dutch leaning against the wall, his hands stuck in his pockets. Since he had promised Dutch a good time, Wynn asked Norma Brownston, his dance partner, to dance with Dutch.

When the couple glided onto the floor, Norma unlocked Dutch's hidden talent. He was a natural! Soon everyone stopped and watched him take Norma through a series of dips, glides, and twirls. Slowly, all the couples left the dance floor allowing them the whole floor. They waltzed, did a fast polka, and ended with a spirited fox trot. When they left the floor, the applause was deafening. By evening's end, women stood in line, begging Dutch for a dance.

Dutch's ability to dance led to more serious problems. He had the feet of Vernon Castle, but sadly, his face was more like Charles Laughton's. This did not deter his female admirers who showered him with invitations. Within a short time, Dutch's transformation from wallflower to lady's man was complete. This short, bespectacled man soon became a legend.

As Wynn sat at the table, he saw something move. He looked again, but it had disappeared. "Must have been a woodchuck." Then he got up and walked toward it. He stopped when he saw movement again. "It's awful big for a woodchuck. Besides it's the wrong color!" Moving closer, he saw it moving up and down.

Then he heard a woman's voice moaning, "Yes! Yes! Yes!"

He stopped short when he heard Dutch's voice shouting, "Ja! Ja! Ja!"

Wynn put his left foot atop Dutch's piston-driven posterior and pushed down firmly. "What the hell are you doing, Dutchman?"

"I'm playing hide the stick, Wynn. Can't you see?"

"Ask a dumb question, and you get an even dumber answer." Wynn turned around, allowing Dutch and his lady-friend to disengage.

Unruffled, the young lady asked, "Would you hand me my dress?"

"Sure," said Wynn.

Then Dutch began to sing:

> In the shade of the old apple tree,
> When Nellie got stung by a bee.
> As she lifted her dress
> She showed me her best.
> It looked like a June bug to me...

Wynn tried to interrupt the doggerel. "Unless you want this to become a team sport, you'd better hurry. There's two more couples coming this way."

As Dutch buttoned his shirt, he moved into the second verse:

> It was hairy and smelled good to me.
> My peter said, "Thanks Mr. Bee."
> With a push and a ram,
> I busted her clam,
> In the shade of the old apple tree.

Dutch's companion murmured, "Tell your friend I'm decent now."

When Wynn turned around, he was shocked. This young lady was not one of Dutch's previous conquests!

Dutch introduced Wynn to Trudie Dankiewicz. Then he added, "I want you to be the first to know. I asked this little lady to marry me. And she's accepted!"

After he had deposited Dutch safely at the mess hall, Wynn walked over to the hospital. He had promised Frank to spell him for a while.

When Wynn walked in, he saw that Frank had spruced up the place. Medical charts hung from the walls, while a manikin lay in a hospital bed. A skeleton sat facing the people outside of the tent.

As a prank, Wynn put on a white coat and placed a stethoscope around his neck and awaited questions from the onlookers.

When people stopped, they asked questions about the pneumonia epidemic. "What treatment did you use?" asked an elderly gentleman.

"Mustard plasters, oil of eucalyptus to relieve congestion, and cupping."

"What's cupping, young man?"

"A type of massage that loosens congestion."

Everyone looked confused.

"Here, let me show you." Wynn turned the manikin over and demonstrated the procedure. After finishing, he sat the manikin up and placed a pillow under its back. Then he added, "There's something else a doctor always practices when treating pneumonia patients."

"What's that?" asked a middle aged woman.

"Plenty of tender loving care."

Impressed with Wynn's responses, two older ladies stopped Frank as he entered the tent. "Sir, I just can't get over how young these doctors are today."

The other woman giggled and pointed at Wynn. "He can treat me anytime!"

When the women had left, Frank motioned to Wynn. "Doctor, there's someone I want you to meet at the education tent."

"Who is it?"

"Find out for yourself."

When Wynn left the tent, he saw a crowd near the creek. Edging his way through the men, he noticed Sergeant Dougherty. "What's going on?"

"Oskowski just moved into the watermelon eating finals," answered Dougherty. Then he walked between Peaches Oskowski and Silent Kylocker. "Ladies and Gentlemen, These two young men are the finalists. Both have already eaten three watermelons." As if he were anointing each man, he put his hands on Peaches' shoulders and then upon Kylocker's. Dougherty pointed to the four watermelons facing each man. "A mountain of watermelons still awaits them."

While Dougherty explained the rules, O'Donnel and Cartwright elbowed their way beside Wynn. "What's the action?" asked O'Donnel.

"It's Peaches against Silent Kylocker in the watermelon eating contest," replied Wynn.

O'Donnel began to laugh when he saw Peaches. "That skinny runt will be lucky if he can eat one of them."

Wynn just smiled knowingly.

"Two bucks on Kylocker," said O'Donnel.

"Me, too," said Cartwright.

When Wynn ignored them, O'Donnel said, "Afraid to part with your dough?"

"Shhhh! I'm listening to Dougherty," said Wynn.

O'Donnel whispered in Wynn's ear. "If you win, you can shoot the works on that twat, Ginny."

Wynn turned quickly and glared at O'Donnel, who waved the money in Wynn's face.

Then O'Donnel said, "Just think of it...You got a hard on...And Ginny's coming down on you..."

"All right! It's my four bucks against yours!" growled Wynn.

While Cartwright nodded, O'Donnel said, "A deal."

"You will notice that each table has a judge," intoned Dougherty. "The judge will cut the melon in quarters so the contestants can handle their job easy." Then he looked at Peaches and Silent, who sat poised over their quarry. "Are you ready?"

Both young men nodded their heads.

"On your mark! Get set! Go!" shouted Dougherty.

As the crowd cheered, the two men plunged into the watermelons. The race was a dead-heat until Peaches slurped up the second melon handily. When Kylocker signaled his surrender, Peaches was attacking a third melon. His face lay buried in seeds, rind, and pulp as he polished off still another melon.

Dougherty yelled, "Oskowski, you won! Stop eating."

"Let me eat the last one," Peaches pleaded. Before waiting for Dougherty's approval, Peaches vacuumed up another one.

Wynn poked O'Donnel and said, "Peaches eats just like a typewriter types, doesn't he?"

Handing the four dollars to Wynn, O'Donnel replied, "The only thing missing is the bell."

"Hey, Peaches," Wynn yelled. "Got room for the pie-eating contest?"

As Peaches wiped seeds from his face, he asked, "Where's that?"

"Over by the mess hall." As Wynn watched Peaches' supporters carry him to the next contest, Wynn waved a five dollar bill in O'Donnel's face. "Want to bet on who'll win that one?"

"My buddy has more important things to do," said Cartwright.

"Like what?" asked Wynn.

"He's fighting for the camp heavyweight championship."

"So?"

"Didn't you fight once?" asked O'Donnel.

"Yeah."

"How come you're not entered against my boy?" asked Cartwright.

"He's yellow," said O'Donnel.

"She...it!" said Wynn as he spit on O'Donnel's shoes.

O'Donnel squared away, but Cartwright cautioned him. "Save it for later."

O'Donnel moved closer to Wynn. "Your little chippy is here." He rubbed his crotch and sneered, "Tonight, I'm going to ride her all the way back to Bradford."

Before Wynn could react, Grabowski's voice came over the public address system. "Would the participants for the heavyweight championship fight please report to my office."

O'Donnel grabbed his crotch again and made a sucking sound. Then he followed Cartwright toward Grabowski's office.

Wynn calmed down as he walked across the compound toward the education tent. Upon entering, he saw an attractive young woman discussing the educational program with the guests. He stayed until the visitors had gone. Then he introduced himself. "Hi, I'm Wynn Odum. Doc told me to come over and say hello."

She smiled and extended her hand. "I'm Ruth Anne Wells."

"You a doctor?"

"I'm a teacher. I'm going to help Doctor Millet with his educational program."

Whistling softly, Wynn replied, "That's going to require a lot of help."

"My friends will teach the regular classes." Then she smiled uneasily. "But the basic reading and math classes will require one teacher for every three students. I'm not sure we've got enough instructors."

Wynn listened attentively. When she had finished, he said, "I've got an idea."

"What is it?"

"First, you'll have to teach people how to teach those basic courses."

"Yes, and I'll need ten volunteers in those workshops."

"Hells Bells, Ruth Anne," he blurted. Immediately after the words tumbled from his mouth, he began to apologize.

"Wynn, I have four brothers."

"That's no excuse for my language."

"What were you going to say?"

Ruth Anne's question set him at ease. He began to feel comfortable again. "I belong to a reading club that Doc has organized. I'm sure every guy in the club will volunteer."

"All right," she said. "You supply the teachers, and I'll do the rest."

"I want to be first to volunteer."

"Your name's at the top."

"When do we start?"

As Ruth Anne explained the program, Ontek and George Higgleston burst into the tent. They looked at Wynn and then at Ruth Anne. After an awkward silence, Ontek winked at Wynn. "You old dog. Got a girlfriend and won't even tell your buddy."

Ruth Anne just smiled.

After Wynn had introduced them to Ruth Anne, he asked, "What's up?"

"The boxing tourney is going down the drain if you don't help," said Higgleston.

"Lieutenant Grabowski has only got two guys, Harry O'Donnel and Jimmy De Lious, for the heavyweight bout," said Ontek.

"Yeah, but here's the rub," said Higgleston. "De Lious was changing a tire this morning and smashed his hand."

"O'Donnel will be champ," added Ontek. "So when Grabowski

146

put out the word for a replacement, I volunteered you."

"With friends like you guys, I don't need enemies."

"C'mon, Wynn," coaxed Ontek.

Finally, Wynn said, "Oh, why not!"

"Thanks a lot, pal," said Ontek as he slapped Wynn on his back. "Higgleston, go over to Grabowski and give him the word." Then, turning toward Wynn, Ontek said, "I brought along some trunks."

"Pretty sure of yourself?"

"I knew you wouldn't let your buddy down."

"Ruth Anne, ever seen a boxing match?" asked Wynn.

"No."

"Do you want to?"

"On one condition."

"What's that?"

"That you take me to the dance this evening."

"A deal," said Wynn. "Go with Ontek while I change into my trunks. I'll see you after the match."

CHAPTER TWENTY-SIX

For the Open House, the men had built a boxing ring on a wooden deck that later would become the floor for Barrack Number Three. Four rows of wooden folding chairs surrounded the ring. A string of lights hung from ten foot poles at the edge of the deck. There was plenty of standing room behind the last row of folding chairs.

While Ontek tied the gloves onto Wynn's hands, Grabowski explained the importance of boxing. "Boxing is an American tradition. It teaches fair play, good sportsmanship and poise to our boys." Although some people laughed at his unintentional rhyming efforts, he ignored them. "They say the future wars are won on the playing fields of our schools." He puffed out his chest proudly. "Let me add, they are won in the boxing ring, too." He moved closer to the ropes and looked at the people in the first row. "Why did America defeat the Germans in the Great War? Because we had Jack Dempsey on our side."

Someone shouted, "If Dempsey was so good, why didn't he join the army and fight the Krauts?"

Ignoring that legitimate question, Grabowski continued mixing politics with boxing. "Right now, the Germans are resurrecting the God of War. Before they strike us, the Huns will send their champion over here to steal from us what is rightfully ours. The heavyweight boxing championship!"

The crowd began to stamp its feet and shout, "We want the fight! We want the fight!"

Grabowski held his hands aloft. "Today is a continuation of the values our forefathers proclaimed on July 4, 1776." When the crowd began to boo, Grabowski moved directly to the introductions.

148

"Ladies...and gentlemen! For the heavyweight championship of Camp One...In this corner, weighing two hundred and ten pounds...In purple trunks...Harry O'Donnel."

Not waiting for the cheers to subside, Grabowski whispered to Wynn, "He's going to beat the tar out of you." Then he shouted, "At one hundred and seventy-five pounds...In white trunks...Wynn Odum."

When Grabowski called the boys together for instructions, O'Donnel interrupted him. "Odum, your twat's going to see me whip your ass."

"Hey, asshole," said Wynn. "This is only an exhibition."

After Grabowski finally finished his instructions, the two fighters returned to their corners and waited for the bell.

When it rang, Wynn moved to the center of the ring. Holding out his gloves ritualistically, he quickly ducked a wild blow by O'Donnel whose momentum carried him into the ropes. While Grabowski helped untangle O'Donnel, Wynn asked, "Don't you know fighting manners?"

Embarrassed, O'Donnel rushed again, but Wynn sidestepped him easily. Then O'Donnel offered a new tactic. Using his weight advantage, he tried to get in close to Wynn, who quickly tied him up and maneuvered him into a neutral corner.

Unleashing a neat combination, Wynn snapped O'Donnel's head back. Quickly, Wynn broke away and backpedaled to the center of the ring. When O'Donnel charged again, Wynn stood fast and dodged roundhouse lefts and rights.

O'Donnel caught his arms under Wynn's armpits and tried to throw him to the floor. Grabowski moved in quickly. "Who do you think you are, Man Mountain Dean?" After the bell rang, O'Donnel scored easily with a left to Wynn's body.

When he returned to his corner, Wynn sat down and closed his eyes. His mind raced back to his fight with Daily. But Ontek jolted Wynn by dumping a bucket of cold water over his head. Sputtering, Wynn leaped up. "What the hell did you do that for?"

"I saw that once in a movie," said Ontek.

Round Two began with another wild charge by O'Donnel. Moving in close, he flailed away, punching air. When Grabowski called for a break from another clinch, O'Donnel connected with a wild left hook that staggered Wynn. Although the crowd screamed at his dirty tactics, O'Donnel only smiled. Then he rushed directly at Wynn, who dodged to the left, making O'Donnel hit the corner post with a wild overhand left.

As Wynn readied for O'Donnel next charge, Wynn shouted, "Enough of this shit, sucker."

"Here! Here! Let's have no talking in the ring," yelled Grabowski.

Wynn ducked under his foe's churning arms and tied him up. When O'Donnel tried to break away, Wynn held him. Chest-to-chest, Wynn positioned his head solidly on O'Donnel's left shoulder. Then Wynn held O'Donnel with one arm and popped him sharply with a series of stinging blows.

As Grabowski tried to force them apart, Wynn growled, "Had to bring Ginny along? I'm going to pound you worse than Red did!"

"One more outburst and I'll take points from you," warned Grabowski.

Wynn glared at Grabowski. "There's no such rule, and you know it." Then Wynn easily broke from the clinch, while Grabowski and O'Donnel wrestled each other in center ring.

Not waiting for another wild rush, Wynn began to stalk O'Donnel. Wynn unleashed jabs and hooks with a machine-like precision, causing a confused O'Donnel to drop his arms. Wynn continued pummeling O'Donnel, but he would not go down.

Wynn looked at Grabowski who signaled for the fight to continue. Shrugging his shoulders, Wynn moved in close and pulled his punches, while holding O'Donnel up. When the bell rang, Wynn guided O'Donnel to his corner.

Before Wynn had returned to his corner, Cartwright tossed out a white towel. Grabowski held Wynn's arm into the air. "Ladies and gentlemen, the heavyweight champion of Camp One...Wynn Odum!"

Wynn did not hear the cheers. He only knew that the black side of fighting had returned. He had tried to suppress it since that night at Greensburg, but it was out in the open again. And he felt good about it. It just felt good, hitting someone.

When Wynn walked to the apron of the ring, Grabowski was

right behind him. "You're not out of the woods, Odum."

"So far, you haven't laid a glove on me," replied Wynn.

"Don't mouth off!"

"Maybe your Uncle Murray can help."

The end of the open house festivities was a square dance. While the orchestra, two accordions, three fiddles, a piano player and two drummers, tuned up, the caller shouted, "Choose your partners."

"I've never done this before," said Wynn.

Ruth Anne led Wynn onto the floor. "Square dancing's a snap."

As the caller continued, Wynn asked, "What's he talking about?"

"Listen to him, loosen up, and go with the music."

When the caller began with "Marching through Georgia," Wynn took Ruth Anne's hands and began to move with the music. Whenever he made the wrong turn, everyone had a good laugh, including Wynn. As the dance continued, he grew more confident. Later, he had begun to request specific dances, surprising even himself.

When the orchestra finished still another set, Lefty Malone shouted, "Let's have some slow dances." A chorus of cheers supported his request.

The orchestra had no choice. It immediately moved into "Blue Skies" and then "Pennies from Heaven."

As Wynn danced with Ruth Anne, he began to laugh.

"What's so funny?"

"I think Red Dawson's picked the music." Wynn enjoyed dancing with Ruth Anne. As he twirled her around, he said, "You're so light. Like a bantamweight." As they danced, Wynn's hands pressed against the small of her back, while her head rested on his shoulder. He closed his eyes and buried his head into her fresh smelling hair.

Then Wynn felt a tap on his shoulder. "Can I cut in?"

When Wynn opened his eyes, he saw O'Donnel. Immediately, Wynn danced away from him.

Following them, O'Donnel asked, "Didn't you hear me?" When Wynn ignored his request again, O'Donnel told him, "That's what a gentleman always says."

"You're not a gentleman!" said Wynn. He released Ruth Anne and confronted O'Donnel. "Didn't you get enough of me today?"

O'Donnel leered at Ruth Anne. "I'd never get enough of her."

When the couples surrounding them stopped dancing, Ruth Anne said, "That's all right, Wynn." She reached toward O'Donnel, who immediately swept her away from an unsmiling Wynn.

Wynn felt another tap on his shoulder. When he turned around, he saw Ginny. His expression remained unchanged.

"It's nice to see you, too," she snapped. Ginny wore a faded red dress with a purple sash wrapped around her waist. "Let's dance."

Stumbling for words, Wynn mumbled, "You look taller."

"Miss Betty put my hair up in a bun." She took his arm and pulled him onto the dance floor. "You wasn't bashful the last time I seen you."

As the dancers flowed around them, Wynn stood there, saying nothing.

"C'mon, one little dance ain't going to hurt you," she begged.

"All those times I went up to see you."

"Yeah?"

"You wouldn't even talk to me."

"I...I...Was...Afraid."

"Of what?

"You."

"I didn't do a thing to you!"

With a doll-like voice, she said, "You was nice to me."

"That scared you?"

"After you and me...Well, you know...And we talked and talked..." Ginny twisted her sash nearly into a rope while teetering first on the balls of her feet and then upon her heels. "Afterwards, I begin to have feelings...Something that I never had before for a boy...I got scared."

When O'Donnel danced by them, he yelled, "Don't be a spoil-sport, Odum. Dance with our little Ginny!"

Wynn tried to catch Ruth Anne's attention, but O'Donnel quickly steered her away.

Hesitating, Ginny asked, "You like her, don't you?"

Wynn became defensive. "I just met her."

"But you like her. I can see it."

"You can't see anything!"

"You're ashamed of me!" Ginny pulled on Wynn's hands. "Dance with me now!" she demanded.

When Ruth Anne and O'Donnel went by them again, O'Donnel said, "Where'd you meet such a nice chickie?" Then he made a sucking sound with his lips.

"What you told me then was all lies?" When Wynn did not respond, her lips began to quiver. "You're nothing but a liar."

As couples around them snickered, Wynn reached out to Ginny. "But you wouldn't talk to me."

She slapped his face. "You're another sorry-assed John looking for tail." She turned then and ran across the floor.

Frank had been at the edge of the platform watching them. When she suddenly left, he called, "Ginny."

She stopped and turned around. "Oh, I thought you was somebody else." Then she asked, "What do you want old man?"

As the orchestra played, "Down in the Valley," Frank walked toward her while extending his hands. "May I have this dance, please?"

"If you want to."

When they began to dance, Ginny danced stiffly, while all the time watching Wynn. Moving closer to Frank, she said, "For an old coot, you dance real good."

"Thank you, Ginny."

O'Donnel waltzed by Wynn and asked, "Where's our Ginny?"

Wynn pointed to Frank. "Over there."

O'Donnel began to laugh. "You lost her to that old goat?" While still laughing, he asked, "Mind if I spin Ruthie around the floor again?"

"Suit yourself."

Then Wynn walked over to Frank and tapped him on the shoulder. "Can I cut in?"

"No," screamed Ginny as tears welled up in her eyes.

"Go ahead and cry," said Frank.

She wiped away the tears with her forearm. Defiantly, she announced, "No guy'll ever make me cry again."

As the three of them walked from the dance floor, Frank softly asked, "Ginny...Ginny...What are we going to do with you?"

She spun around and shouted, "Nobody's going to make me over, that's for sure!"

Frank said, "Nobody even suggested that."

She pointed to Wynn. "He did!" She loosened her hair, allowing it to fall below her waist.

"You have such beautiful hair," said Frank.

"And I know how to use it, too!" Pointing at Wynn, she said, "Ask him!" While everyone stared, she ran out into the darkness.

"Wynn," said Frank. "Go to her."

Wynn looked at Ruth Anne who was still dancing. "I can't, Doc. I just can't."

"I know who and what she is," Frank said.

"You do?"

"I check Miss Betty's girls periodically for venereal disease," explained Frank. "It's part of my job. I've been particularly concerned about Ginny, because she's so fragile." When Wynn turned away and started to look for Ruth Anne, Frank spun him around. "How can you be so bright but yet so stupid? Ginny doesn't need a lover. She needs a friend!"

O'Donnel brought Ruth Anne to Wynn. Acknowledging her, O'Donnel said, "You got great wheels, doll. Thanks for the spin."

"Wynn, are you going?"

"No, Doc. I can't."

"Then somebody must." While Wynn stood there with Ruth Anne and O'Donnel, Frank left the dance floor.

"We're even now."

"What to you mean by that, O'Donnel?"

"This afternoon, you made me look like a fool."

"It wasn't hard."

"How does it feel when the shoe's on the other foot, buster?" O'Donnel bowed stiffly to Ruth Anne and said, "Goodnight, my sweet woman."

"Who's that?" asked Wynn.

He waved beyond the row of lights that illuminated the dance floor. "Our little Ginny," he answered. "Who else?"

154

When taps blew, signalling the end of the day, Danny Witkowski shouted, "Let's have one more dance!"

Grabowski came onto the dance floor. "Thank you for coming. It's my pleasure to announce that the last dance will be a slow one. A very slow one, fellas."

While the orchestra broke into the familiar strains of "Good Night Ladies," Ruth Anne stood there with her arms folded.

"You want to dance?" Wynn asked.

She did not reply.

Wynn took a frowning Ruth Anne and led her onto the floor. As they danced stiffly, Wynn said, "Your hands are cold."

"Your friend...O'Donnel."

"He's not my friend."

"He says Ginny's a..."

"A what?" demanded Wynn.

"Ahh...Whore."

Wynn enjoyed dragging the words from Ruth Anne.

"And you know her real well. Is that true?"

Although the music had stopped, Wynn continued to hold her hands. While the crowd drifted away, he finally admitted, "Yeah, I do."

She pulled her hands away and folded her arms across her body.

"Can I see you again?"

"I'll be teaching here two nights a week."

"Ah c'mon."

"I'm running the workshop for the volunteers."

"Then I'll see you?"

"Only in class," she said as she walked toward the bus.

Wynn caught up with her quickly. "Let's talk."

"No."

While someone turned off the lights, one by one, Wynn stood there alone and watched Ruth Anne get into the bus. When she sat down, Wynn waved at her.

She did not wave back.

CHAPTER TWENTY-SEVEN

Rushing into Wynn's tent, Frank shouted, "Wynn, get out of bed."

"Cut it out," Wynn said sleepily.

"C'mon. Wake up!"

"It's my day off." Then Wynn slowly opened his eyes. "What's the matter?"

"It's Ginny. Last evening when she ran away from us..."

Fully awake, Wynn asked, "What happened?"

"When I couldn't find her, I went down the bridge. She was standing naked, screaming at the men who surrounded her."

"Why'd she do that for?"

"She had had sex with them."

"Them?"

"At least twenty. When no one else accepted her invitation, she called them, 'Pansies and queers.'"

As Wynn pulled on his boots, he asked, "Where's she now?"

"With O'Donnel."

"Wouldn't she listen to you?"

Frank shook his head. "I gave her my jacket and offered to take her home. Then O'Donnel showed up. They ran up the road to a parked car. When I got there, they were gone."

"It's my fault, Doc. What you called me at the dance was right."

"We both made mistakes," said Frank. "Professionally, I've known Ginny for the last two years, and you're only a small part of her problem. She's quite ill."

"Like the measles?" asked Wynn.

"She's had a nervous breakdown," answered Frank.

"Will she get better?" asked a concerned Wynn.

Mousy Gray interrupted them. As he charged into the tent, he said, "Cookie needs to see you, Doc."

When they reached the mess hall, Cookie was waiting. "My car's missing."

"Who took it?" asked Wynn.

Mousy answered immediately. "When I went to the can around midnight, I saw O'Donnel getting into Cookie's car."

"Here's the worst part," said Cookie. "My pistol's gone, too."

"Was it loaded?" asked Frank.

"I always keep a full clip in it."

A telephone rang in the kitchen. When Cookie answered it, he said, "Miss Betty, what can I do for you?" As he listened, he kept saying "He what?" Then he said, "My God, Miss Betty. That's awful!" Finally he said, "We'll be right up." After hanging up the phone, he stood there without saying anything.

"For God's sake, man, what's wrong?" Frank asked.

"O'Donnel beat up Ginny right in front of Miss Betty's. When Sam intervened, O'Donnel shot him in the arm. Then he forced Ginny back into the car and just took off."

"Who's Sam?" asked Mousy.

"A colored man who works for Miss Betty," said Cookie.

"Have the police been called?" asked Frank.

"Yeah, and she gave them a description of the car."

"Was it yours?" asked Mousy.

"Yeah," replied Cookie.

Frank turned to Mousy and said, "Tell Grabowski that Cookie, Wynn, and I are going to Bradford. We've got to find O'Donnel before he hurts Ginny."

When they had reached Lindy's, Sam was waiting for them. He had his left arm in a sling. "You guys are a sight for sore eyes."

"How do you feel?" asked Frank.

"Fine. The kid just grazed me, that's all."

As they entered the restaurant, Miss Betty gestured to them. "I'm glad you're here." She hugged Cookie and then shook Frank's hand. Looking at Wynn, she said, "Don't I know you?"

"Yes, ma'am. I was here a while back."

Miss Betty grimaced. "Oh, it's you who caused the problem."

"All I wanted to do was talk."

She bristled as she said, "Talk's a waste of money in my business." Then Miss Betty motioned for them to sit down. "The cops are coming back, so's you might as well sit tight and wait for them." As they sat down, Miss Betty said, "I'll have Sam get breakfast."

"I'm always glad to eat somebody else's cooking," said Cookie.

"The cops call your boy, 'armed and dangerous,'" said Miss Betty.

"Up until now, he just been a big pain in the butt," offered Wynn.

"What really fries me," said Miss Betty, "is that the cops found out about Ginny's record."

"What record?" asked Cookie.

"She walked out of prison in New York," said Wynn.

"Looks like both of them's in a heap of trouble," said Cookie.

They had just begun eating when Sheriff Dale Boggs interrupted them. Accompanying Boggs was his deputy, Bobby Joe Thompson. After Miss Betty introduced them, Boggs asked, "Which one of you boys had the car stolen?"

"I did," said Cookie. "But I ain't pressing charges."

Boggs began to laugh. "Car theft is a petty charge now."

"What do you mean, sheriff?" asked Frank.

"For starters, assault with a deadly weapon, intent to kill, and let's add on kidnapping." He looked at his aide, Thompson. "Did I forget anything?" Then he remembered. "Oh, yeah! your boy took the whore..." Boggs stopped and nodded toward Miss Betty and said, "Excuse me, darling." Then he said, "He took the <u>girl</u> over the state line into Limestone, New York. Then he brought her back to Pennsylvania. Now he's holed up at Farnsworth Station, twenty miles south of Warren."

"How do you know?" asked Frank.

"Got a positive ID from Jimmy Adams, a lease worker."

"What about Ginny and O'Donnel?" asked Wynn.

"Is O'Donnel the Mick that kidnapped her?" asked Boggs.

"We're going to grab a Mick, too," sung out Thompson.

"You guys coming for the capture?" asked Boggs. "Because we got to move fast before the Feds close in."

"You've called the FBI?" asked Frank.

"Had to. The kid made a fatal mistake by crossing the state line."

"And even though the gal is a whore, it's still kidnapping," said Thompson.

Sheriff Boggs hitched up his trousers and peered through the window. "Hate those Feds. But this time me and Thompson's going to make the collar. Got ten men outside..."

"...And another ten already up at Farnsworth," said Thompson.

"What's your plan?" asked Cookie.

"We'll smoke them out or carry them out feet first. Don't matter which way," said Boggs.

Frank looked at his friends. "We'd better go along."

"If you want to," said Boggs. After hitching up his pants again, Boggs went out the door with Thompson closely behind. Before ordering the posse into their cars, Boggs hooted, "A Mick and a whore. We'll bag them both."

Cookie said, "He sounds like a big game hunter."

"Let's go!" Frank said.

When they got to Farnsworth Station, the deputies had already surrounded a small stone house. "The Mick was outside when my boys showed up," said Boggs. "When he flashed a gun, my men opened fire."

Shouting over the gunfire, Frank tried to reason with Boggs. "For God's sake, man. There's no reason to kill them."

Cookie ran over to Frank. "Doc, these guys are nuts. They're shooting at each other. They think O'Donnel's returning the fire, and I know he ain't."

Boggs shouted, "What makes you so sure?"

"Because I'd recognize the sound of my own pistol."

"Call a cease fire!" shouted Frank.

Waving his arms, Boggs motioned for the firing to stop. When the posse finally obeyed, he looked pleased. "Doc, if you got any ideas, I'll listen to them. Otherwise we're going to charge the building."

"Allow me to negotiate with O'Donnel."

"You're a stubborn one." After pausing, Boggs said, "You got fifteen minutes! If you fail, we'll blast them out!" As Frank and Wynn walked toward the house, Boggs shouted, "Don't you want to carry a white flag?"

"He's not going to shoot us."

"What should we tell them?" asked Wynn.

"The truth, Wynn. That's the only way we're going to get them out alive."

As they approached the porch, O'Donnel shouted, "Stop where you are!"

"We're here to help you," said Frank.

"Bullshit," screamed O'Donnel.

When Wynn saw Ginny at the window, he asked, "How's Ginny?"

Before she could reply, O'Donnel knocked her down. "Don't tell them nothing, you little bitch!"

Wynn screamed, "Ginny!" He ran for the door and kicked it down, knocking it and O'Donnel onto the floor. When Wynn saw O'Donnel had dropped his weapon, Wynn shouted, "Ginny, pick up the gun and let me have it!"

She reached under the table, took it into her hands, and pointed it at Wynn. "Yeah, I just might," she said.

"Wynn," Frank shouted, "are you all right?"

"Yeah, Doc."

"Can I come in?"

Ginny screamed, "No!"

"You've wasted two minutes already," Boggs yelled.

Wynn looked at Ginny. "You aren't going to shoot me?" he asked.

"Don't bet on it, you damned liar."

Then Wynn looked at O'Donnel, who had regained consciousness. "You took her across the state line. That's a federal charge."

"Screw the Feds! I'm going to take Ginny back to Philly."

Ginny waved the gun toward the two young men. "Cut the shit and sit down!"

As Wynn sat down at a kitchen table, he said, "Ginny, be careful with the gun."

When O'Donnel shuffled around looking for a chair, Ginny shouted, "Find a chair, stupid!"

"There ain't none around," whimpered O'Donnel.

"Sit on the goddamned floor!" While walking behind Wynn, she rubbed her breasts against Wynn's shoulders. When he reached up to touch her, she nearly kicked his chair over. Then she saw O'Donnel edge toward the door. "Move again and I'll blow off your head. " Pacing in front of Wynn, she began to unbutton her blouse. "You want to see these, Wynn baby?" With a sing-song voice, she teased, "You haven't seen them for a while. Remember the first time you saw them? You thought they was so small." While squeezing a nipple, her voice became gruff as she said, "It ain't the size, buster, it's what you can do with them that counts." She pointed the gun straight at Wynn's head and resumed her child-like voice. "Oh, I forgot. You don't have a good memory." She rubbed the barrel of the gun from her wrist, up to her elbow, and finally across her breasts. She caressed her nipples with the gun barrel and then pointed the gun against her chest before asking, "Did you ever play Russian Roulette?"

"Give me the gun," pleaded Wynn.

Calmly, she said, "Naw, I'm not going to waste myself." Turning the gun toward O'Donnel, she asked, "What do you think of a guy who buggers a woman, Wynn?"

"You balled half the company last night before I ever touched you," said O'Donnel.

"Yeah, you're like George Washington, O'Donnel. First in war, first in peace, and then he married a widow! It don't matter how many guys I screwed last night, because that was my choice. But you gave me no choice. You humped me front and back. Whenever you wanted."

She swung the gun toward Wynn. "But a liar is worse! When you said that you'd buy me a cup of coffee in Kane even though people knew what I was, I believed you. But at the dance...That was different. You were ashamed of me and wanted nothing to do with me. I knew it. Everyone there knew it. You hurt me more than that buggering O'Donnel ever hurt me."

161

"A whore with feelings," hooted O'Donnel. "That's a laugh."

Ignoring him, she said, "Let's see, where should I shoot you, Wynn?" Smiling that same crooked little smile that Wynn immediately recognized, she said, "In the balls, of course! That's what you think with." Her hand began to waiver and she reached over with her left hand, placing it around her right wrist. But the increased tension from her finger was enough to discharge the gun. The bullet splintered the stone fireplace directly above Wynn.

Rock segments exploded, striking Wynn's head and knocking him down.

In the confusion, O'Donnel rushed to the window.

Boggs yelled, "He's getting away. Fire at will!"

Amidst the deafening noise, Wynn saw Ginny fall. He crawled over to her immediately, but she did not move.

When he turned her over, blood oozed from her chest. Then she shuddered violently. She was dead.

Wynn took cover behind an overturned oak table. Dragging Ginny's body onto his lap, he wrapped his arms around her and began to rock her, as if comforting a child. "You killed her! She's dead! All I wanted to do was to talk with her."

When the shooting had stopped, Boggs started to laugh. "We got the whore, boys. Now let's get the Mick."

Frank ran to the door. "Wynn, are you all right?"

"Yeah, Doc. But Ginny's gone."

"What about O'Donnel?"

"He's hiding somewhere."

"Can you come out?"

Wynn pushed open the door and carried Ginny onto the porch. As he blinked in the sunlight, he saw rifles pointing at him. "Haven't you done enough killing for one day?"

When he started to walk down the steps, O'Donnel raced out the door and threw a stranglehold around Wynn's neck. With the other hand, he pressed a gun to Wynn's head. "One wrong move and Odum's dead!"

O'Donnel's strong grip caused Wynn to drop Ginny.

Her body tumbled down the steps, coming to rest on the path.

Wynn saw Bobby Joe Thompson aiming his rifle at them. "Don't shoot," stuck in Wynn's throat as he watched a small white puff from a gun barrel and then heard an ugly hiss near his head. He felt O'Donnel's grip suddenly tighten and then immediately loosen.

The bullet caught O'Donnel directly above the left eye, shattering that side of his head. Its impact knocked him against the railing. Then he toppled forward, falling beside Ginny.

Frank looked at O'Donnel and shook his head. "He's gone, Wynn." Then he looked at Ginny. Her blouse lay open, revealing a blood-covered chest and stomach. Frank took off his jacket and gently covered her exposed body. Before closing her eyes, he straightened her black hair that lay twisted and matted over her face. As he stood up, he said, "You deserved so much more."

The posse immediately surrounded the bodies. Amid joyous hooting, Boggs congratulated his deputy. "Great shooting!"

"Hell, I've had tougher shots shooting a deer," replied Thompson.

Another posse member marveled, "Did you see her tits all covered with blood?"

"S'pose they got it on before she died?" drooled Thompson, as he nudged Ginny's body with his foot.

Enraged, Wynn punched Thompson in the belly, doubling him up. Then, with a strong uppercut, Wynn knocked Thompson to the ground. Instantly, Wynn straddled him and smashed his head into the soft earth, again and again. Then he began to rain blows upon the deputy's chest and face while shouting, "You goddamned pig! You killed her without giving her a chance! Why didn't you kill me? She never really hurt anybody! I'm the one who hurt her!. Why didn't you shoot me?"

Wynn was still screaming when three other deputies dragged him from the dazed lawman's chest.

Boggs spoke directly to Frank. "Get rid of this young man before I press charges."

Frank exploded, "Your men have murdered two people!"

"Pick up the bodies," ordered Boggs. "The county will want autopsies."

Frank pushed aside the first man who moved toward Ginny.

"I'll sign the death certificates," he said. "That will make these executions legal."

Frank's willingness to slash red tape pleased Boggs, who promptly raised another bureaucratic problem. "What about the slut...?"

Wynn screamed, "If she's a slut, you're an asshole of the whole world!"

Boggs smiled and taunted Wynn. "What's wrong boy? Did I offend your sensibilities?"

Turning to Frank, Boggs said, "Since the young lady has no kin, it'll cost the county a ton just to bury her."

"I'll pay for it," said Frank. "As least she deserves a decent funeral." Motioning to Cookie, Frank said, "Drive back to Camp One. Bring a truck to pick up the bodies. We'll stay here."

"Well, c'mon boys," said Boggs. "The excitement is over. Let's go home. Besides, I got a lot of paperwork I've got to do."

When the last patrol car disappeared down the dust-covered road, Frank and Wynn remained with the bodies.

Wynn stared at the bodies, feeling responsible for this tragedy. "God, it so quiet now. I wish at least one bird would sing," he said. "It might make me feel better." When Frank put his arm around Wynn's shoulder, Wynn said, "If I'd listened to you, maybe we could have saved them."

"It's not your fault."

"But she kept standing me up at Lindy's."

"That's understandable, Wynn. She stirred feelings within you that you had never experienced." Frank took out his pipe, tamped tobacco into its bowl, and lit it. He sat down on the steps while Wynn continued to stand near Ginny's body. "I've watched you help Peaches and Dutch. You're responsible for their staying in the C's. And you've got to take a lot of credit for pulling the boys through the pneumonia crisis."

"But, Doc. If I just would have gone after her..."

Frank interrupted him. "Your response to Ginny was natural. You had no way to know that she was unbalanced."

Wynn sighed deeply and walked to a tiny field of wildflowers, growing on the edge of the clearing. He knelt down and picked a daisy. Slowly, he plucked the petals from it and put them into his hat. Then he repeated the process again and again until the white petals spilled out from his cap. After that, he picked a bouquet of forget-me-nots before walking over to Ginny's body. He removed Frank's coat that covered her. Tenderly placing the spray of blue flowers in her hand, he sprinkled the white daisy petals from her head to her feet. After carefully covering her with the coat, he stood there in silence while tears ran down his cheeks.

CHAPTER TWENTY-EIGHT

Immediately after Open House, the completion of the Lamonaville Road became the chief priority of Camp One. This twenty mile stretch through the wilderness was an important route into the Bear Creek area that still posed a fire threat. Officially, the Forest Service called this strategic road, "Truck Trail Number One." The men who worked on this project, disdainfully referred to it as, "The Road to Nowhere in Particular From Nowhere at All."

Road-building was hard, hand labor. After the road had been surveyed, the men had to move in and clear-cut the right-of-way. Then a tractor pulling a grader crudely shaped a road bed. When a boulder obstructed the road's path, shooters dynamited it. A crew of about twenty boys loaded the rubble rock from the boulders onto trucks. After the trucks had dumped their loads on the road bed, crew leaders assigned every man a sixteen by twenty foot section of the road bed. Each man's task was quite simple---smash those rocks into fist-sized stones in an eight hour day.

As the road building season progressed, the work did not become any easier. The men just became tougher. Red Dawson, their foreman, saw to that. Helping Red were Wynn, who had become Red's assistant and Ontek, Wynn's assistant.

As their crew began another day, Red called Wynn and Ontek together. "We got to push the men harder."

"Why?" asked Wynn.

"Orders from the Supervisor."

"What's he got? A bug up his ass?"

"He wants the road done by winter."

"Can't we get any bulldozers in to help us?" asked Ontek.

"We're lucky we've got trucks," said Red.

166

"I'm working the butts off my crew now," said Wynn.

Red turned and watched the crew who had begun pounding rocks. "Who's the biggest goof-off?"

Just then, Joe Shudjinkuski called to Wynn, "Hey, Sarge, I got to piss."

Wynn and Ontek immediately pointed to Shudjinkuski.

"I agree," said Red.

"Jeez," said Wynn, "if I hear that lunkhead call me one more time, I'm going to kill him."

"Let's make an example of that tall-drink-of-water," said Red. "It might make everyone work just a little bit harder."

Joe Shudjinkuski, everyone called him Tarbo because nobody could pronounce his last name, hated work. The only job that interested him was finding ways to dodge work. His laments to Wynn echoed throughout the work site. "Sarge, let me take off my shirt...Sarge, I got stones in my shoes...Hey, Sarge, I just broke my hammer handle."

By the next day, Red had devised a plan that included the cooperation of the leaders and most of the men. When it was in place, he called Tarbo over him. "Tarbo, we've got a problem only you can solve."

"What kind of problem?"

"Know what a board stretcher is?"

"Sure, I do," said Tarbo, while running his hands through a shank of blond hair that grew wildly from his head.

"Good," remarked Red, "because the other guys couldn't know one if it dropped on their toes."

"My old man used one, once," offered Tarbo.

"I want you to go to Jack Warnick's crew," said Red. "He's got one. Bring it back as soon as possible."

"Where's Warnick?" asked Tarbo.

"A mile up the grade," answered Wynn.

Wynn suppressed his laughter as Tarbo looked at Red and then at Silent Kylocker, who continued pounding rocks.

"Silent?"

"What do you want, Tarbo?"

"You hid some big rocks under the smaller ones." Pointing to

Wynn, Tarbo said, "Don't want Sarge to find them, do you?"

"Sheee...it!" muttered Silent. He turned around and began smashing rocks with such a force that the smaller chips began to spray against Tarbo's legs.

"Silent?" When Silent refused to answer, Tarbo called again. Then he turned away from the sweating young man and sauntered up the road.

As Tarbo disappeared, Red called to Wynn. "Follow that yardbird. See what the hell he's up to." As Wynn left, Red yelled at his crew, "Wipe those smiles from your faces and get back to smashing rocks!"

After walking three hundred yards, Tarbo took off his shirt, wrapping it around his waist. Stopping, he cupped his hand to his ear. "Sing along little birdies," he shouted. Then he began to count the birds. "One...Two...Three...Seven...Ah...Three...Four...Five...Six." He finally threw his hands in the air and moaned, "She...it! Stop moving so fast! I'm not a good counter."

After another thirty minute walk, Tarbo reached Warnick's crew. "Where's the foreman?"

Warnick saw Wynn following close behind. "Is he with you?"

Tarbo turned around and saw Wynn. "Maybe the Sarge's going to help me carry the board stretcher back to Red."

"A what?" asked Warnick.

"A board stretcher. Got one?"

"We just busted it. The next crew has one, though."

"Where're they at?"

"Two miles up the road."

With Wynn following close behind, Tarbo resumed his quest. He stopped near a tiny stream and stared into it. "Lookie at the fishes," he shouted. Taking his shoes off, he waded into the stream and tried to catch them. After three futile attempts, he crawled up on an embankment and plopped down, his feet pointing skyward.

When a red-tailed hawk whistled sharply, Tarbo leaped up and shouted, "Ain't she a beauty, Sarge?" As the bird rode the air currents, Tarbo yelled, "I want to fly, too!" He began by flapping his arms, while galloping toward Wynn. Then Tarbo leaped from a small knoll before rolling to a stop in a gully, filled with dandelions. When Wynn reached him, Tarbo held his stomach with his hands.

"Are you hurt?"

"Don't you hear something?"

Wynn shook his head.

"My belly says it's time to eat."

"It wouldn't look good if you starved out here."

Startled with that possibility, Tarbo's eyes became big as saucers. "We ain't going to die out here, are we?"

Wynn began to chuckle aloud. "Don't worry. The Dutchman's up ahead with something for us to eat."

"Good," said Tarbo, and he turned and began running toward the next crew, and more significantly toward his next meal. When Wynn failed to keep up with him, he stopped and said, "C'mon Sarge, it's just over the next hill."

When Wynn caught up, he said, "How do you know that?"

"Because I can smell the food a mile away."

When they arrived at the work site, the other men had begun eating. Everyone acknowledged Wynn, but some snickered when they saw Tarbo.

"Hey Dutch, got any vittles?" Tarbo shouted.

"Vittles?"

Wynn interceded. "Food, Dutchman."

"Oh," said Dutch, "we always got enough for a couple of more guys." Then he asked, "Where's your mess gear?"

"I don't got any," said Tarbo.

Dutch rummaged through a large box and came up with utensils and a plate. "You like macaroni and cheese?"

"I sure do," said Tarbo.

Dutch filled Wynn's plate and then Tarbo's.

"You got any java?" asked Tarbo.

"Need a cup, too?" asked Dutch.

"Sure."

When Dutch pulled a cup from his box and filled it up with coffee, Cartwright exploded. "Don't you own anything, you big lug?" He turned to his crew and said, "While we're eating out of tin cans, take a look at good old Tarbo! He's got everything excepting napkins and a goblet." As Tarbo continued to stuff his face, Cartwright yelled,

"What the hell are you doing here?"

Tarbo did not answer immediately, because his mouth was full. Finally, he said, "I'm looking for a board stretcher."

Choking, Cartwright replied, "The shooter's took it. Guess you'll have to go back without it."

When Tarbo shrugged his shoulders and looked into the heavens, Wynn said, "Don't take it so hard, kid."

"I'll give you a lift back," said Dutch.

"Naw, I'll go on Shank's mare." Then Tarbo looked at Wynn. "Is that all right, Sarge?" When Wynn nodded in agreement, Tarbo cleaned his utensils, waved good-bye, and headed back to his crew. Then Tarbo turned around and said, "C'mon, Sarge. Let's go back together."

Wynn shrugged his shoulders. "Why not?"

The sun had risen higher, making it more uncomfortable. Whenever Wynn tried to hurry, Tarbo worried aloud about heat stroke and immediately sat down.

"Why were you able to run to lunch?" asked Wynn. "It's not a lot hotter now as it was then."

"Don't the doctors say you should do nothing for at least one hour after you ate?"

"That's swimming," said Wynn.

"Well, I'd better be careful anyway," said Tarbo.

Regardless of Wynn's protestations, the trip back took the rest of the afternoon.

When Wynn and Tarbo had returned, the men were in the trucks, awaiting the long ride back to camp. "Hey Tarbo," shouted Red. "Where's my board stretcher?"

"Nobody's got one."

Then the men exploded with laughter. Ontek pointed his finger at his forehead, making a circular motion. "You dumb cluck. There ain't no such thing."

As his tormentors laughed, Tarbo said, "I know that. But while you guys was smashing rocks, me and my Sarge was having a nice walk through the woods, listening to the birds, counting clouds..."

Wynn interrupted Tarbo. "Don't forget trying to fly."

170

"Yeah," said Tarbo, "I got to work on that for a while."

Later, work on Truck Trail Number One almost slowed to a halt. At least it became much less efficient. A few young ladies from Hallton frequented a small swimming hole adjacent to the road site. Their swimming and sunbathing usually coincided with the road crew's lunch break, making it difficult for the men to focus on their work.

On a particularly humid August afternoon, Marygold Halke, finally forced Red's hand. As Marygold crawled out of the stream, she loosened her halter and laid down in the sand. Then she said loudly, "I wish someone would rub suntan oil onto my back."

Instantaneously, Ontek, Cartwright, and Newt Blaustine jumped into the water, fully clothed. While the other men cheered them on, Ontek and Newt churned their way toward Marygold. Ontek hit the shore first, but Newt pulled Ontek back into the water, vaulting ahead of him.

In his haste to help Marygold, Cartwright had forgotten that he did not know how to swim. As Cartwright went down for the second time, Wynn yelled, "Grab him, he's drowning."

Marygold leaped into the water, reaching Cartwright quickly. When she pulled him to safety, she turned an unconscious Cartwright over and assumed the proper position for artificial respiration.

"Why not me, dear Lord?" groaned Timmy Nedshe.

Ontek yelled, "He's faking it."

Newt shouted, "He is not!" Reaching over, he shoved Ontek into the creek. Newt's forward motion caused him to fall on top of Cartwright, who instinctively jumped up, tossing Marygold into the stream.

As more men rushed to help, Red shouted, "The next joker into the water has KP for a month."

Amidst a chorus of moans, Ontek and Marygold scrambled from the water. Then she stood there as everyone ogled her.

"What about the suntan lotion?" Wynn asked.

"Odum, you're just making it worse!" said Red.

Picking up the lotion, Marygold poured some into the outstretched hands of Newt, Cartwright, and Ontek. Then she lay down on a blanket. "Now each of you may rub some on me." When all three men reached out to her simultaneously, she shouted, "One at a time, please."

Newt went first. He rubbed her back so quickly that Wynn jeered, "Jackrabbit!"

Cartwright was next. Unfortunately, he still had sand on his hands. As he rubbed the lotion onto her shoulders, she complained, "What's on your hands? Sandpaper?"

When it became Ontek's turn, he rubbed his hands together and said, "Got to make sure there's lots of lotion on my hands." He put his thumbs on each side of Marygold's spine and moved them gently to the base of her skull, while softly massaging each side of her neck with his fingers. Allowing his hands to slip down slowly between her shoulder blades, he repeated the whole procedure. He massaged each side of her spine and the length of her neck. Then he began to rub her temples in a circular movement.

While everyone watched in silence, Red broke the spell. He bellowed, "All right, lovers! Back to the stone pile!"

As Newt and Cartwright crawled up the bank and walked slowly back to the crew, Ontek lingered, getting Marygold's name and address.

"Adamchunk," yelled Red. "Get over here, now!"

Ontek kissed Marygold's hand, jumped into the creek, and quickly rejoined his crew.

Work progressed slowly the rest of the day. By late afternoon, no one had smashed his quota of rocks. While the men sleep-walked through the last hour of work, Red disappeared.

"Where'd the boss go?" shouted Wynn.

"Why ask me?" bitched Ontek.

"Because your nose is usually up his ass," said Newt.

"Up yours with a wa-wa brush," countered Ontek.

"Oh shit! I busted another handle," added Tarbo.

"What else is new?" screamed three others.

"The appearance of Kulack's truck averted a possible dispute.. When he pulled up beside them, he shouted, "Quitting time!"

"Damned truck driver," muttered Cartwright. "Wish to hell I had his job."

"Come on," said Timmy Nedshe. "Get on the truck. Just be glad it's quitting time."

Kulack stuck his head out the window. "Everybody here?"

"No," said Wynn.

"Who's missing?"

"Red."

"Where is he?" asked Ontek.

"Let's not start that again," moaned Wynn.

Just then, Red reappeared. Smiling, he motioned for quiet. "Listen up, men! I think we'll agree that your work on this project has not been up to snuff." While a few of the men swore under their breath, Red continued. "It's those girls, right?" As cheers and whistles greeted his question, he raised his hand for silence. "I think I have solved our little problem."

Holding his hands over his chest, Newt said, "I hope so, because I got it real bad."

"Where you got it," snapped Cartwright, "is between your legs!"

"Gentlemen, please!" cautioned Red. "I just returned from Hallton where I talked with a teacher friend of mine. He knows all the young ladies we have...Ahh...Gotten to know over the past few weeks. Anyway, he and I and the girls have agreed to hold dances at the town social hall for the next four consecutive Saturdays. As the men cheered, Red raised his hands again. "There are a few strings attached, however. And the first one is that the girls will stop swimming near the work site." While the men groaned, Red announced the second provision. "Each man must smash his daily quota of rocks. If one person fails to meet the requirement, there will be no dances. It's as simple as that." Then Red looked at Tarbo.

Dumbly, he asked, "Do I got pimples or something?"

"You'd better not screw-up," threatened Ontek. "Because I'm going to light up the night with Marygold!"

"There's only one thing better than goofing off," said Tarbo.

"What's that?" asked Red.

"A girl," said a grinning Tarbo. "Any kind of girl."

CHAPTER TWENTY- NINE

Winter came early to the Allegheny in 1933. The first killing frost occurred in late August, and snow flurries became common throughout October. By Armistice Day, eight inches of snow covered everything. A perpetual northwestern wind chilled the men, and the snow stabbed at their faces and hands, making frostbite a real threat.

With the onset of winter, road building had stopped, because the rocks were to hard to split. Instead, the crews worked on Truck Trail Number One's right-of-way. As difficult as smashing rocks, the work was, at least, different. Clearing and burning of underbrush became the standing order as the men traded their knapping hammers for saws, rakes, and axes.

Because driving had become treacherous, Cookie stopped the delivery of hot lunches. Instead, his staff prepared "wonder" sandwiches and distributed them in the mess hall after breakfast. These sandwiches soon became the major topic of conversation.

As everyone sat around a roaring fire at lunchtime, Bert Jones, a new arrival from Harrisburg, pulled a sandwich from his knapsack and looked at it.

"What's wrong?" asked Wynn.

"I've never seen a sandwich like this before."

"That's a 'wonder' sandwich," said Ontek.

"How'd it get that name?"

"Ever see the cooks make them?" asked Wynn.

"No, Sarge, this is only my second day here."

"Your education is about to begin," said Wynn. "First, Cookie lines up six tables in a row...Sort of like an assembly line." Then Wynn stuck his sandwich on a stick and began to toast it. "It takes the whole mess crew to make them. The first guy walks down the table flipping out bread, just like a card dealer. Then the next guy comes behind, dabbing every other slice with butter or maybe lard."

Jones lifted up the edge of his sandwich and peered inside it. "You mean, there's lard in this?"

"Then the Dutchman comes by and smears peanut butter on all the slices he can reach."

"Who's the Dutchman?"

"The world's best sandwich maker."

"Then it's Cookie's turn," said Ontek. "He's carrying three or four different kinds a meat. Depending on his mood, he throws on a piece here and another piece there until he runs out of meat."

Wynn removed his toasted sandwich from the fire. "Here's the best part, kid. The KP's splash on mustard, catsup, or relish."

"Anything to add color," said Ontek.

"And the head KP guy was a house painter before he was laid off, so he knows what he's doing." When Wynn finished his sandwich, he said, "Then they squish them together and give them to us. And when you sink your teeth into one of these delights..."

"And you wonder what to hell you're eating!" yelled the crew in unison.

When Jones bit into his sandwich, he wailed, "It's froze!"

Wynn handed the young man a toasting stick. "Stick this through the sandwich. Then put it over the fire."

When Jones stuck his sandwich into the fire, it immediately turned black and caught fire. Then it fell into the coals.

"Try another one," offered a sympathetic Wynn.

Jones lost that one, too.

Then Wynn reached into the fire with a long handled wire tool.

"What's that?" asked Jones.

"Something Kulack invented." While Wynn retrieved the sandwich, he said, "You better get used to eating burnt bread. Especially on these cold days."

Although the work was still hard, the men worked at a slower pace. As a result, they discovered a way to stretch their lunch hour. This happened innocently enough when Cartwright hit Ontek with a snowball during lunch. He retaliated with a direct hit upon Timmy Nedshe, who then fired snowballs at everyone, drawing the entire crew into the fray. As the snow balls zipped back and forth, Red Dawson, who had lost a sandwich in the fire, became a victim of an errant toss.

Red stopped fishing for his sandwich and scooped up snow in his hands. Quickly making a snowball, he threw it, scoring a direct hit on Wynn. Red immediately followed through with two more solid hits on Nedshe and Ontek. This marked the beginning of the Snowball Battle of Truck Trail Number One, a conflict that lasted another twenty minutes before Red called a halt to it.

As the men trooped back to work, Nedshe called out, "Where'd you learn to throw like that, Red?"

"Just comes natural," replied Red.

"You should be in the big leagues," added Wynn.

"Why don't you pitch for Camp One next year?" asked Nedshe.

"Not a bad idea," said Red. Then he lobbed another one toward Nedshe.

After that, if the men wanted an extended lunch time, all anyone had to do was to throw a snowball at Red. Within minutes, there would be a friendly conflict, involving the whole crew.

The best winter job was burning the large piles of underbrush that lined the road. At least, nobody ever complained of getting cold when doing this job. Two men took care of a dozen brush heaps. They used long poles and rakes to rearrange the piles so the wet wood would burn faster. By quitting time, the brush heaps had been reduced to glowing hot coals and ashes.

Wynn and Ontek got this choice job on an early December day, because Red was shorthanded. After they had everything burning, Wynn asked, "What are you doing tonight?"

As Ontek moved around the fire to avoid the smoke, he replied, "Got a mechanics class."

"I hear you're pretty good at fixing engines."

"Hope so," said Ontek as he rearranged some green wood that had begun to smoke.

"I got a night off," said Wynn.

"First one in a long time, ain't it?"

"I've been as busy as a one-armed paperhanger. But since I finished my night school classes, I only work two nights teaching reading to some of the fellas here."

As Ontek moved on to another brush heap, he yelled, "Hey, Mr. High School Graduate. Your pile is going out on you." Ontek ran over and helped rearrange the brush. As the fire began to spread, Ontek reached down and threw a snowball at Wynn.

Dodging it, Wynn joked, "That's no way to treat an edju-ma-cated man."

Ontek threw another one but it missed, too. Then he leaned on his pole and watched the smoke spiral upward. After a while, he said, "Have you seen Ruth Anne?" When Wynn nodded, Ontek asked, "Where at?"

"At her class."

"Do you talk?"

"Only about my reading class." Thoughtfully, Wynn added, "She's not cut out for me."

"Oh." Then Ontek asked, "What about college?"

"Doc's helping me. We just sent a letter to Penn State."

"You'll be leaving the C's, won't you?"

"Thirteen months to go."

Ontek remained silent while he threw a large log into the fire. Then he moved away from Wynn toward another brush heap.

After repositioning some branches that had refused to burn, Wynn walked toward Ontek, who still had not spoken. "What's bugging you?"

"You're my very best friend..."

"Hey, I'm only going a hundred miles east of here."

"Yeah, but you'll be a college man..."

Wynn threw a wet handful of snow at Ontek. "You'll be the one with a good job while I'm still on the dole."

A wet snow had began to fall, making it more difficult to burn the green wood. The two men used their tools to rearrange the hot spots, but as they worked, the snow came down ever harder, knocking down the flames. Dense clouds of smoke rose up and then sunk back down upon the ground, held there by the high humidity.

As Wynn looked down the road, he saw columns of smoke rising above each side of the road. Staring hypnotically at the walls of smoke, he said, "Looks like the smoke's closed in each side of the road, making it go on forever."

Walking over to Wynn, Ontek asked, "What are you looking at?"

"I think my eyes are playing tricks."

As Ontek studied the phenomenon, he said quietly, "I can see your future out there."

"What?" said Wynn.

"You heard me," said Ontek.

Wynn began to laugh. "Jeez, another one of your old country superstitions?"

"I'm not joking, Wynn. The smoke tells me everything."

Wynn decided to humor his friend. "Well, tell me about my life."

Cupping his hands over his eyes, Ontek slowly answered, "I see a long life ahead for you with a nice wife and lots of kids."

"And do you see your future, too?" While Ontek remained quiet, Wynn grew impatient. "Tell me what you see."

Rubbing his eyes, Ontek said, "Mine ain't out there."

Growing nervous, Wynn said, "C'mon, good buddy. Quit pulling my leg."

Ontek turned away from the smoke and looked directly at his friend. "There ain't nothing out there but your life."

Irritated, Wynn jabbed Ontek in the chest. "So help me, sometimes I think you're as nutty as a fruitcake."

Kulack interrupted them by blowing the horn sharply. As Wynn and Ontek picked up their tools and walked toward the truck, Kulack blew the horn three more times. Then he shouted, "Get your asses in gear before I leave you guys out here in the boonies."

Concerned that Kulack was serious, they ran toward the truck. Neither young man wanted to walk twenty-five miles back to camp.

CHAPTER THIRTY

The winter of 1933-34 was the coldest Allegheny winter on record. During February 1934, the mercury had dipped below zero on eighteen days. Eight of those days saw the temperature plunging to more than twenty below zero! The outlying areas routinely reported temperatures at forty below.

Fortunately, the men at Camp One no longer lived in tents. Four barracks, each housing fifty men, had been completed before Christmas. Ugly, but utilitarian, the barracks were covered with tar paper and furring strips. Each barrack had crude indoor toilets, shower facilities, and hot and cold running water.

A large coal stove, located in the middle of each barrack, provided heat. Recent arrivals slept farthermost from the stove and the shower room complex. A two-man fire detail patrolled the barracks each night. If a barrack stove went out, this detail had to contend with fifty hostile young men.

Carmine Pompodura and Sollie Bondurusso, both from Trenton, New Jersey, barged noisily into Barrack Number Three, carrying buckets of coal to bank the stoves. When Carmine forgot to shut the outside door, a few obscenities greeted him.

Cartwright, who had just taken a shower, screamed, "You born in a barn, asshole?"

Matters became worse when Sollie forgot to open the stove's damper before putting coal into the stove. A large puff of coal smoke spread throughout the building. Now the obscenities became personal.

Coughing badly, Silent Kylocker shouted, "Do you guys know your ass from a hole in the ground?"

"Up yours, Kylocker," snarled Carmine.

"Let the fire go out tonight, and I'll personally string y'all up by your balls!" threatened Newt Blaustine.

Sollie shook down the ashes from the stove and ignored his critics. "It's as cold as a witch's tit," he said.

"Over at the mess hall, Cookie was listening to Admiral Byrd," added Carmine.

Villic was half asleep when he heard Carmine's reference to Admiral Byrd. Bolting upright in his bunk, he asked, "Vat happened to Grabowski? Vas he canned?"

"You dumb Hunky! Grabowski's still here," responded Carmine.

Villic looked to his friend, Howie Petrosky, for an answer. "Then why vas Cookie listening to this here navy guy?"

Petrosky shrugged his shoulders and pointed at Carmine.

"Admiral Byrd's exploring the South Pole." While shoveling the cinders into a bucket, Carmine continued, "Tonight, Byrd broadcast directly from the bottom of the world."

"Big frigging deal," grumbled Kylocker.

"Byrd said it was twenty-six degrees below zero at his base camp. Then you know what?"

"I'm sure you're going to tell us," said Kylocker.

"Cookie checked his thermometer outside the mess hall door."

"It was down to thirty-three below!" interrupted Sollie.

"She...it! Looks like the admiral better bring in his brass monkeys," hooted Ontek.

With a straight face, Sollie offered, "Just before I came in here, I saw a dog frozen to a tree!"

"Y'all don't really know cold," countered Newt. "Down in Georgia, it got so cold once that I saw a lawyer with his hands in his own pockets."

Just then, the stove belched another black cloud of smoke, prompting a chorus of hacking to ripple throughout the building.

As Carmine went over to check it, he threatened, "You guys had better be nice, or we're going to let the fire go out."

"Yeah," agreed Sollie, "accidentally on purpose."

Wynn was lying in his cot listening to the discussion. Turning over, he leaned on one elbow and said, "C'mon, let's have some news from the other barracks."

"Yeah," said Ontek. "Is the big fight still on between Dutch Osterman and Bill Shaftoe?"

"Right after chow, tomorrow" answered Carmine.

"Shaftoe's going to kill the Dutchman," added Sollie.

"Don't bet on it," said Newt. Pointing at Wynn, Newt said, "He's training the Dutchman."

"Yeah, but Dutch's giving away eighty pounds to Shaftoe," said Carmine. Holding a dollar bill up in the air, he shouted, "My money says the Dutchman won't last a round!"

Wynn rolled over in bed and closed his eyes. Once again, he felt responsible for Dutch's problems. "If the Dutchman had been a lousy dancer, he wouldn't be in this pickle," he groaned.

Wynn remembered that the fight between Dutch Osterman and Bill Shaftoe had been brewing for some time. When Shaftoe came into the outfit, he had teased Dutch about his accent. The ribbing turned mean when Shaftoe took Clarissa Culpepper to the Christmas Frolic at the Marienville Fire Hall. After three dances with Shaftoe, Clarissa suggested that he should see Dutch about lessons.

Open conflict between the two men occurred later when Shaftoe made a vile comment about Trudy Dankiewicz, one of Dutch's fiancees. Enraged, Dutch leaped over the serving table and squared off against the big man. Peaches got between them and kept them from fighting until Wynn had arrived from the kitchen.

"What the hell's going on?" Wynn asked.

"He called my Trudy an awful name."

"How in hell would he know," snapped Shaftoe. "He don't know English."

"He called my little Trudy a, a, a..."

"I called her a slut!" bellowed Shaftoe.

"You can't duke it out here," cautioned Wynn.

Then Dutch got an idea. "You know those books that Peaches reads? They're always having duels over something. Since Shaftoe called my Trudy an awful name, I think we ought to duel."

"With guns?" asked a wide-eyed Shaftoe.

"Hell no!" interrupted Wynn. "In the ring with boxing gloves."

Dutch reached up and tapped Shaftoe's cheeks with his open palm.

"What did you do that for?" asked Shaftoe.

"I fight for my Trudy's honor," answered Dutch.

"For God's sake, Dutch. Be serious!" pleaded Wynn.

Shaftoe reached down and slapped Dutch's left cheek. "When I get done with you, there'll be nothing left except a spot of wiener schnitzel."

As the men began shouting, Wynn bowed to public interest. He announced, "All right. The fight's on for Wednesday night. Right after evening mess."

Kylocker raised a point of order. "It'll be no fun to watch the fight outside. We'll freeze to death!"

"We'll set up the ring in here," suggested Wynn.

The men agreed and began talking excitedly about the fight.

Wynn's only recourse was to step-up Dutch's lessons. First off, Wynn had his student do some shadow boxing. When Dutch tripped and fell down, Wynn complained, "How come you're such a good dancer but yet have such awful footwork as a boxer?"

"Because when I dance, nobody's going to hit me."

Exasperated, Wynn threw his hands in the air. "Good God! A lover not a fighter."

Then Wynn had Peaches hold a flour bag in front of Dutch. "Pretend that's Shaftoe," coaxed Wynn. When Dutch hit the flour bag twice before stopping, Wynn yelled, "What's wrong?"

"It hurts my hand."

"Lookie here, Dutch. It's lights out if Shaftoe tags you. He's bigger and will knock you ass-over-tincups." Pausing, Wynn added, "Shaftoe doesn't have speed. We have to work on your footwork. That way you can take advantage of his size."

Wynn showed Dutch a basic boxing stance. Then still another. Finally, Wynn physically set Dutch's hands and feet in a correct position.

Dutch caught a glimpse of himself in a mirror. Smiling, he puffed out his chest and then looked at his friend Peaches. "Just like that Sullivan fella, eh?" Still caught up in a fighting mode, Dutch swung wildly with a roundhouse-right.

Wynn ducked easily under the blow and screamed, "The power of a boxer comes from his feet not his hands." Wynn gently lobbed a right to Dutch's chest. "Think I'd lie to you?" Then Wynn tried another approach. He took a two foot cord and tied each end around Dutch's ankles.

"What are you doing that for?"

"You can't strike a hard blow if your feet's splayed apart like you're doing a polka. Now punch the flour bag while I watch."

A lunging Dutch tripped over his tether. Missing the bag completely, he hit, instead, Peaches, who dropped to the floor, as if hit with a sledge hammer.

Untying the rope from Dutch's feet, Wynn looked at Peaches, who did not know what had happened. Then Wynn peered at a worried Dutch. "That's the end of the lesson, boys. Maybe we should burn a candle."

"Is one going to be enough?" asked Peaches.

Shrugging his shoulders, Wynn said, "Maybe a box of flares might get His attention!"

After lights out, Wynn could not sleep. He still worried about the upcoming fight. There must be a way out of this mess, he thought. As he stared into the darkness, an idea began to take shape. Sitting up in bed, he said aloud, "It's so simple. Even Dutch can't screw it up."

At least four men shouted, "Shut up."

Excitedly, Wynn got up, opened his foot locker, and rummaged through it until he found a canteen, full of water. Then he put on his clothes, walked quietly out of the building, and headed toward the mess hall.

The cooks slept in a small building next to the mess hall. Cookie had a separate room while Dutch and Peaches shared one. Everyone was snoring loudly when Wynn walked in. He went straight to Dutch's bed and touched his arm. When Dutch did not respond, Wynn began to shake him. Finally, Wynn awakened his friend.

Startled, Dutch said, "What are you doing here?"

"I've got a plan for your fight with Shaftoe."

Dutch smiled and said, "You bet your life...For my Trudy!"

Wynn showed him the canteen. Going to the window, he opened it slightly and placed the canteen on a hook outside the

183

window. As he closed it, he said, "By morning, it'll be froze solid and here's what I want you to do." When Peaches began to awaken, Wynn whispered the rest of his plan into Dutch's ear.

Upon hearing it, Dutch bolted upright in bed. "But won't that hurt?" he asked.

Wynn pushed Dutch down into bed. "It's either that, or you're going to be dead."

As Wynn began to leave, Dutch raised up on his elbow. "Thanks, friend."

Wynn waved at him. "Just don't forget the plan."

The next morning was bitter cold. Thirty-three degrees below zero! While the men hurried into the mess hall, they showed no inclination to go back outside. "Ain't no way in hell I'm going to work today," shouted Carmine as he filled his coffee cup for the third time. Then he turned to Shaftoe and yelled, "You got the fire detail today. Better get over to Barrack One. The fire's damn near out."

"Keep your shirt on," responded Shaftoe.

In the meantime, Dutch had put on his winter gear. He went to the refrigerator where he had stored the frozen canteen. Carefully, he wrapped his scarf around the canteen before hiding it under his jacket. Then he slipped out the back door.

Wynn shouted at Shaftoe, "You'd better get going. The men over at Kelletville beat the shit out of a guy just because he let a fire go out."

When the other men agreed with Wynn, Shaftoe quickly gulped down his coffee and headed for the door. Upon opening it, he allowed a bitter blast of cold air to blow into the room.

"Shut the damn door!" Wynn demanded.

Muttering obscenities, Shaftoe closed the door behind him.

Staring at the door, Higgleston complained, "That bastard better not let any fires go out today."

Then Dutch barged through the mess hall doors. "Shaftoe fell on the icy steps. We got to get him to the Doc!"

While two men took an unconscious Shaftoe to the infirmary, the men in the mess hall marveled at Dutch's concern. "Three cheers for the Dutchman," shouted Sollie.

As the cheers reverberated throughout the building, Wynn

stood behind the serving line, rubbing his chin. "Some of the best ideas are the simple ones," he said.

Then Cookie yelled, "Hey, Wynn. The Doc wants you over at the hospital on the double."

"What's going on, Cookie?" asked Wynn.

"Something big! That's what," answered Cookie.

Wynn shivered as he put on his cap. Then he made sure his ear flaps were pulled town. Wrapping a scarf around his nose and mouth, he opened the door slightly and squeezed through it as fast as possible. Once outside, he started to trot toward the hospital. When he reached the hospital, he heard Frank and Dutch talking.

"Will he be all right, Doc?"

"He'll have a headache for a while, but I want Shaftoe to stay here for the next day," said Frank.

"Can I stay with him?" asked Dutch. "I want him to see my face when he comes around."

Frank pulled up a chair next to Shaftoe's bed. Then he motioned for Dutch to sit down. While closing the examining room's curtain, Frank looked up and saw Wynn. "Seems you and I are going to a trial, Wynn. Fifty-one colored men at the Highland Camp refused to work because of the cold. The army's going to court-martial them."

"How does that affect us?"

"I'm their legal counsel."

"But you're no lawyer."

"This will be a summary court-martial. Any U.S. military officer can do it."

"How many days do you have to prepare?"

"The case is scheduled for 1530 tomorrow!"

"But why include me?"

"Since the preparation time's so short, I requested that you help me."

"What do I have to do?"

"I want you to gather background information for me."

When Shaftoe began to come around, Frank said, "You've had quite a blow to your head, young man."

Shaftoe looked up and smiled at Dutch.

"You're going to be good as new," offered Dutch.

Looking at Frank, Shaftoe said, "Dutch is a true friend, ain't he? We're going to be best buddies from now on."

"Does that mean we won't have to fight?" asked Dutch.

Wynn kicked Dutch in the shin and then looked at Frank for reenforcement.

"With that blow on the head, you will do no fighting for some time," said Frank.

"I wouldn't ever fight my buddy, Dutch," said Shaftoe. "And I'll brain anyone who ever makes fun of him again."

Beaming, Dutch said, "That's my friend."

"They'll be calling you the Two Musketeers soon," said Wynn.

"Wynn," Frank said, "you'd better go pack enough clothes for a two days. This is going to be an interesting experience."

"I don't like the way you said that, Doc."

"Major Anderson has already decided that the men are guilty."

"Looks like we're all going to get a lesson?"

"I'm afraid so, Wynn."

CHAPTER THIRTY-ONE

While Frank warmed up the car, Wynn came from the infirmary carrying four army blankets. As he climbed into the car, he said, "If you haven't noticed, it's only five above zero."

"Son, this automobile is a Packard. Not to worry!" Frank pulled the car from the parking lot and drove slowly out of camp. While driving up the hill, he hit a terrific pothole, making the car groan. "I hope this isn't a hint of what's to come," he said.

"How far is it to the camp?"

Twenty-five miles," Frank answered, "but the final seven miles are on dirt roads."

The paved road was snow-covered and icy in spots. Complicating matters were the huge drifts that had blown out onto the road. Frank had to approach them with caution.

"Can't ever tell how wide and how deep they really are," groaned Frank.

"Don't the snow fences work," asked Wynn.

"The snow drifts over them very fast," said Frank.

"As far as I'm concerned, this winter driving up here is downright dangerous."

"Certainly not for the inexperienced," said Frank. "I had one patient who was stuck on a back road. He nearly died of exposure."

When they left the hard-top, the frozen ruts threw the car nearly into the ditch. After Frank had regained control, he said, "Now the adventure begins."

When the road worsened, Frank found some high ground and parked the car. Then he gave Wynn a lesson on how to put on the car chains. After completing this winter ritual, Frank admitted, "I sure am glad you brought along the blankets."

As they continued toward Camp Four, Wynn noticed that the side windows were completely covered with frost. "Jeez, it's like driving in a tunnel."

"Winter driving is a constant battle," said Frank. Then he reached under the seat and gave Wynn a tiny cloth bag. "Use this," Frank said. "It should do the trick."

"What is it?"

"A salt bag. Rub it on the window. That should improve your vision."

As the car bounced along, Wynn rubbed the frost from the window and looked outside. Apprehensively, he said, "I don't even see a house."

Frank had no time to respond. Suddenly, he shouted, "Hang on!" The car almost stalled as it bottomed out in a frozen mud hole that stretched across the road. Pieces of brown ice flew up over the hood and onto the windshield. As the car settled into the muck, he quickly down-shifted and gassed the engine. The car shot from the morass as if an unseen hand had propelled it. "We almost had it that time," he admitted. While Wynn hung on, Frank skillfully kept the car moving forward. When Frank finally saw the sign for Camp Four, he joked, "Nothing like a wintertime jaunt through the Pennsylvania woods."

When they pulled into camp, Wynn saw a fat army officer approaching the car. Wynn muttered aloud, "Looks like one of them Japanese wrestlers."

When Frank rolled down the window, the officer said, "I'm Captain Moore. You must be Captain Millet."

While Frank acknowledged the greeting, Wynn mumbled, "Now I know how Stanley must have felt when he met Dr. Livingstone!"

When they arrived at Moore's quarters, a colored man with bandages covering his eyes opened the door. Captain Moore said, "That's Lincoln Peacock. He's blind." Before asking Frank to sit down, More turned to Lincoln and said, "Take Captain Millet's aide into the pantry. Wait there until further orders."

The pantry was a tiny room adjacent to the kitchen. As Wynn sat down, he saw a mirror in the kitchen. Looking into it, he could see into the dining room. "How long must we stay here?" Wynn whispered.

"When the Man says for us to leave."

As Moore and Frank sat down at the dinner table, Wynn stared at a white tablecloth that nearly reached the floor. He had never seen fabric that white before.

While waiting for his food, Frank commented, "This tablecloth certainly enhances regular army utensils."

"That's a war prize," said Moore. "I got it in France. The owner was unhappy when I took it. But what the hell, we won, didn't we?" When Moore clapped his hands, two Negroes brought in food and began to serve it. After they had finished, Moore said, "That will be all, boys." Then Moore began to talk about his new command. "This is my first experience commanding colored boys. But having been reared in Virginia, I've had lots of experience with them. My family owned a dray business near Lynchburg. The good niggers did the heavy work for us. Daddy always treated them like children. That's the correct way to work them."

When Frank mentioned the historic role black soldiers played at the Texas border before World War I, Moore responded, "Look who commanded them, John J. Pershing!"

"Why do you suppose they called him, 'Black Jack,'" Frank said. When he had completed eating, Frank pushed his chair away from the table. Then he accepted a cigar from Moore.

"You'll find these Virginia cigars better than the big Cuban ones," said Moore.

After lighting it, Frank took a deep puff and said, "Hmmn, not bad. Not bad at all." Then he asked, "What happened to the young man who had bandages over his eyes?"

"Lincoln? He was a shooter on a road crew. An explosion nearly killed his partner."

"He's under treatment, I presume?"

"We don't have a camp doctor. But a local doctor saw him once."

"What will happen to him?"

"If his sight doesn't come back, I'll discharge him."

"I'd like to examine him," offered Frank.

"One less to look after," sighed Moore.

"He's very young to have handled explosives!"

"Hell, Doctor, somebody had to do it. But the Almighty just didn't parcel out brains to those boys." Moore leaned forward in his chair. "Darwin was right when it came to the colored. But that don't mean that we can ignore them. Not on your mother's tintype! The uppity ones are dangerous. Go around and give the others ideas! Just like the case you're going to prosecute tomorrow."

Frank interrupted his host's tirade. "You realize, of course, that I'm defending them."

Moore laughed. "I've got them niggers dead to rights on insubordination."

"Over in Europe, I worked with Negro doctors. They were a credit to the medical profession."

Moore hooted loudly and slapped his knee. "Bet they had white blood in them."

Frank excused himself. "It's getting late. Could you show me my room, please?"

Captain Moore clutched the edge of the table and the veins in his neck began to protrude. "Those coons that get an education. They're the dangerous ones."

"In 1917, I saw those 'dangerous ones' perform surgery around the clock within earshot of the gas shell explosions."

"Don't get me wrong, Doc. I don't want no bloodshed. Just put them aside, where they can't do no harm. You know what I mean?" Moore's voice had risen in pitch and his accent got thicker as he ranted about Negroes. Suddenly, he stopped and looked at Frank, whose face had remained expressionless. "I'm deeply sorry, Captain Millet. Apparently, we do not share similar viewpoints about the racial problems afflicting our sovereign nation." Rising from his chair, he bowed deeply and clicked his heels. "Sir, you are my guest. I'm sorry if I have offended you."

When Moore took Frank down a narrow hallway, Wynn could no longer see them, but he could still hear them.

Moore said, "This room is mine. That one over here is the guest room. If you need anything, just yell. I got a boy who stays here all night."

190

Frank said, "Captain Moore, our discussion this evening reminded me of some German colleagues I had met in New York."

"How's that, Captain Millet?"

"Their attitude toward the Jews is similar to your feelings about Negroes."

"I can't say those Krauts are all bad!" replied Moore.

Wynn heard a door close and then he saw Moore walking toward them.

"Lincoln?"

"Yes, Sir?" responded the young man.

"Take Dr. Millet's aide to the mess hall so he can eat. Then you two'll bunk with the cooks."

Lincoln motioned for Wynn to follow him. As they reached the door, each young man offered a quick good night to Moore. Then Lincoln opened the door, and they plunged into the darkness.

The sharp wind made Wynn inhale deeply. "Where's the mess hall?"

"You forget, boy, I'm blind." replied Lincoln. He extended his hand and said, "What's your name?"

"Odum, Wynn Odum. And yours?"

As they quickly walked through the compound, the young man replied, "Lincoln Peacock, at your service."

"How do you know where we're going?"

"Nothing to it! It's nine steps from Moore's quarters to the gravel sidewalk. From there, it's another fifty-two steps to the mess hall. Once I get near the mess hall, I let my nose do the walking." As they came to the mess hall steps, Lincoln stopped. "Here we are. Turn right and watch the fourth step. It's a higher than the others."

"How did you get us here?"

Laughing easily, Lincoln said, "Us darkies can talk and count at the same time, boy!" There was no malice in his comment. It was a statement of fact. "Now will you answer a question for me?"

"Fire away."

"Sure there ain't some African blood in you?"

It was Wynn's turn to laugh. "Naw! My father came from Austria. Why would you ask?"

"Because you got the moves of a brother!"

"What do you mean?"

"C'mon in the mess hall, and I'll show you."

As they entered the warm building, Lincoln shouted to the cooks, "I'm going to put on a little parade for this white boy." Letting go of Wynn's arm, he walked ten paces and then returned. When Wynn started to laugh, Lincoln asked, "What are you laughing at?"

"At you, Lincoln. Got a poker stuck up your ass?"

Peacock grinned from ear to ear. "That's how white folks walk. Tight-assed! But you're different. You got music in your walk. You're positive the boat that brought your daddy didn't dip toward Africa?" Then he felt Wynn's face and then his cheek bones and his jaw. As Lincoln ran his index finger over Wynn's eyebrows, he said, "You got a scar there. Did you ever fight?"

"A little."

"I knew you weren't no ordinary white boy!" Softly, he asked, "Did you beat up any of my brothers?"

"A few."

"Fair fights?"

"Always."

Turning to the three young men who stood behind the serving line, Lincoln announced, "I'd like you to meet my friend, Wynn Odum. He's here to help us."

Lincoln sat down at a table and motioned for Wynn to join him. Then he shouted, "Come on boys. Let's eat!"

Willie Mann brought food left over from the evening's meal. Similar to Camp One's menu, it included meat loaf, plenty of mashed potatoes and gravy, and carrots.

As Wynn ate, he noticed one man had an army pistol strapped to his pistol belt. "What's he carrying a gun for? That's against regulations."

Lincoln said, "That's Sarge Dixon. He always totes that, because there's some mean mothers here!"

Accepting this explanation, Wynn attacked his food. "Jeez, I'm hungry."

"Where's the damn salt?" exploded Peacock.

"I'll get it."

"Tell me where it is. At two o'clock or nine o'clock?"

192

Pausing, Wynn said, "It's on your left at three o'clock."

While reaching for it, Lincoln knocked the salt shaker over. "Damn," he said, "being blind is a real pain."

Uneasily, Wynn asked, "How'd it happen?"

"Say it man. It ain't no disease!"

"Your not being able to see."

As Lincoln ate the mashed potatoes, he grimaced and said, "Needs more salt." This time, he found the salt shaker easily and sprinkled some into his left hand before dropping it onto his potatoes. "Jersey Moreland needed an assistant at shooting rocks. It sounded a lot easier than busting stones by hand. We were doing real fine until we got some bad dynamite. A stick went off right after we set it. I lost my hearing and my sight. A week later, my hearing came back, but I still don't know if I can see yet."

"What happened to Jersey?"

"They cut off his legs."

Both young men remained silent for a short time.

Finally, Lincoln spoke. "What do doctors do after they cut off a guy's legs?"

The question made Wynn uncomfortable. "Hell, man, I don't know."

"S'pose they said any prayers over them?"

"Naw. I doubt it."

"Why?"

"Because that's not the most important part of Jersey."

"Not important! He's a cripple."

"What's important is his soul, and since Jersey's alive, his soul is still with him."

"That makes sense," said Lincoln.

"I bet they sent his legs to a medical school for study," offered Wynn.

Slowly, a smile formed on Lincoln's face. "That way, folks could study them and get to know more about the body, couldn't they?"

"Yes."

Lincoln remained silent. Then he said, "Thanks man."

"For what?"

"You know. About Jersey."

Wynn noticed that Lincoln still seemed troubled. "Something else bothering you?

Lincoln's lips became contorted as if he were ready to cry. Finally he blurted, "I'm scared! I lay awake at night and think about seeing again. I want to rip the bandages right off and find out. But I just don't have the guts to do it." He clenched his fists and pounded them on the table. "I'm never going to see again."

"Who said that?"

"A doctor. He thought I was sleeping. But I fooled him. I heard him say that." Lincoln punched his fists together. Then he drummed the table with his fingers. Finally, with an unsteady voice, he asked, "Will you help me?"

"Do what?"

"Be with me when they take my bandages off."

"No problem."

"Thanks, brother."

As they ate, Lincoln told Wynn about what had happened at Camp Four. Slowly, Wynn gained a picture of life in a Negro camp. It was much different than his experiences at Camp One.

"My last commanding officer was a drunk," said Lincoln. "That was the start of our trouble."

"Grabowski's a lot of things, but he ain't no rummy."

"Mine was so drunk all the time that he even forgot to order winter clothes for the guys. A bunch of older enrollees ran the camp. When Captain Moore took over, the leaders thought nothing would change. Was that a mistake. Poor old Ickie Jones was the first cat to feel Moore's sting. Seems that Ickie stole a camp truck. When the cops brought him back, Moore was waiting. He made Ickie strip down naked in front of the whole company. After poor old Ickie stood in the snow bare-assed for fifteen minutes, Moore put him in a barrel outside the mess hall for twenty-four hours. He screamed all night long. The next day, Moore took Ickie out of the barrel and made him run ten laps around the snowy compound. The only thing Ickie had on was a pair of shoes. Then Moore shipped him out on the evening train."

"What happened yesterday?"

"Yesterday was a test between Moore and the men who used to run the camp. The last four days were so damn cold that nobody worked. When Moore came to the barracks and ordered the Timber Survey crew to work, we all knew trouble was coming."

"It was thirty below at Camp One."

"Made no matter to Moore. The trucks took fifty-one boys to work. We pooled our winter gear so the fellas would have some protection. But by ten in the morning, the guys quit. That's when Moore filed the charges."

"Even Grabowski thought it was too damned cold to work."

"It was the ring leaders who talked the rest of them into quitting."

Dixon's voice boomed out, "It's almost three in the morning. Because of you guys, I'll have to make another pot of coffee."

Lincoln stood up and said to Dixon, "Don't bother, Sarge." Then Lincoln offered his arm to Wynn. "Come on brother, I'll show you to your cot."

CHAPTER THIRTY-TWO

Facing Major Oliver Anderson when he walked into Camp Four's Recreation Room were fifty-one young black men who sat in neatly arranged rows of folding chairs. The court stenographer sat ten feet in front of the defendants. On either side of the stenographer was a large table and chair for the counselors. At Anderson's right sat Captain Frank Millet, who represented the accused. Captain Lawrence Roper represented the army.

Anderson cleared his throat and began to speak. "My superiors have ordered me to preside over the trial of fifty-one enrollees accused of insubordination. The defendants are not members of the United States Army. Instead, they are members of the CCC, a civilian agency regulated by the United States War Department. Therefore, the basic rules of a summary court-martial will apply. I will hear the case and decide the outcome. Since this is not a formal military trial, there will be no appeal." As he sat down, he added, "The court has sworn in the witnesses to expedite the legal process. Both counselors have agreed with this procedure." Then he leaned forward and asked, "Will the counselors approach the bench?" When they had complied, Anderson said, "Let's end this charade, gentlemen." Turning to Frank, he said, "Have them plead guilty."

"I thought this was going to be a trial."

"If that's what you wish, counselor, but let's not drag this out all afternoon." Anderson then nodded to Roper. "Please begin."

"Your honor, the War Department charges these fifty-one boys with insubordination, that is a complete unwillingness to submit to proper authority. I will show the court that these boys defied a direct order on three separate instances from their designated superiors. The entire army system is built on authority..."

"I object your honor," said Frank. "These men are not in the Army."

"Objection denied!" said Anderson. "The men are in an agency controlled by the War Department. They must submit to proper authority, in this case, the War Department."

Roper resumed his opening remarks. "Discipline is the glue that holds the entire army system together. If we allow anyone to break that code, we will destroy the very fabric that enables an army to function!"

After Roper had finished, Frank argued that the weather had been so bad that no one should have worked on that day. He did not deny that insubordination had occurred. Then he asked if he could approach the bench. After Roper had joined them, Frank said, "Sir, I want to strike a bargain with the court."

"State your position," replied the judge.

"I have determined that four men led the insubordination. They will plead guilty and place themselves at the court's mercy. Will the army drop the insubordination charges against the other men and allow Captain Moore to discipline them under existing camp rules?"

Major Anderson shook his head. "Call your first witness, Captain Roper."

"Superintendent Stone to the witness chair, please." When Stone sat down, Roper asked, "Mr. Stone what was the nature of the boy's work on 28 February 1934?"

Stone was a short, beefy man who had been with the Forest Service for less than a year. He constantly squirmed in his seat while on the stand. "They were conducting Timber Stand Improvement under my supervision on the Seven Mile Road."

"How cold was it when the men left camp at 0800 on the day of question?"

"Only fifteen below. It had warmed up ten degrees in the past hour."

"What was the temperature at 1030 when the men walked off the job?"

"Twenty degrees above zero."

"What was your reaction when the men laid down their equipment?"

"When I told them to get back to work, Corporal Lewis Christmas said, 'Bullshit!' Then Corporal Marvin Donnelly yelled, 'Let's get the hell out of here and go back to the barracks.'"

"What happened next?"

"When they left the job, the whole crew followed."

"Now don't be nervous. We're here to ascertain the truth," said Roper. "Mr. Stone, did you ever tell the men to leave their jobs during that morning?"

"No, Sir."

"Your witness, Captain Millet."

"Superintendent Stone, describe the clothes you wore on February 28th."

"I had on a wool hat with ear flaps. A good pair of gloves and a heavy mackinaw coat that reached below my hips. Let's see...I had two pairs of woolen socks and a pair of high top boots. Also a woolen pair of trousers plus a pair of long johns."

"Were you cold?"

"My face was."

"What did the enrollees wear?"

"Some didn't have gloves, but most had coats, though."

"Not all the men had coats?"

Stone kept looking at Roper. "Some did not."

"What did the men do the four days before February 28th?"

"They didn't work outside, because it was too cold."

"What was the temperature for those days?"

"Between twenty-five to thirty-five below zero."

"What made the 28th any different from the other?"

"Captain Moore was falling behind his goals. So he wanted me to take the boys out."

"Doesn't the Forest Service control the work outside the camp?"

"Oh, yes, but we cooperate very close with the army."

"Thank you, Mr. Stone."

Then Captain Roper called John Givens, the foreman of the project. A heavyset man, he had a large chew of snuff under his lower lip. He refused to look in the direction of the accused men.

"Did the men work when they arrived at the site?"

"No, Sir. They just sort of milled around and complained."

"Did you give them a direct order to go to work?"

"Yes, I did."

"And their response?"

"Corporal Christmas called me a dirty name."

"What did he call you?"

Barely audible, he said, "It's too awful to repeat."

"What did the boys do after he called you that awful name?"

"They agreed with him."

"Your witness, Captain Millet."

"Mr. Givens, did you tell the men not to work that morning?"

"Never! But I tried to stop them from leaving. That's when one boy threatened me."

"Can you identify the young man who allegedly threatened you?"

Givens peered at the fifty-one men. After two minutes of silence, the judge repeated Frank's question. Finally, Givens mumbled, "I can't pick him out. They all look alike!"

"That's all, Mr. Givens."

Captain Moore was the next witness. Unable to contain himself, he bounded to the front of the room and had barely seated himself before Roper had completed his name.

"Captain Moore, when you got to the work site, what were the boys doing?"

"They had built a huge fire and were standing around it."

"What did you do?"

"I tried to persuade them to return to work."

"And their response?"

"Corporal Christmas called me an 'old fart'. And Corporal Grey pushed me."

"Did you offer any concessions?"

"I told them there would be punishment handed out, but it would be just."

"And their response?"

"At that point, someone shouted, 'Back to camp, men'"

"Can you identify that person?"

Pointing at Corporal Donnelly, Moore said, "That's him."

"Then what happened?"

"As they walked off the job, I went back to the camp and waited. When they had arrived, I warned them again of the consequences of their actions."

"What happened?"

"Private Wilbur Elmore pushed me and walked back to the barracks."

"Your witness, Captain Millet."

"What is your idea of just punishment, Captain Moore?"

Moore sat up straight in his chair, and closed his eyes as if trying to remember his personal book of rules. "Restriction to camp...No leaves for three months...Fines totaling three dollars a month for two months."

"Oh, you wouldn't put anyone in a barrel nude and confine him like an animal for twenty-four hours..."

Roper shot up from his chair. "Objection...This is irrelevant to the case."

Without looking up, Anderson muttered, "Sustained."

Frank shook his head. "Captain Moore, have you had any disciplinary problems at the Highland Camp?"

"Objection. This has no bearing to this case."

"Sustained."

"Your honor, I am trying to show there was just cause for the actions of these men."

"Captain, you have been overruled. Get on with the proper line of questioning, please!"

"Did you go into the barracks on the evening of the 27th and tell these men they would work the next day, regardless of the weather?"

"We were weeks behind schedule because of my predecessor's poor administration. I told them we would work if the weather broke..."

"...Twenty-five degrees below zero means the weather broke?"

"Let me remind you, Captain Millet. It was twenty-five degrees above zero later that day."

"That's all Captain Moore," said Frank. "You may step down, please."

The judge looked at Frank and said, "You may call your defense witnesses, Captain."

The first person to testify for the defendants was Red Dawson. As Red got comfortable in his chair, Frank asked him his position at Camp One. "I'm a foreman for the Project Superintendent at Camp One."

"What did you do with your crew on the 28th?"

"Nothing, Sir. It was too cold."

"What was the temperature."

"Twenty-seven below zero. Nobody went out in the field. We had assignments for the men ranging from studying reading to helping in the mess hall. While some men hauled coal to the barracks, others kept the fires going."

"Nobody worked outside?"

"No, Sir. At least not for but a few minutes. Exposure to that kind of weather can hurt a person just like that." To emphasize his point, he snapped his fingers as he completed his statement.

"That's all, Mr. Dawson."

Now it was Roper's turn to cross examine Red.

"Mr. Dawson, have you worked in below zero weather?"

"Yes."

"It doesn't look as if it had harmed you."

"I was dressed for it. I know the danger signs that would tell me to get out of it as soon as possible."

"But have you worked in below zero weather?"

"Many times."

"For how long?"

"Up to a couple of hours each time."

"And you survived?"

"Certainly, but..."

"Step down, please."

As Red walked back to his seat, he mumbled loudly that he did not have a chance to continue his statement. Anderson gaveled for order, while Frank called Clarence Hufnegle to the stand.

"Private Hufnegle, what camp are you assigned?"

"The Kelletville Camp, Sir."

"Where are you from, young man?"

"Huntly, Alabama, Sir."

"How do you like our weather?"

"Not fit for man nor beast, Sir!"

"Private Hufnegle, how cold was it at Kelletville at 0500 on Feb 28th?"

"Thirty-eight below, Sir."

"What was your reaction to work that day?"

"No way was I going to work in that cold!"

"What happened when the trucks pulled up to your barrack door that morning?"

"None of us budged. After a while, all of the drivers joined us, too."

"Why?"

Laughing, he said, "Their engines stalled. And they couldn't restart them."

"What happened when Captain Haines came to your barrack?"

"He huffed and puffed a lot, but no one went outside. Finally, he left. We stayed there all morning. Then he reappeared and said that he was going to punish us for insub...Insurb...For disobeying an order."

"What was the punishment?"

"Captain Haines is a physical fitness nut..."

"Objection."

"Sustained. Strike the last statement from the record."

"He led us in physical exercises. That was our punishment. After thirty minutes of jumping up and down in the snow, he had enough and dismissed us to our barracks."

"Then what did you do?"

"After lunch, we went out in the field to work."

"What was the temperature then?"

"A regular heat wave, Sir! Must have been twenty degrees, anyway."

"Thank you, son."

The next witness Private Leroy Green jogged to the witness stand. A few giggles from the boys made Anderson look up sharply.

"Private Green, are you from this camp?"

"Yes, Sir."

"Did you refuse to work?"

"Yes, Sir."

"Why?"

"I was freezing to death!"

"Objection...The statement is not specific enough!"

"Sustained."

"How cold were you?"

"I lost the feeling in my feet."

"That's all." Frank turned to Captain Roper. "He'll ask you some questions."

"Private, do you drink?" asked Roper.

Frowning, Green said, "Once in a while, Sir."

"Do they drink methano in your barrack?"

Private Green did not answer. Desperately, he looked around as if he were looking for a way to escape.

"Answer the question, boy!" snapped Roper.

"I object," shouted Frank. "The last question has no relevance to the case."

Major Anderson replied, "Objection denied. This could have a bearing on the case!"

"You took a drink of methano before you went to work that morning, didn't you?" demanded Roper.

"Some did," mumbled the young man. He fixed his eyes on his shoes and would not look at anyone.

"Speak up, boy!" demanded Roper.

"But not me!" Green whispered. "That stuff killed a CCC brother over at Croyland last month."

Roper looked at Green and said, "That's all, boy!"

Next to testify was Private Jomak Littleton. When he sat down, he twisted his shirt tail into a tight knot until the buttons were ready to pop.

Quietly, Frank said, "Now, son, we're not here to hurt you." Then he handed the distraught young man a glass of water. "Take this and just relax."

The frightened young man took it from Frank's hand and gulped it down without taking a breath.

"Tell us when you're ready," said Frank.

203

When the young man nodded, Frank asked, "Why did you quit working on February 28th?"

"M-M-My hands was cold."

"Why were they cold?"

"Because I don't have no g-g-gloves."

"Tell the court why you had no gloves."

"Ah...I was n-never given none."

"How long have you been in camp?"

"F-F-Four months."

"Your witness, counselor."

"No questions," mumbled Roper.

As Private Woodward Charles came to the stand, several of his friends patted him on his back.

"Why did you stop working on February 28th?"

"I was cold, Sir."

"Why?"

"Because I was wearing summer underwear and a thin pair of summer pants."

"Any reason for this, son?

"I got one pair of winter underwear and it was so cold in the barrack...It couldn't dry."

"Have you been issued winter underwear?"

"No, Sir. The pair I told you about came from my Aunt."

"How long have you been here at Camp Four?"

"Six months."

"Thank you...Counselor?"

"No questions."

"My next witness is Private Tyrone Pickney."

As Pickney walked past Charles, he winked at him and said, "Good job, Woody!"

"Private Pickney, what did Mr. Stone tell you at 0800 about the cold?"

"He said we should build a fire and just try to stay warm."

Since all the defendants are under oath, may I have a show of hands from the others who heard that statement?"

"Objection! This can't be entered under formal testimony!"

"If you wish," said Frank, "I'll call every one of these boys."

"Please, Doctor, please!" said Major Anderson. "The objection is overruled."

"Did others hear that statement?" asked Frank as he looked at the accused young men. When seven young men raised their hands, Frank said, "Let the record show that seven boys heard Mr. Stone make that statement." Then he turned back to Private Pickney. "Later on in the morning, did the temperature increase?"

"Maybe it did, but we was awful cold. My face felt like little daggers was being pushed through my cheeks."

"Did you complain?"

"Yes."

"To whom?"

The young man pointed to Givens.

"What was his response?"

"He said it was too cold to work, and he was going to ask the Captain to bring us back in."

"Did others hear it?"

"Yes, Sir."

Looking at the accused young men, Frank asked, "Please raise your hands if you heard Mr. Givens make that statement." When four men raised their hands, Frank said, "Let the record show that four men verified Private Pickney's testimony."

As the trial progressed, Anderson had become increasingly impatient. Making no effort to hide his feelings, he drummed his fingers on the table loudly. Finally, he asked the counselors to approach the bench. "Gentlemen, enough is enough! Let's get to the summation. Captain Roper, you go first."

"Your honor, the case is clear. These fifty-one men disobeyed a direct order and refused to work on the morning of February 28th. This is insubordination. This refusal to work occurred with three witnesses present, all of whom testified to that fact. The defense claims that the Project Superintendent and the foreman encouraged the defendants to stop working. Mr. Stone and Mr. Givens have had long and distinguished careers. To have had their profession questioned by less than reputable witnesses is a despicable act! I ask you to find for the prosecution."

Major Anderson said to Frank, "Begin closing arguments."

"Your honor, consider the weather factors on that bitter morning. I have testimony showing one camp did not work outdoors that day. Another camp worked only in the afternoon when the temperature had risen to twenty degrees above zero. The men have testified that the Project Superintendent and the foreman had doubts about working on that frigid day. In addition, I have shown that these men were not properly dressed for working in such frigid weather. Please consider these factors when making your decision."

After Frank had completed his summation, Anderson rose from his chair and spoke directly to the counselors. "Thank you, gentlemen! I will retire to the next room where I shall make my decision. Everyone will stay here until I return." Then he pivoted smartly and strode from the room.

While some defendants got up to stretch their legs, Frank remained seated. Turning to Wynn, he said, "Thanks Wynn. Without the information you uncovered, I couldn't have put up any defense. As it is, I feel used by the system."

"Looks bad, doesn't it?"

Frank replied, "Those young men don't have a chance."

Suddenly, the door into the Recreation Room opened and Major Anderson briskly walked into the room. Upon reaching his desk, he remained standing. Staring at the accused, he waited for complete silence. "I find the fifty-one boys accused of insubordination guilty as charged."

Moore and Roper beamed, while some of the convicted men muttered aloud. Anderson gaveled for silence. "Their penalty will be immediate dismissal. Since their act of insubordination occurred on the 28th February 1934, they will forfeit their entire pay for the month!"

Pickney yelled, "It ain't fair, Sir. That's money my folks needs!"

Rising above the din was Marvin Donnelly's voice. "A setup! Now Moore can get credit for all the money he's saved Uncle Sam!"

"Order in the court," shouted Anderson. He gaveled sharply before the noise began to subside. Then he glared at the men until they became quiet. "The convicted boys shall receive only train fare to their homes. A truck will pick them up in one hour. If they do not leave on the transportation provided, they shall also forfeit their train ticket. This court is adjourned." Anderson turned sharply on his heels and left the room.

Immediately, Captain Moore walked over to Frank. "Sir, I trust you harbor no hard feelings! Those boys received due process, and the system spoke loudly and clearly." He reached his hand out to Frank.

Not responding to Moore's hand, Frank said, "These are terrible hours for the nation, but there's change in the air. I can feel it." Instead, Frank grabbed Moore's forearm. "Presently, there's a black attorney named Thurgood Marshall who is working with the NAACP. I hope that you and I will live to see the revolution he causes."

Ignoring Frank's comments, Moore said, "By the way, remember young Peacock?"

"Yes."

"I thought you might take him with you. Perhaps you might help him."

"Thank you, Captain Moore."

Just before making an about-face, Moore said, "I hope to see you again this summer."

"In what capacity?" asked Frank.

"At the CCC boxing tournament. "I hear your boy, Odum, is pretty good with his dukes."

"He knows his way around the ring."

Wynn tapped Frank on the shoulder. "Excuse me, Doc, we've got another passenger back to Camp One?"

"You heard Captain Moore, Wynn. Are you interested in the tournament?"

"Sure, but Grabowski isn't going to buy training equipment."

"I'll bring down my gear from Kane," said Frank.

Smiling, Wynn said, "You'd do that for me?"

"Certainly."

"It's a deal!"

"Don't get your hopes up," Moore said. "I got two boys who'll take Odum easily." Then Moore saluted Frank, spun on his heels, and disappeared into Major Anderson's office.

When Frank saw Lincoln, he said, "You're going on temporary duty with me."

"To help me with my eyes?"

"I'll do what I can, son."

While Frank explained the treatment to Lincoln, Wynn went over to a window and looked out. Frost had begun collecting on the inside of the windows, creating a wintery mosaic. The sun had already dipped behind the tops of the maple trees that surrounded the building. He watched the little whirlwinds of snow blow through the compound, causing those men outside to bury their hands deep within their pockets. Wynn could already feel the chill of another bitterly cold Allegheny night.

Then Frank called to Wynn. "Let's get moving before it gets dark. It will be much easier to teach Lincoln how to put on car chains in the daylight."

CHAPTER THIRTY-THREE

Immediately upon returning from Camp Four, Frank began his examination of Lincoln. While Wynn watched, Frank took off the bandages from Lincoln's head.

"Can you see anything?" asked Wynn.

Dejectedly, Lincoln answered, "Nothing." Then he added, "I haven't seen a thing since the explosion."

"Son," cautioned Frank, "we've just started." While examining Lincoln's corneas, Frank said, "I can't see any damage in either one. That's a positive sign."

"How can you tell, Doc?" Lincoln asked.

"There's no scar tissue evident." Then, after looking into the interior of Lincoln's eyes, Frank said, "As I suspected, I can't see the retinas."

"Why, Doc?"

"The sudden flash from the explosion caused blood vessels in your eye to hemorrhage. Right now, I can only see blood."

"Will I see again, Doc?"

Frank placed his hand on the young man's shoulder and said, "A tincture of time will restore your sight. There is no functional damage to your eye. It will heal itself."

"How long will it take?"

"As the blood inside your eyes dissolves, your sight will gradually come back. I've seen similar cases during the war."

A large smile spread over Lincoln's face. "When can I ditch these bandages?"

"About four weeks. In the meantime, it's bed rest for you."

"Bed rest?" moaned Lincoln.

"I'm the boss, now!" said Frank.

"Four whole weeks!" protested Lincoln.

While bandaging Lincoln's head, Frank explained his plan. "I assure you, this is not a boring place. Wynn's reading group meets here daily. And it's about time you got back into some type of formal education."

"That don't sound half bad, especially if Wynn's going to be here."

"Give Lincoln a rundown of our plans, Wynn."

"During the day, each fella from the reading group will take turns reading to you. Then, after supper, we'll meet here to talk about what we read. And I have to warn you, Doc expects you to take part in the discussions."

"What are we reading?"

"Right now we're doing the modern American poets, Whitman and Dickinson up to Frost and Sandburg."

Lincoln remained silent as he felt the fresh bandages on his head. Then he asked, "What do you do for fun around here?"

"Like what?" asked Wynn.

"Like what kind of sports do you play?"

"Baseball and softball in the summer. In the winter, we play basketball up in Marienville. We swim a lot in the summer, and then there's ice-skating when the creeks freeze over."

"Those game's for kids," said Lincoln. "There's nothing like prize fighting."

"We had a tournament last summer," said Frank.

"Was Wynn in it?"

"Yeah," said Wynn.

"Lincoln leaned forward and asked, "Did you win?"

"Yeah."

"There's going to be a big boxing tournament coming up this summer. Guys will be coming in from the whole CCC district. If you like to box, why don't you enter, Wynn? After the Doc fixes me up, I can work your corner."

"That might work out!" exclaimed Wynn.

Lincoln asked, "How does that sound, Doc?"

"An excellent idea," answered Frank.

Wynn remembered his dream of training in a real gym. "You

won't forget to bring down those two punching bags along with all your other equipment?"

"Everything will be here by the end of the week," said Frank.

"Then my friend is going to be the next champ, huh?" asked Lincoln.

Smiling, Wynn said, "Hey, just a minute."

Frank looked at his watch. "Gentlemen, first things first! Wynn, would you please tell Cookie that we'll need to have meals sent over here daily, until further notice."

"Sure thing, Doc." Once outside, he began to trot slowly toward the mess hall, a hundred yards away. When he reached the building, he quickly bounded up its steps. As he entered its warm interior, he saw Dutch and Peaches setting up the serving lines.

Upon seeing Wynn, Cookie bellowed, "Hey kid, come on over here. I got someone who wants to meet you."

Henry Zukowski gradually turned around in his chair and stared at Wynn. "My God, a ghost of the past," said Zukowski.

Wynn looked stunned. "I haven't seen you since..."

"...That day in my English class."

Whistling softly, Wynn said, "Seems like a hundred years ago."

"Ten months and sixteen days ago," said a grim-faced Zukowski. He got up and walked over to his former student, stopping at arm's length from him.

They stood quietly, staring at each other. Neither man averted his eyes.

As Wynn leaned against a mess table, he said, "What are you doing here?"

"I'm the Education Advisor."

"What's that?"

"I'll organize and run Camp One's educational program."

"Wynn's already been working with Doc teaching some of the fellas how to read and write," said Cookie.

"Doc's got a great program in place," said Wynn.

"Lieutenant Grabowski's told me about it," said Zukowski. "It's heavy on the academics. I'm going to emphasize vocational education."

"That will change a lot of things."

"I promise not to tell the Doc how to run his infirmary as long as he stays out of my classrooms." While Wynn grimaced, Zukowski added, "By the way, Murray sends his regards. He's become a power in Pittsburgh politics."

"Does he have a last name yet?"

"Murray Halderman, Vice Chairman of the Democratic Party."

"Still in charge of vice?"

"He's still got his eye on you."

"Murray's old news, like the war."

Zukowski felt his jaw. "I still remember that day."

Grinning, Wynn said, "They paying you in script for this job?"

"That still isn't any of your business."

"It's a different world up here, a place to begin again. What happened between us is in the past." He extended his hand to his former teacher, "Welcome to Camp One, Mr. Zukowski."

Zukowski would not accept Wynn's hand. Instead, he put on his coat, pushed open the mess hall door, and walked out into the compound without ever looking back.

"Phewy, Wynn. That was some kind of scene," said Cookie. "I do believe he don't like you"

"I can't blame him."

"What did you ever do to him?"

"Something I've always regretted."

Just then, Peaches dropped an armload of dishes. Plates, cups, and saucers crashed in all directions. An unbroken saucer twirled crazily before stopping at Cookie's feet.

"Jesus H. Christ, Peaches!" yelled Cookie, "are you trying to put us out of business?"

Wynn looked first at Cookie and then at Peaches, who had tears in his eyes. After helping Peaches pick up the broken dishes, Wynn relayed Frank's message. "Never a dull minute around here," muttered Wynn as he left the mess hall and went outside into the darkness.

CHAPTER THIRTY-FOUR

Frank read to Lincoln during their evening meal. After completing SPOON RIVER and MY ANTONIA, he began to read LADY CHATTERLY'S LOVER. When word leaked out about the nature of Lady Chatterly, Frank and Lincoln found themselves dining with the entire club.

During one session, Lieutenant Grabowski overheard the tale of "Sir Mortar and Lady Pestle." Then he barged through the door, shouting, "What the hell are you teaching these lads?"

"LADY CHATTERLY'S LOVER."

"That's a dirty book!"

"Have you read it?" asked Frank.

"Goddammit it! I don't have to. It's got filthy words in it."

"Lieutenant Grabowski," Frank said, "I'm sure everyone here knows all the dirty words found in the book."

"Doctor, that bastard who wrote it married the sister of the Baron von Richthofen. I watched him shoot down our boys from the sky."

"What does D. H. Lawrence's brother-in-law have to do with the literary merit of the novel?"

"It's not American," Grabowski blustered. "Besides, the book's contraband."

"It's from my personal library," said Frank.

"Well, I don't want the Feds swooping down on my camp because of some dirty book."

"The boys are sworn to secrecy."

"Reading the book might turn some of these boys into sex maniacs," whispered Grabowski.

The young men who had been listening to this exchange began

to giggle.

"See, Doctor Millet! Discipline is already breaking down."

"Lieutenant, you have my solemn oath as an officer and a gentleman. I'll be responsible for any sexual excesses these boys might have."

"If I have your word, Doctor."

Winking at the boys, Frank said, "I ordered Cookie to spike their meals with a liberal dose of saltpeter. That should take care of their raging hormones."

"Will that work?" asked Grabowski.

"You have my word," said Frank.

"Say, Doc, suppose twenty pounds of that stuff might keep Dutch Osterman's buttons from unbuttoning?" asked Grabowski. "The thought of a less virile Dutchman has brightened my whole day." Then he motioned to the young men, "Come on to the mess hall. I'm buying."

As the men got up, Frank asked Grabowski, "Do you mind if Wynn stays with me? I'm taking Lincoln's bandages off."

"Moral support, eh?"

"Precisely."

Before leaving the tent, Grabowski said to Lincoln, "Good luck, son. Although I question the Doc's literary tastes, I know you're in excellent medical hands."

When Frank had begun loosening the bandages from Lincoln's head, Lincoln grabbed Frank's hands and said, "Please, stop."

"Certainly," responded Frank.

Lincoln reached one hand toward Wynn who grasped it tightly. Then Lincoln said, "Go ahead, Doc."

After removing the final bandage, Frank asked, "Can you see?" When Lincoln blinked several times without answering, Frank continued, "Focus your eyes on something in the room!"

Lincoln slowly fixed his eyes on Wynn, who was still squeezing Lincoln's hands. Softly, Lincoln said, "I can see you, Wynn. You're uglier than I even thought."

"Hey pal, you're not going to win any beauty prize yourself," replied Wynn.

"Doc, I see big, black blobs."

"Not to worry," said Frank. "They're called floaters,"

"Yeah," said Lincoln. "They do sort of float, don't they?"

"Floaters are unabsorbed blood. They'll soon go away." Using the ophthalmoscope, Frank studied Lincoln's retinas. "They're looking good. We won't need the bandages anymore, but you're still confined to the infirmary. I don't want you to risk a fall or suffer any sharp blows."

"Doc?"

"What, Lincoln?"

"That Captain over at Number Four was ready to toss me out on the streets. I was dead meat!"

"Not everyone in the world is like Captain Moore."

"You and Wynn's the only white folks who's ever been nice to me."

"Thank you, Lincoln."

"Am I going to stay here?"

"For awhile."

"Could I ask you something if you promise not to get mad?"

"Fire away!"

"Could you get some books about my people?"

"Certainly, Lincoln. But why?"

"I don't know much about my history."

"Lincoln," said Frank. "You're a bright lad. With help, you're going places. But it's a world dominated by the white man. In order to make it, there's a body of knowledge you must learn. Some of it is the 'white man's' literature."

"But Doc, us colored folks have done things, too."

"Certainly! Booker T. Washington, Frederick Douglass, W.E.B. DuBois, and Langston Hughes. Just to name a few."

"I never heard of any of those guys except that Washington cat."

"I have books written by those men," said Frank. "I'll expect you to read them."

"After I came here," Lincoln said, "I laid awake at night, wondering if I'd ever see again. I'm almost ashamed of what I thought. It began to chew away inside me. I'd get to feeling that I was an animal in a cage, like in a zoo. And all you white folks just came to look at me. Sure, you helped me, too. I'm not denying that." As Lincoln paused, his face became contorted. "If there was more of my brothers here? Would you still be willing to help?"

"I would, Lincoln."

"Me too," added Wynn.

"God knows us colored are poor. But I was scratch poor! Nobody knows what poor is about unless you're colored. The last hired and the first fired. And all the time walking on eggs so's not to rile the white folks."

"Poverty and ignorance keep people down. If you overcome them, things will fall into place," said Frank.

"But right now, Doc, I don't have two nickels to rub together."

"That's why I want you to read DuBois' book. He's got an answer, and I believe you can find it."

As Lincoln's eyesight improved, Frank kept him under observation for an additional four weeks. Then he insisted on keeping him another month. After that, Lincoln became an aide in the infirmary, while Frank struggled to find a valid reason to keep him at Camp One.

CHAPTER THIRTY-FIVE

On a warm, spring morning, Frank walked into the recreation room just as Wynn had begun using the heavy punching bag. After watching for a few minutes, Frank tapped Wynn on the shoulder and asked him to stop. Then, taking a piece of chalk from his pocket, Frank traced a man's silhouette on the bag. "What's the most vulnerable position on the body?" he asked.

"Straight on the button," answered Wynn.

Frank drew a number one on the upper part of the bag corresponding to the point of the chin. Next he drew a two that represented the ribs. Quickly, he numbered three more positions, the stomach and the right and left side of the jaw. "These are the five points I want you to concentrate on when you work with the big bag."

"Hell, Doc, that'll be easy."

"I've been watching you. You've got good straight-away power, but your combinations are slow."

Incredulously, Wynn asked, "And you're going to teach me?"

"We've got a lot of work to do. Right now you're not prepared to meet someone better than you."

"And where'd you get all this boxing know-how?"

Smiling softly, Frank said, "Before the war, I spent a number of years in Paris. I studied ancient languages and practiced medicine for the university students."

How's that going to help me?"

"I didn't spend all my time buried in the libraries, Wynn. I had boxed as a student and had never lost my interest in that sport. In my time off, I attended boxing bouts. Eventually, I began treating fighters who had been hurt in the ring. To understand why they'd submit their bodies to such punishment, I began to study boxing as an art as well as a science. My speculation as to how I might help a fighter led to my becoming a cut-man, probably the only doctor in Paris who practiced that avocation. That's how I met Jack Johnson."

A wide-eyed Wynn responded, "You knew the heavyweight champion?" When Frank nodded his head, Wynn said, "I heard that he didn't hit it off with white people."

"He had an insatiable intellect and possessed a marvelous ear for language, self-taught in French and German." When he discovered that I knew Sanskrit, we became friends. For almost a year, I taught him the ancient language, while he schooled me on the finer points of boxing."

Pointing to the numbers on the bag, Wynn said, "So that's where those came from."

"At training camp, he had a heavy punching bag with large numbers on it, just like the one before you. While his trainer shouted out the combinations, Johnson pounded the bag ruthlessly."

"Do you think the numbers might help me?"

"I'm going to shout combinations of numbers. You hit those spots with hooks, jabs, and uppercuts. Got it?"

Assuming a normal boxing stance, Wynn said, "Give me the word."

Frank stood behind the bag. "Let's start with a left jab, a straight right, and a left hook." After pausing for a few seconds, he shouted, "One, three and five."

Wynn responded with an average left jab, a crisp right hook, and a left jab that propelled the bag backward by almost a foot.

"Now reverse that combination." Then, without pausing, Frank shouted, "Four, two, and three. Now, back to the original combination. Watch your feet. Keep them closer together!"

As Frank held the bag, Wynn slugged it until heavy drops of perspiration dripped from his head and face down to his shoulders and chest, making them glisten under the lights. His punches struck the bag with such a fury that the veins in his neck soon became distended.

After fifteen minutes of that heavy workout, Frank stopped the exercise. "Tomorrow," he said, "we'll work on more combinations. I want you to cool down by doing three minutes of shadow boxing.

Then take a one minute breather before working out on the speed bag for another three minutes. Then a one minute rest before you go back to the rope for three minutes."

"Why three, three, and three?"

"Because in boxing, everything is done in intervals of three minutes. After completing those intervals of three minutes, then straight to the barrack for a shower and bed, young man."

Three more bouts separated Wynn from the regional championship, scheduled for Labor Day 1934. The first one was a tune-up for the Allegheny National Forest Heavyweight Title. He easily defeated Monroe Givens from Camp Four by knocking him out in the second round. The next fight was for the ANF title where Wynn faced Boyd Harris, another Negro opponent.

Harris, a southpaw, was Wynn's first real test. Wynn looked bad in the first round as he walked into a couple of strong lefts thrown by Harris. By the round's end, Harris' fans were on their feet, cheering.

When Wynn returned to his corner, Frank would not allow him to sit down. Instead, he used his body to maneuver Wynn against the ring-post. Then Frank began to teach. "I've yet to see a good southpaw. It's an unnatural way to fight."

"He's mixing me up," complained Wynn.

"Whenever he jabs with his right, he drops his hand slightly. Parry his jab with a left across his body. That will neutralize his power. Then come over his left with your right. It'll keep him off balance."

Using that information, Wynn took the next two rounds easily. Then, with seconds left in the fourth round, Wynn tagged Harris with a right cross and followed up immediately with a hammer-handed left uppercut to his chin. The bell rang when Harris hit the floor. There was no count.

When Harris could not answer the bell for the next round, the referee awarded a TKO victory to Wynn. He had eliminated the last Negro boxer from the Allegheny National Forest.

As Wynn prepared to leave the ring, a colored fan yelled, "Hey, Whitey. You'd better watch your ass in the finals."

Lincoln elbowed his way through the crowd while Frank and Wynn trailed behind. When they made it to the dressing room, they still heard the taunts.

Lincoln wiped the perspiration from Wynn's shoulders and said, "There's still a lot of mean cats out there."

While Frank was cutting the tape from Wynn's wrists, he heard a chair smash against the door. Looking at the two younger men, he said, "Let's hear it for mom, apple pie, and the good old American Way."

"Hell, Doc, I don't blame them, said Wynn. "I cost a lot of them a month's pay."

"They really thought that Harris was going to be the champ," said Lincoln.

"This place is tough on colored men," said Frank.

Lincoln shook his head. "As bad as below the Mason-Dixon Line."

Frank had begun to examine Wynn's right hand. "I saw you flinch when you connected with this hand."

"Naw, Doc, it's nothing."

Frank grasped Wynn's hand with his thumb and forefinger and exerted pressure on every bone from the knuckles to his wrist. "Tell me if it hurts," he said sternly.

"Feels normal, Doc."

Satisfied, Frank released Wynn's hand. "Think you can make it to the big one?"

"Who's lined up against me?"

"A colored kid by the name of Jimmy Henry Smith," said Lincoln.

"Know anything about him?" asked Wynn.

"Only that he's stationed at the Penfield camp," answered Frank.

"He comes from Michigan," said Lincoln. "But I'll check him out through my buddies over at Camp Four."

Just then, Tommy Carleson, a local fight promoter, burst into the room. Like a beam of light, he streaked over to Wynn and grasped his hand. "Can't wait to see you in the finals in two weeks."

"Where will the fight be?" asked Frank.

"I've rescheduled the finals for the armory in Kane. We'll be able to attract a lot more fans."

"What's a ticket cost?" asked Frank.

"Three bucks."

"That's pretty steep," said Wynn.

"This fight will put Kane, Pennsylvania, on the map," said Carleson. "There will be reporters from all over the state covering this fight."

"But the ticket cost is going to keep a lot of my friends from attending the fight," said Wynn.

"Odum, you just don't see the big picture," snapped Carleson. When he turned to leave, Carleson said, "Just show up. Leave the business matters to me."

After Carleson had left, Lincoln said, "I don't like him."

"Yeah," said Wynn. "He reminds me of Murray," Then he added, "And that spells big trouble."

CHAPTER THIRTY-SIX

An hour before the championship bout, Wynn kept calm by trying to remember the lines from a popular poem, "Ode to a Deserted Elementary School Teacher."

> So rare...So rare
> As a day in June when in retrospect
> Time permits measuring her life in coffee spoons
> For a lifetime of facing unadmiring bogs...

Frustrated, Wynn stopped and said, "I forgot the next line."
"I'll give you a hint," said Frank.
"C'mon, Doc, you know the whole thing."
"How about sack and axe?"
"That's it! Now I've got it," said Wynn."

> Of clods
> Most of whom had ugly bods
> Totally rotten in the sack
> Undeserving of a dull axe.

Lincoln interrupted Wynn's recitation by barging into the dressing room. "Who's this Halderman cat?" he asked.
"Sonnavabitch!" was Wynn's only reaction.
"He's brought in a ringer from Detroit City."
Wynn said, "That doesn't surprise me. He's got connections all over."
"Talk over at Camp Four is that Smith fought Joe Louis when

they was amateurs!" said Lincoln. "And Smith went the distance with him."

Wynn walked around the table. "Now what's that next line?" he asked before lying down.

"Try shoveled under."

"Zukowski and Haldeman's set you up!" said Lincoln. "Something about what you done to them in the past. Lordie, Wynn! If Smith is good enough to go up against Louis, he could really hurt you!"

"Should we bring the Marines?" asked Wynn.

"I knew you'd say that!" said Lincoln. " So I've done the next best thing."

"What's that?"

"Geechy Brown's our new employee."

"What the hell's a Geechy Brown?" asked Wynn.

"Old Geechy came to Camp Four from Carolina. He learned black magic from his Mama. And for two bucks, he's going to put a spell on Smith. As soon as Smith enters the ring, old Geechy's going to stand up and point at him. He won't stop pointing until Smith leaves..."

Wynn's opponent interrupted Lincoln by bursting through the closed door. Shoving his left index finger toward Wynn, Smith screamed, "I'm going to whup you so bad that when you shit you'll have to wipe between your toes!"

Frank remained at the dressing table and continued to massage Wynn, who did not acknowledge Smith.

Lincoln, however, rushed between the intruder and his two friends. "Get out of here, man!"

Brushing Lincoln aside, Smith continued scowling. "Don't forget, Whitey, after our little business is over, I'm walking out of the ring victorious." Then, pointing at Lincoln, he shouted, "And your little nigger buddy's going to haul your ass out feet first."

Frank asked, "Remember those lines, Wynn?"

> Let alone being shoveled
> Under at Shiloh and Verdun.
> Charged with low crimes and misdemeanors

> She could not have been less mean
> Facing someone's faceless son...

"Thanks, Doc," replied Wynn. "The next lines go like this, don't they?"

> Conceived in a cramped rumble seat
> A product of passionless drippings
> A mere afterthought
> Of booze-filled recollections...

Smith's mouth remained opened, but no sounds came out. First he stared at Wynn and then at Frank. Finally, he blurted, "She...it! What are you talking about, man? Doncha know I'm going to pound the shit out of your boy?" He shook his fists while his voice rose to a shrill falsetto. "See these, tight-ass! This one is lighting and the other's thunder." Spitting on the floor, he said, "You ain't got a chance, boy." When Smith went to the door, he gave Wynn one more nasty glare, and stalked out into the hallway.

As Lincoln closed the door, he said, "That was some kind of noise!"

Wynn sat up on the table. "That's just a show. I'll get his respect by popping him hard early on."

"He was just trying to psyche-out Wynn, that's all." As Frank began wrapping gauze around Wynn's right wrist, he said, "In Paris some of the best shows occurred in the dressing room when one fighter would confront another, just as Smith did."

After Frank had completed taping Wynn's right hand, Wynn clenched his fist and wriggled his fingers.

Turning to Lincoln, Frank asked, "Please get the gloves in the box that's under the table."

When Lincoln showed Frank the gloves, Frank said, "Hmmm. Six ouncers this time." After completing the taping, Frank ran his fingers over the gloves. Then he held them to Wynn's face. "Smell them. There's no aroma as distinctive as the fragrance of brand new leather"

"The gloves I used before were old and had nicks in them."

"They were soft, Wynn. This pair isn't broken-in." As he slipped them onto Wynn's hands, he continued, "New leather is hard and leaves welts on your body."

Wynn said, "Jeez, both you guys are certainly loaded with good news." When Frank had completed lacing up the gloves, Wynn jumped from the table and went through a routine of shadowboxing. Then he stopped in front of Frank. "Doc, I just want to say thanks. I've learned a lot because of you. It's been a good run, but this is my last fight. After fire season is over, I'm headed for Penn State."

Frank asked, "You've been accepted?"

"I got the letter today," said a smiling Wynn. "Doc, it's not like I don't want to compete anymore. I like boxing a lot, but a fella's got to grow up and move on to his life's work."

"I understand."

"When I go to Penn State, you're going to be proud of me."

"I'm proud of you now, son."

Someone pounding on the door reminded them of their immediate task. Then, from the hallway, a man's voice shouted, "Time to go, gentlemen."

Lincoln opened the door. Frank went first, followed by Wynn with Lincoln coming behind, carrying the corner supplies.

When Wynn's fans saw him, they shouted, "We...in! We...in! We...in!"

Wynn remembered his dream of long ago and felt good about it.

CHAPTER THIRTY-SEVEN

The pre-fight activities were a blur to Wynn. Kathy Carleson, the promoter's rotund daughter, sang all the verses of the National Anthem, a cappella. It took forever. When she concluded her interpretation, the crowd applauded more in relief than in appreciation.

Miss Carleson's rendition sounded good in comparison to the ringside introductions. Eddie Cox, the ring announcer, had to wrest the microphone from the CCC Regional Commander, Brigadier General Owen Sandstrom, who had launched into a speech. After that, Cox kept the microphone firmly in his hand while introducing other luminaries. The crowd hooted and jeered whenever another local dignitary climbed into the ring.

The loudest cheer occurred when a local school board member tumbled down the steps into the lap of an amply endowed dowager, sitting at ringside. Nonplused, she gave him a big kiss, patted him on his rear, and sent him back to his seventh row seat.

The fans gave her a standing ovation.

Finally, it was the fighters' turn. The announcer somberly intoned the camps they represented, their names, the color of their trunks, and their weights. Wynn remembered only that Smith outweighed him by twenty-two pounds.

When Wynn returned to his corner, Frank told him, "Take it slow. Feel him out. Don't get into a slugfest with someone who weighs so much more than you."

As the scheduled six round bout began, both fighters came to the center of the ring and touched gloves. Then each backed away two steps before Smith flicked out a right jab and fired a looping left. Wynn moved in quickly and scored with two jabs, both on target. Surprised with his success, Wynn tried to repeat the same move.

This time, Smith shuffled backward, while waiting for an opening. When Wynn threw a flurry from the outside, Smith stepped inside and rifled a stiff right cross, catching Wynn directly on the mouth. As Wynn countered with an ineffective right jab, Smith answered with a right cross and a strong left uppercut followed by another left hook and a solid right uppercut that froze Wynn's legs. Then Smith followed through with a solid left hook that put Wynn on the canvas.

The noise in the gymnasium was overpowering. The referee tapped Wynn on his shoulder three times, giving him the count. Then the referee began at four, making sure that Wynn could see his lips.

At a nine count, Wynn got up and faced a charging Smith.

Still woozy, Wynn took a hard left to the stomach before falling into a clinch. He pinned Smith's arms against his body and held on.

While the referee wrestled to pull them apart, Smith cursed incessantly. "Bastard, let me go! Afraid to take a licking, prick?" Smith was still cursing when the bell sounded, ending the round.

When Wynn sat down on the stool, Frank immediately looked into the young man's eyes. "They're clear!" he shouted to Lincoln, who poured warm water over Wynn's neck and shoulders. Frank knelt in front of Wynn and gave him a mini-boxing clinic. "Crowd him. Keep your hand cocked, ready for the opening. Keep moving to the left. When he comes at you, grab him and jerk him to the left. Stay away from his right. Fight from a crouch, keeping your left high. And stay away from his right."

The brief respite had cleared Wynn's head. As Wynn stood up and waited for the bell, he felt renewed confidence. He had taken Smith's strongest punch. He was confident the next round belonged to him.

Fighting out of a crouch, Wynn circled Smith, who stood in the center of the ring, attempting to figure out his opponent's strategy. When Smith moved in close, Wynn simultaneously jerked Smith to the left and popped him with a stiff right jab to the chin. Then Wynn moved inside, chest-to-chest with his chin riding Smith's shoulder.

"That all you got, Whitey? Shee...it!" screamed Smith. "My old lady hits me harder when we rock 'n roll!" When Wynn tried to stay in close, Smith retreated to an arm's length distance. When Wynn refused to advance, Smith dropped both arms to his side and screamed, "Goddamned mother-clutching Honkey! Come here so's we can mix it up."

With a smile on his face, Wynn moved back into short range again, shooting out a left jab. It had no leverage, however. Then he stepped back, feinting a left jab. Smith took the bait. Wynn's right hand was at his side. Imperceptibly, he hesitated, starting the blow from belt buckle level. His right arm turned ever so slowly as he brought the fist over Smith's left arm and hand, catching him squarely on the jaw.

Smith's eyes' rolled back into his head, and he fell to the mat on his left side. He took an eight count.

When he got up, Smith used his weight advantage and hung on doggedly until the light-headedness left him. Steadily, he pushed Wynn into the ropes, working them to his benefit. Skillfully, he hooked his left arm around Wynn's head and raked his adversary's eyelids over the upper rope.

When Wynn dropped his arms, Smith thumped Wynn with a stiff overhand right, stunning him. But before Smith could follow-up, the bell rang.

As Wynn stumbled back to his corner, Frank immediately examined Wynn's eyes. "It's good this isn't a ten rounder," he said.

"Where's old Geechy?" Wynn asked.

"Right behind us," answered Lincoln.

"Have him change his tactics, will you?"

"I don't get your drift, Wynn."

"You paying him to use one hand?"

"Yeah."

"Tell Geechy to use both of them, because one's not doing the job."

The next two rounds belonged to Smith as his experience began to show. Altering his tactics, he fought in a straight-up stance, while other times he switched to a modified bob-and-weave style. Whenever Wynn made a move, Smith easily parried his blows. By the middle of the fourth round, Smith had opened cuts above and below Wynn's right eye.

When the fourth round ended, Wynn's right eye had swollen shut. The referee came over to Wynn's corner. As he examined Wynn's eye, the referee asked, "Want to quit, son?" When Wynn refused, the referee said, " I won't let that cut get worse."

Frank worked feverishly upon Wynn's eye to arrest the bleeding, but the swelling alarmed him. He took a quarter from his pocket and pressed it down on the swollen eye.

As it broke the blood-blister, Wynn screamed in pain. Then he shouted, "I can see, Doc. I can see!"

"It's a miracle," sighed Lincoln.

"Worked for me in Paris, too," said Frank. Quickly, he knelt down and cupped Wynn's face in his hands. "The last time you feinted him out of his jockstrap, you nailed him real hard. Stay in close. And watch for an opening. He's ripe for a feint again, I'm sure."

Round Five began the same way the last round had ended. Smith went directly for Wynn's head. But Wynn ducked under Smith's blows and stabbed Smith with two well-timed jabs that were as sweet as the first bite from a blueberry pie. Seconds later, Wynn delivered a solid combination that caught Smith moving forward.

This offensive outburst enraged Smith, who snarled, "I'll make you pay, asshole!"

As he wrestled Smith into another clinch, Wynn grunted, "Go to it, jazzman." The clinch allowed Wynn a short breather, while making Smith more frustrated. Recognizing Smith's anger, Wynn determined to have it work in his favor. Confident that Smith could not put him away by concentrating on his midsection, Wynn decided to goad Smith into changing his attack. Suddenly, Wynn broke free and pulled back, out of range. A smile spread over his battered face. Dropping his guard, he pointed to his belly. "Come on, nigger! Come and get me!"

Smith immediately charged at Wynn, aiming his assault at his opponent's solar plexus. As they came in close, Smith snarled, "You'll pay, you white bastard!"

Disdainfully, Wynn tied him up. As they continued to struggle, Wynn said, "That all you got, <u>boy</u>?" After the referee had pulled them apart, Wynn stung Smith with a sharp left and a hard right to the ribs.

Smith countered with a flurry of body blows that had negligible effect. One blow fell clearly below the belt. As the referee barked out a warning, Smith reached out his gloves as a <u>mea</u> <u>culpa</u>.

Wynn just smiled.

Then Wynn muscled his way inside again, scoring with a left hook and a right uppercut in rapid succession. Neither man backed away as they stood toe-to-toe, firing short but telling body blows. During one flurry, Wynn instinctively realized that Smith dropped his left slightly after using it. Seconds later, Wynn feinted with his left. Smith countered with his left. Only this time, Wynn came over top, scoring directly on the button. While Smith's knees began to buckle, Wynn followed up with another hard right before Smith fell into Wynn.

As Wynn wrestled to free himself, Smith butted him. Blood poured into Wynn's right eye, nearly blinding him. Every time Smith came in close, blood spilled onto him. When they exchanged punches, it splattered onto the fans, sitting in the first row. As the bell sounded, blood covered both men.

Over the crowd noise, Lincoln whispered to an exhausted Wynn. "My friends just told me that Halderman's set to drop ten grand if you finish the fight."

Frank cleaned off Wynn's face and put an astringent on the new wound. It stopped bleeding in a few seconds. Then he gave Wynn his final instructions. "Stay away from his jabs."

"Tell me, Doc. It feels like he's screwing a light bulb into my nose and then smashing it!"

"Stay inside. Don't let him get outside. Tie him up! Hang on him!"

As the bell sounded for the last round, the fans stood and cheered. Neither man would touch gloves. Smith spit on the canvas, while Wynn reciprocated with an Italian arm signal. After a second futile attempt at bringing them together, the referee shrugged his shoulders. "Let's get at it, gentlemen."

Although each man was physically spent, neither one was content to allow the other to carry the assault. Smith scored the round's first blow, a left jab that reopened the cut over Wynn's left eye. He followed up with a razor-sharp right hook to Wynn's jaw.

Wynn clung to Smith's arms, pulling them to his side. Somehow, Wynn connected with a right uppercut that sent Smith reeling backwards. Then Wynn plodded after him. There was nothing scientific about his assault. His furious barrage forced Smith against the ropes, but Wynn lost his edge when he allowed Smith to fall into a clinch.

After the referee broke them apart, both men moved to center ring where Wynn began to circle Smith slowly. Then, taking a full step backward, Wynn motioned for Smith to come and get him.

He accepted Wynn's invitation.

Each man stood flatfooted, throwing knockout blows. Covered with blood, they looked like two wounded cannoneers lobbing broadsides at each other. Wynn concentrated on Smith's body while Smith redirected his attention to Wynn's head.

After Smith had scored with a quick succession of blows, Wynn's knees began to buckle. Somehow, Wynn caught Smith's body, and both men dropped to their knees. When the referee separated them, Wynn fell to the canvas, while Smith remained on his knees.

Smith took a two count, but Wynn stayed down until nine.

Less than thirty seconds remained when the referee cleaned off their gloves. Then Smith let out a tigerish yowl and pounced at Wynn, throwing a barrage of punches. The more he attacked, the louder he shrieked. "You bastard! You sonnavabitch! Don't you know when to quit?"

Wynn covered up and hung on.

Smith was still pounding Wynn and screaming at the final bell.

Frank and Lincoln rushed into the ring. Lincoln threw an oversized towel around Wynn's shoulders. Peering anxiously into Wynn's eyes, Frank held up two fingers. "How many fingers do you see?" When Wynn did not respond, Frank repeated the question.

Finally Wynn mumbled, "Two."

"Good."

"My right hand hurts."

"Only your hand hurts?" Frank cut off the glove and unwrapped Wynn's hand. "You've got a swelling behind the middle knuckle."

Moving to the center of the ring, the announcer raised Smith's hand while intoning, "Ladies and Gentlemen! The winner by unanimous decision in this evening's pugilistic attraction is Jimmy Smith."

A large roar reverberated through out the building. Now the colored men had a champion. They continued to cheer as Smith danced around the ring before stopping briefly to shake hands with Wynn. Then Smith climbed through the ropes and disappeared into a group of well-wishers.

Ontek and Higgleston jumped into the ring to assist their friend. As they helped him down the steps, Wynn asked, "Where were you when I needed help?"

Ontek placed his hand on Wynn's head. "You did good, pal."

"I saw Zukowski and Grabowski going at it hot and heavy in the hallway," offered Higgleston. "Both of them's going to have a lot of explaining to do."

"How so?" asked Wynn.

"You going the distance cost that Halderman guy ten big ones!" said Ontek.

Once inside the dressing room, Frank examined Wynn. Finding no serious aftereffect of the beating, he placed a butterfly dressing on the cut below Wynn's eye. Then Frank stitched up the gash caused by Smith's head butt. "I want you to stay in the infirmary with me. After all, you took some wicked shots to the head."

"Can I take a shower?"

"Sure."

Wynn removed his trunks and went into the shower room. Turning on the hot water, he allowed it to pour over him. As it ran down his body, the water soothed the surface pain caused by the discolored welts that covered his midsection and his chest. When he began to lather himself with soap, he winced as the suds irritated every bruise on his body.

When he came from the shower, he decided to look at himself in the mirror. Wiping the condensation from it, he sucked in a deep breath when he saw his face. It was crooked! His right eye was closed. A large welt, a size of a quarter, rose from under his skin in the middle of his forehead. His left jaw was swollen. The edema from his right eye had displaced his nose, making it appear as if it were on the left side of his face. He looked as if he were a character from a painting by the most bizarre of artists, Hieronymus Bosch.

"It isn't pretty, is it?" remarked Frank.

"I hope Smith hurts half as much as I do."

"He knows he was in a fight."

"Think I'll be ready for the fire season, Doc?"

"You'll be as good as new within a week, Wynn."

When Wynn had finished dressing, he said, "No more fighting. From here on, I'm going to hit the books."

"I just hope they don't hit back," quipped Ontek.

As they prepared to leave, Lincoln came into the dressing room, smiling. "Zukowski's gone. I heard him and Grabowski fighting. Then Grabowski told him, 'Pack your bags and get to hell out of here. I'll get Odum myself!'"

Through swollen lips, Wynn mumbled, "I guess our war's still on."

When they walked out into the bright evening, Frank said, "Wait here, and I'll go around and get the car."

As the young men stood on the street, a well dressed woman, old enough to be their grandmother, slowly approached them. Her white hair, tinted blue with a Bulldog Rinse, remained firmly in place though a soft breeze blew down the street. She glanced warily at Wynn before briskly walking by him. Then she virtually stopped in midstep and turned sharply toward him. "You poor dear. Were you in an automobile accident?"

"No, ma'am."

"You look terrible."

"Yes, ma'am."

"How did it happen?"

Politely, Wynn said, "I'm a boxer, ma'am."

While studying his swollen face, she sniffed, "A boxer, you say?"

"That's right, ma'am."

"You mean that you...Ah...Fight with your fists?"

"Yes, ma'am."

"Does your poor mother know of your vocation?"

"She's passed away, ma'am."

This response caused her to arch her eyebrows. "Your profession...Did it?...Ah...Cause her death?"

"No, ma'am."

She touched Wynn's arm and said, "If I had a son, I wouldn't permit him to engage in such a barbaric sport!" Then she turned on her heels and continued her march up the street.

As the elderly woman disappeared into the darkness, Frank drove the car to the waiting young men. Wynn gingerly eased himself into the front seat, while his friends piled into the rear seat. He closed his eyes and rested his head against the top of the seat. When Frank began to drive down the street, Wynn said, "Watch the potholes on the way back, Doc."

"Son, don't you remember?" proclaimed Frank. "This is a Packard!"

Everyone laughed except Wynn as they began their trip back to Camp One.

CHAPTER THIRTY-EIGHT

October 1934 had been the worst fire month in the young history of the Allegheny National Forest. Weather conditions were perfect for a major fire. The summer had been exceptionally dry, and the temperatures routinely rose to the low nineties. September and early October saw the temperatures fall somewhat, but there was still no significant rain to dampen the tinder-dry forest floor.

By early October, Red's original crew had become a veteran team, knocking down more than thirty fires since Labor Day. Now each man led a fire team numbering up to twenty men. This caused Red's position to change also. He and Wynn, his assistant, were on the move continually, supervising the individual line crews.

When Red and Wynn pulled into a Sinclair station, south of Warren, for gas, the attendant ran toward truck and asked, "Heard of the big fire down on the Allegheny River, near Tionesta?"

"No, we haven't," Red replied.

"It's the granddaddy of them all."

"Fill her up quick!" Then he shouted, "Where's the nearest phone?" When the attendant pointed to the station, Red jumped from the truck, his long legs nearly tripping over the gas hose before he disappeared into the building. When he returned, Red looked pale. "It's on Jamison Run, twenty miles south of here." Settling uneasily behind the steering wheel, he nervously turned a tiny gold ring that he wore on his right hand little finger. As he started the truck, he worried aloud. "It's filled with ravines and draws with lots of dead-ends."

"What crews are available?" asked Wynn.

"Here's the worst part of it, Wynn. Simpson gave Grabowski a crew. There was nobody else available."

"Is Grabowski qualified?"

"Seems Grabowski had fire fighting experience down in Texas."

"Any of our guys with him?"

"Ontek."

Wynn looked a bit relieved. "My old buddy can handle a fire."

"Yeah, but can he handle someone who wants to be a hero?" After scribbling his name on an expense slip, he started the engine, and double-clutched the truck, roaring out onto the highway. Normally, Red drove fast. Now he laid on the horn, passing everything in sight.

The road south to Tionesta bordered the Allegheny River and had as many curves in as the river itself. Small farms with drab little houses and unpainted barns pockmarked the area. Some houses still showed the high water mark from last year's flood.

As Red weaved in and out of traffic, Wynn said, "Cripes, I've been chasing fires with you for almost two years, and it's still a lot more fun laying down backfires than racing off with you to a fire."

After getting around a horse-drawn wagon, Red asked, "Ever see such a beautiful team of horses?"

"Not in Pittsburgh." When Red slowed down, Wynn asked, "Is it really true you lost a government truck in a fire?"

Over the engine's roar, Red hollered, "Back at the Bear Creek Fire in 1926, I had a Dodge truck." He passed two more cars, while barely missing an oncoming truck. "And I told them it was a piece of junk. That a Ford was more reliable. But no! They wouldn't believe me." As he down-shifted to make it around a sharp turn, Red continued his story. "Jim Simpson was with me. You remember him from the big Clarion River fire, don't you? We were trying to outrun a fire, but the Dodge just died, dead as hell right in the middle of the road with the flames ready to singe my butt. Good thing there was a culvert nearby. Jim and I shared it with a fox and two very nervous skunks."

"What about the truck?"

"Burned up."

"Then it is true. You <u>really</u> lost a Forest Service truck."

"Yep," Red nodded, "and Uncle Sam hasn't forgiven me yet."

"Is that why you hate fires so much?" When Red did not answer, Wynn said, "Fighting fires is a job for me." Then he paused before asking, "Why's it like a war to you?"

Red did not answer the question immediately. He remained quiet for the next two miles. Finally, he said, "A house fire killed my parents when I was twelve. I saw the smoke from down the road. When I got to the yard, I heard them screaming. I kicked in the front door, but the flames blocked my way. All I could do was stand out front and listen to them. Then after a while there was no sound except the crackling of the fire." Reaching his right hand over toward Wynn, Red quietly said, "See that ring? That's all I have left of mother."

Neither man spoke again until they reached West Hickory, only seven miles north of Jamison Run. By now, the smoke was billowing high over the river, covering the hamlet with a brown pall.

Breaking the silence, Wynn said, "I've never seen anything like this before." Then he saw noticed small fragments floating from the sky. "Those look like something from a house roof."

"If that's the case, we're driving into a helluva fire."

As they rounded a bend, they saw a barn burning vigorously. The forest behind the barn was also in flames. Red turned into a long driveway, leading to a farm house, only fifty yards from the blazing barn.

As Red stopped the truck, a screaming woman ran out of the house, waiving her arms. "My boy! He's missing! Help me, please!" I can't find my little boy!"

The house was an unpainted, frame building with a tar paper roof. A porch wrapped around three sides of the building, and latticework enclosed the porch to the ground. Leaning against the house was a large wood pile. At the rear of the house stood six large evergreen trees that towered over the building.

Red just shook his head. "That latticework can trap the gasses from the fire. After a while, the whole thing will blow. I've seen it happen before." As pieces of burning tar paper fell around them, Red got out of the truck and talked to the woman. Then he turned to Wynn. "I'll go find the boy. You turn the truck around in case we have to make to make a run for it."

When Red and the woman disappeared from view, Wynn backed the truck toward the driveway. Seeing a couple of spot fires, he jumped from the truck, grabbed a spray can, and tried to extinguish them. As more fires began to erupt, Wynn realized his efforts were futile. He turned toward the house and yelled, "Red, this place is getting dangerous." Then he saw the woman peering anxiously through a hole in the latticework. "Is my boss under there?" When she nodded and pointed under the porch, Wynn ripped away a large chunk of the decorative wood and looked into the darkness. "Red, get to hell out of there! This place is about to go."

"I'm coming," acknowledged Red, who emerged from under the porch dragging a screaming little boy. Dirt and cobwebs matted Red's hair while perspiration streaked down his blackened face. "I found him way back near the foundation. Had to pull him out." Handing the child to Wynn, Red said, "Take him back to the truck while I get his mother."

Clutching the child, Wynn moved toward the truck. When he looked back, he saw the woman running toward the house.

"I've got to get my pocketbook," she wailed as she ran up the porch steps.

While putting the child safely into the truck, Wynn looked through the truck window and saw Red dragging the hysterical woman from the house. "Dammit, Red, get...," yelled Wynn. His last words were drowned out by an explosion.

During the explosion, Wynn thought his eyes were playing tricks on him as everything seemed to move in slow motion. Transfixed, he watched stone, wood, and glass rubble form an arc high over a foundation where a house had once stood. Simultaneously, he saw Red clinging to the woman as the explosion lifted them along the ground, rolling them like a hoop toward a huge oak tree. Wynn cringed when the woman's body hit the tree causing her body to stretch to its full length before Red slammed into her. Wynn's cries of concern were drowned out when the debris began falling upon the cab, creating a deafening roar as if angry persons were hitting the cab with a thousand ball-peen hammers.

Quickly, Wynn locked the child in the truck and ran over to Red, who was unconscious. After checking him for broken bones,

Wynn muttered, "Except for that knot on your head, you're one lucky man."

When Wynn looked at the woman, he saw that she had not been so fortunate. A wood splinter, somewhat thicker than an arrow, had entered the rear of her left thigh, almost coming out the other side. Wynn could feel the sharp end of the fragment directly under the skin, four inches above her knee. He placed her in a prone position, making sure that nothing touched the protruding shaft. Taking off his shirt, he put it under her face as a shield from the dirt.

As Wynn felt the intense heat, he looked up and saw the fire moving closer. Immediately, he got up and dashed through a tiny corridor between the flames toward the truck.

When he opened the door, a screaming child pounded him in the face. The child howled, "You hurt my mama!"

Wynn held the child at arm's length, allowing the child to flail away, harmlessly. "Can't you see, I'm trying to save your mother," he explained. As the child calmed down, Wynn lifted him up and put him behind the driver's seat. "Now stay put," Wynn warned. Fumbling with the keys, he finally started the engine, put it into low gear, and plowed through a yard that was beginning to smolder.

When the child threw his arms around Wynn's head, he pinned the child against the cab while he tried to steer with the other hand. Finally struggling free, Wynn grabbed the steering wheel with both hands and swerved the truck violently, narrowly avoiding the boy's mother who still lay under the tree.

Jumping out of the truck, Wynn immediately tended to the unconscious woman. He placed the woman in the rear of the vehicle and covered her with a blanket. Then he threw a tarpaulin over her to shield her from the burning debris. "The fire be damned. I've got to get you to the Warren Hospital!"

"I agree," said Red, who had regained consciousness.

"You don't look so hot either," said Wynn.

"Nobody's hit me this hard since I got cow-kicked back when I was a kid."

"When we get to the hospital, they'd better check you out, too." As he helped Red into the passenger's seat, Wynn said, "Hold the child's head down. I don't want him to see what's facing us." Upon starting the truck, Wynn realized that the fire had encircled them. "Got any suggestions?"

"I remember going through a flower garden."

As Wynn turned the truck around, he saw truck tracks. "If we came in this way, it must be the way out." Carefully, Wynn edged the vehicle through the smoldering garden before stopping.

Red looked at Wynn and admitted, "For the first time in my life, I'm hearing choir music."

"I can't see a damned thing," was the only admission Wynn would make. While smoke began to seep into the cab, Wynn sat there with the engine idling, nervously tapping his fingers on the steering wheel. Suddenly, he gave a high-pitched cry like a cowboy riding an out-of-control bucking bronco. While grinding the gears into low, he slammed the accelerator to the floor, and popped the clutch, causing the Ford truck to lurch forward into the dense smoke.

"I can't see a thing," shouted Red.

"The hell you say," shouted Wynn as he swerved to avoid hitting a tree. "Where did that come from?" he asked as the truck jolted to a halt.

"What did we hit?"

"Missed a tree, but hit a large rock."

"Think the truck's damaged?"

"Naw," said Wynn, "but now I know how to get out of here. I saw that rock when you drove in." He repositioned the truck for another escape attempt, and then he tramped on the accelerator. Going through the flames seemed like an eternity. He heard a strange hissing sound coupled with the smell of burnt paint. Doggedly, he clung to the steering wheel, while screaming, "I'll be damned if I'm ever going to lose a truck!" Wynn did not slow down until he saw daylight. Then he drove another half mile before stopping.

When Red looked back on the blazing farmyard, he said, "Barnie Oldfield would have been proud of you."

Wynn still gripped the steering wheel. Finally, he relaxed and asked, "Red?"

"What?"

"I heard the choir music, too."

When they had reached the hospital, Wynn handed the woman

and her son over to the staff. Then he insisted that the doctors also examine Red.

While waiting for his friend, he inspected the truck. He ran his fingers over its body from the front to the rear. "Got a few dings in it," he announced proudly. "The front bumper's shot and the left fender's a little scorched." As he reflected upon his near-death experience, he said, "It could have been a lot worse."

When Red came out of the hospital, Wynn ran up to him. "Is everything all right?"

"Got a clean bill of health. So let's head for Jamison Run."

Wynn looked nervously at his feet while kicking up a small cloud of dust. "Red, I've got to ask you a question."

"What is it?"

"Were you scared?"

"Yes, I was damned scared," admitted Red.

Surprised, Wynn said, "You were?"

"I guess I don't show it as much," Red replied.

"This one was a lot worse than back on the Clarion," said Wynn. "I really thought we were goners."

"Fighting fires is a war," said Red. "And even though you're undefeated, the very next fire could be your last."

Wynn shook Red's hand warmly, and began to smile. "I want to show you something." As he and Red walked around the truck, Wynn pointed at the truck's blackened fender and then he kicked its tires. He stopped and put his arm around Red's shoulder. "Just as you always said, 'They don't build a better truck than a Ford.'"

CHAPTER THIRTY-NINE

When Red and Wynn wheeled into Jamison Run base camp, they saw everyone milling about. Red jumped out of the truck and shouted, "Let's get moving! There's work to be done."

Nobody moved.

Frank came out of the medical tent. Walking over to Red, he motioned for Wynn to join them.

"What's going on, Doc?" Wynn asked.

"It's Grabowski, Ontek and their crew. They're up there."

Red looked at the hillside enveloped in smoke and flames. "Up there?"

"Let's get them," demanded Wynn.

"We can't. The fire's cut them off," answered Frank.

"They can still make it to the top, can't they?"

"We just don't know," said Frank.

"Let's go, Red," pleaded Wynn.

"Who's up there with Ontek and Grabowski?" asked Red.

"Nine other men," replied Frank. "Blaustine, Peaches, Dutch, and Lincoln Peacock..."

Enraged, Wynn interrupted Frank. "Peaches and Dutch never fought a fire before!"

Quietly, Frank responded, "Neither has Lincoln."

"Who else is up there?" asked Red.

"Tarbo, Nedshe, Mousy Gray, Silent Kylocker, and Selig."

"Goddamned Grabowski!" screamed Wynn. He ran to the edge of the clearing and stared up the hill, while shaking his fist. "You rotten bastard! You're going to kill the whole crew."

While Frank tried to calm Wynn, Red scanned the slopes with

his binoculars. "I surveyed this section back in 1927, and there are trails that funnel into a seventy-foot rock formation." As he scanned the hill again, he said, "I don't see anything but smoke and flames." When a massive whoosh caught his attention. "My God! The wind has switched and it's driving the fire from the south over to the north rim of the hill." When he saw the flames converging into a massive horseshoe configuration, an ashen-faced Red quietly asked Frank, "Have you notified the hospitals?"

As Frank discussed his emergency plans with Red, some onlookers began to cheer. Frank looked up and asked, "What's happening?"

Wynn yelled, "Someone's coming out of the woods."

As the men drew closer, Red said, "It's Lincoln and the Dutchman."

Lincoln was leading Dutch by his arm. Then he shouted, "Doc, we need help."

When Frank reached Lincoln, he saw huge welts on the young man's chest. "What happened?"

"I've been stung by bees."

Upon seeing Dutch's swollen face and eyes, Frank ordered, "Bring him into the medical tent immediately."

Lincoln sat down on a folding chair outside of the tent. "I need some water."

After giving him a drink, Wynn asked, "What happened out there?"

"Nothing but craziness, man. Grabowski's going to kill everybody. He marched us straight through a blueberry thicket. After that, he knocked Peaches down when the kid began to cry. Then Grabowski got shooting pains down his left arm. He told Nedshe to take the point. We ended up by going from the blueberry thickets straight into a blind draw. Grabowski got so mad that he started to crawl up the steep ridge, hand-over-hand! Took him fifteen minutes. When he got on top, he yelled, 'Nothing to it. Chop! Chop! Let's go!' Dutch and Peaches led the way up. When Peaches nearly reached the top, he slipped, smashing into Dutch and Nedshe. Rakes, spray cans, and saws, slid and fell to the bottom of the draw. You should have heard Grabowski cussing us out! That's when me and Dutch got stung by the bees. When Dutch began to swell up real bad, Grabowski sent us back to base camp."

"What's his plans?" asked Red.

"He ordered Ontek to the top of the hill to hunt for some possible escape routes."

What about Newt Blaustine?" asked Wynn.

"Grabowski sent him out to scout the north edge of the fire."

"Jeez, he's divided the crew," moaned Wynn.

"The only thing we do know is that there are still nine men out there," said Frank.

"Yeah, and led by that nut, Grabowski," said Wynn.

"How are we fixed on this end, Doc?" asked Red.

"Stretcher bearers are ready to go. The ambulances are enroute, and the Kane and Warren Hospitals are standing by."

"We're not going to do anything?" asked Wynn.

"There's nothing we can do," said Red.

"Damn it, Red. Let's drag pumps up there."

Shaking his head sadly, Red turned away and surveyed the hill again.

"Let's go on the other side. We'll reach them that way." When Red would not respond, Wynn looked through his binoculars and the hillside. As the flames licked up the hill, Wynn saw movement on the south side of the fire. "Red, take a look over there at three o'clock."

Peering through his field glasses, Red said, "Yeah, I see something."

When the wind blew the smoke up the hill, away from the edge of the fire, Wynn caught a clear view. "Somebody's coming out!" He quickly refocused the binoculars. "It's Newt Blaustine!"

"The way he's walking, I'd say he's not injured," said Red.

Training the binoculars on Newt, Wynn said, "God, look at him. His pants are torn, and his shirt's in tatters. He looks like he's been to Hell and back."

As Newt staggered into the base camp, he rubbed his bloodshot eyes and said, "The Hallton fire was a cakewalk compared to this one."

"How bad is it up there?" asked Red.

"I never thought I'd see any of y'all again," replied Newt. Then he shook Red's hand and hugged Wynn. "After drinking a glass of water, he said, "All hell's busted loose up there."

"Where's Ontek?" asked Wynn.

"On the top of the mountain, I hope."

"What do you mean?" asked Wynn.

"There ain't no other way out now."

"Where's Grabowski?" asked Red.

Newt turned away. His voice cracked when he said, "Dead! And so's Peaches."

"Oh, God, that sweet, innocent kid. He never hurt a fly!" Then Wynn grabbed Newt by the arm. In an accusing tone, Wynn said, "But you made it?"

"Wynn! Watch your mouth!" said Red.

Wynn touched Newt's shoulder. "I'm sorry, man."

"Grabowski sent me out to scout the fire. When I got back, only Peaches and Nedshe was with Grabowski."

"Where were Kylocker and Mousy?" asked Frank.

"Grabowski sent them up the hill to find Ontek."

"Jeez, there's two more gone!"

"Wynn, get hold of yourself!" snapped Red.

"But, Grabowski's killing everyone!"

Red gave Newt another drink of water. When Newt had gulped it down, Red said, "Go ahead, son."

"Then I heard this hellish roar below us. I knew it was the wind changing." He turned to Wynn and asked, "Mind, the noise of the fire exploding at the Hallton fire? Only this was worse. The flame-front came flying toward us. Grabowski told Peaches and Nedshe to run straight up the hill. I stayed with Grabowski who was real sick. I tried to carry him, but he was dead-weight. We must have covered only forty feet when I could feel the heat on my backside. Grabowski wasn't able to stand up so he told me to run while I still had time. I reached down and put a poncho under his head and sprayed a tankful of water over him and left another full tank beside him. I ran toward the edge of the fire and climbed a tree. Then Grabowski started to scream." Grimacing, Newt continued the story. "Must have screamed for three minutes before he stopped. Then I saw Peaches. He was on top of a big rock. He was praying and calling to his mother. Then the fire went straight for him. When I looked again he was gone."

"Maybe he jumped off the back of the rock and escaped," said Wynn.

Newt shook his head sadly. "There was fire all around."

"How'd you get away?" asked Red.

"I thought I was a goner until I saw a narrow path that wasn't burning yet. When I looked up the mountain, I caught a glimpse of Mousy running down the hill. I yelled and yelled! Then I ripped of part of my shirt and waved for him to see. But he was running like crazy, as if the Devil was right at his heels. He flew straight into the flames without ever slowing down." His voice faltering, Newt said slowly, "The flames just gobbled him up." He gulped down some more water and stared at the smoking mountain. When Frank patted him on his shoulders, Newt said, "I shinnied down that tree and hightailed out of there as fast as I could." He pointed proudly to his trousers. "Scorched them when the flames reached out to eat me.."

After the fire had burned itself out, Frank, Red, and Wynn led the rescue team up the steep hill. For the first few hundred yards, they found nothing. Then they came across Grabowski's body. They identified him because of the scorched water tank lying beside him.

Continuing their search, they saw fire fighting equipment scattered over the hill. Frank discovered a spray tank lodged between two saplings. Wynn found a burned shoe, while Red kicked a water canteen down the edge of a steep draw. High in a sapling was a scorched shirt.

Then they began to find the bodies of the other men.

The first one looked peaceful. But when Wynn turned it over, the victim's face was charred with strips of skin hanging from his forehead. Fighting back the urge to retch, Wynn cried, "Who's he?"

Frank replied, "We'll need dental records to identify him."

Wynn pointed toward a cluster of three small boulders twenty feet in front of them. "There's two more bodies," he whispered.

When Red walked over from the opposite side of the boulders, he said, "No, there are three of them."

One body, leaning against a tree, stood supported on his knees

Michael Schulz

as if in prayerful thought. Another rested on his hands and knees while his head lay on a large rock. The third victim had been impaled on a charred and twisted snag. The body dangled there, neither the hands nor feet touching the ground.

Red motioned for the litter bearers. Then he and Frank tenderly lifted the body from the snag and placed it on a litter. After covering the corpse with a blanket, Red said, "God, that must have been Mousy because he's so little."

Frank took Red's arm and gently pointed him toward the top of the mountain. "Were not finished yet."

Further up the hill, Wynn yelled, "Stop! I heard something." When everything had become quiet, he shouted, "It's coming from that rock pile."

The men converged upon a large mound of shale. Wynn leaped in and began to dig with his hands. When he stopped, he heard another weak call. Intensifying his digging, he yelled, "Here's a leg!" When he had removed more rocks, Wynn saw the young man's face.

"It's Timmy Nedshe!"

Frank examined the young man who was barely conscious. "No broken bones, lots of contusions, and probably dehydrated. He's a lucky young man!"

"At least we saved one," said Red.

"Ask him about Ontek," said Wynn.

"Not now," said Frank. "Nedshe's got to go to a hospital."

"But we must find Ontek."

Quietly, Red said, "We'll find him, Wynn."

When the rescue team neared the summit, Red looked around and shook his head. "Is this what they mean by a scorched earth program?"

"No, it looks more like the aftermath of the Battle of the Marne," said Frank.

The smoke still clung to the ground that was so hot that the heat radiated through the boots of the men. Whenever a breeze wafted over the afflicted area, embers glowed a bright red. Reaching down and picking up a belt buckle, Red dropped it quickly because it was too hot to touch. A badly bent sprayer, its paint burned completely off, hung from a charred sapling. Blackened trees reached toward the

In The Shadow Of The Trees

sky, becoming silent sentinels for the dead. A five foot pine tree, completely devoid of limbs, stood askew, like a pole half-driven into the ground. Its top tailed smoke in the warm breeze.

When the team reached the summit, its search ended. Another body lay thirty feet from the cliff. Then Wynn and Red spotted a rope dangling from the precipice, thirty feet from the ground. At the base of the cliff, directly beneath the rope, they found Ontek.

Red called softly to Frank. Then Red rolled Ontek's body over, placed his hands together on his chest, and closed his eyes. When the others arrived, Red pointed to the rope hanging from the cliff. "The fire didn't get him! Ontek must have climbed part way up the cliff, and something caused him to fall."

Wynn kneeled beside Ontek. "Look at his neck, it's swollen something awful!"

Frank turned Ontek's head slightly. "There are pin pricks on either side of his juggler vein."

"Good God!" exclaimed Red. "A rattlesnake must have got him when he was climbing the cliff"

When the other men came over to look, Wynn got up and screamed, "Get to hell out of here! Haven't you seen enough already?"

As they backed away, Wynn began to regain his composure. When Frank put his arms around him, Wynn asked, "Would you mind if I stay alone with Ontek for a few minutes?"

Red and Frank withdrew a few steps.

Wynn knelt beside his friend. "I'm glad the fire didn't get you." He sighed deeply and said, "At least your mother'll know you."

He reached down and smoothed Ontek's hair. Then he buttoned his shirt and straightened his lapels. "No sweat passing an inspection now, friend." He took Ontek's hand and cupped it into his large hands. Remaining silent, he looked at Ontek's bruised face. As tears rolled down his face, Wynn whispered, "I'm sorry. I'm so sorry." While placing Ontek's hand back on his chest, Wynn picked up Ontek's pocket watch. He noticed it had stopped at 1645. "You old bugger! Always liked Retreat. The best part of the day. I'm going to have the bugler blow the sweetest Retreat you ever heard. It'll be for you, buddy!" Wynn got up, took two steps backward, and saluted Ontek. He held it for a full minute, while saying a silent prayer.

Frank, Red, and Wynn remained at the summit while the men carried the dead men down the hill. They stood in silence as the last litter bearer disappeared into a deep ravine.

"Wynn, I said it was a war," said Red. In a self-deprecating voice, he continued. "Here's how it's done, boys!" He threw his hat to the ground and kicked it through the grimy, ash-covered ground. When he continued, his voice quavered with emotion. "Listen to this old bird. He can get you through. He knows everything."

"Red, you trained only Ontek! You had no control over anything else," counseled Frank.

"Seven people died needlessly," said Red.

"Ontek died trying to save their lives," said Wynn.

Frank added, "He was following your teaching to the end."

"A helluva a teacher I am!"

"That's a damn lie," snapped Wynn.

"I know I couldn't teach all the boys, but I thought if I trained my crew hard, then each fellow..."

Interrupting him, Frank asked, "There are too many intangibles in life, Red."

"Like Grabowski leading a fire crew?" Wynn asked.

"Yes," said Frank.

Red's face began to relax. He unclenched his fists, closed his eyes, and breathed deeply. His anger and frustration began to ebb. But the terrible sense of loss remained. Slowly, his resolve started to crack, as tears began to run down his dirt-stained cheeks.

Frank put his arm around Red's shoulder. Softly, he said, "Sometimes, crying is all that we can do."

Rubbing his eyes, Red looked out over the charred hillside, "This will never happen again," he announced. " I'll make sure of it!"

Frank and Wynn nodded in agreement. Then, with Red between them, they began their difficult journey down into the valley.

CHAPTER FORTY

Six weeks had elapsed before the Forest County Coroner's Jury finally released the results of the Jamison Run tragedy. Testimony revealed that four young men had received no fire training at all, and the remainder of the team had not received enough rest between fire fighting duties. Grabowski's army records showed that his claim of previous fire fighting experience was false. This disclosure softened the criticism of James Simpson's selection of Grabowski as fire boss. Despite the damning nature of the testimony, the Coroner's Jury ruled that "...unintentional laxity and negligence contributed to the deaths."

It recommended that no further action be taken.

CHAPTER FORTY-ONE

The mess hall was unusually quiet as Red and Wynn read the report of the Jamison Run tragedy. When Red had finished, Wynn was staring through the window out onto the compound. "What do you think?" asked Wynn.

"It won't bring back the dead."

"It got Simpson off the hook."

"Yeah," said Red, "but he's being transferred to Montana."

Wynn laughed softly. "He's going as a ranger."

"That's being promoted the hard way."

Wynn nervously twisted the tiny gold ring on his index finger. "I miss them guys, especially Ontek and Peaches.

"That's Ontek's ring, isn't it?"

"Yeah, his mom gave it to me after the funeral."

"It will give you something to remember him by."

"As if I'll ever forget that big lug."

After finishing another cup of coffee, Red said, "The only good thing to come out of the Jamison Run Fire was me being appointed head of fire training for all the C's in the Region. And I'm going train them here at Camp One. Just like I did for your crew, Wynn. Remember?" As Wynn smiled, Red got up and said, "I'll be seeing you next spring when you come back from school."

"Aren't you going to make it to Doc's Christmas party?"

"Shaking his head, Red said, "Naw, parties always make me nervous." When Wynn reached out his hand, Red shook it warmly. Then he hugged Wynn quickly before retreating to an open door. "By the way, Wynn. I expect nothing but straight A's from my best student."

As Red walked down the stairs, George Higgleston and Danny

Witkowski barged through the door. "You're missing a great party." said Higgleston.

While bowing formerly from the waist, Witkowski said, "And the Doc requests the pleasure of your company."

"Let's get some of that terrific food before the rookies scarf it all down," urged Higgleston.

When Wynn walked into the Recreation Room, Lincoln shouted, "Three cheers for Wynn!"

While the cheers echoed throughout the room, Frank walked over and stood beside Wynn. He asked Lincoln to join them and then embraced each young man warmly. As the applause from their friends subsided, Frank said, "When I came here, something was missing in my life."

"Yeah, a lot of goldbricking enrollees," shouted Cartwright, the only remaining member of the River Rats.

After the laughter had died down, Frank continued. "I've found two sons, Wynn and Lincoln. I've watched them grow, and I'm proud of them, as any father would be. Wynn leaves for Penn State tomorrow. Lincoln will leave next spring after helping me set up the new hospital here at Camp One."

"Where's Lincoln going?" asked Higgleston.

"He'll study with my colleague, who teaches at Howard University."

The remainder of the party was a blur to Wynn, a blur of so-longs and good-byes. He had lived with these young men, worked with them, fought with them, and had even witnessed death with them. Now he knew that he would never see them again. With each, "See you later, buddy," Wynn hurt just a little more.

The next day, Frank drove Wynn from Camp One for the last time. As they passed a column of young men struggling to keep up with Red Dawson, Frank stopped the car so Wynn could get out.

"You're here to keep the little fires from becoming big ones," shouted Red. As one young man started to fall out, Red ran beside him, offering him encouragement. As another young man showed signs of faltering, Red shouted, "Kid, you've got to lose some of that baby fat before a fire renders it down, until you're nothing but a grease spot." As he trotted by Wynn, Red acknowledged him with a wink and a big smile.

Wynn stood and listened to Red's voice fading into the distance. "A big part of me will always be out there, running with Red." Finally, Wynn slid into the passenger's seat. "C'mon, Doc. If we don't meet the bus in thirty minutes, I'll have to hoof it all the way to State College."

"Son, you keep forgetting," said Frank. "This is a Packard!"

ABOUT THE AUTHOR

Michael Schultz is a native of Camp One CCC territory. He was born and raised in Wilcox, Pennsylvania, not many miles from Camp One's location. After serving in the army for three years, he attended Indiana University of Pennsylvania on the GI Bill before beginning his teaching career at Gateway High School in Monroeville, Pennsylvania. During that time, he received his MEd from IUP and then a Ph.D from the University of Pittsburgh. In addition to teaching three decades at Gateway, he also taught for Penn State University, The Citadel, and the University of Pittsburgh.

He is the author of THE NATIONAL EDUCATION ASSOCIATION AND THE BLACK TEACHER (1972) and co-authored SEARCH THE HEART(1990) with Grace Gunderman.

He and his wife, Marie, were Campground Hosts for ten years at Loleta, a recreation site, in the Allegheny National Forest. During that tenure, he met and interviewed hundreds of CCC veterans, who became the inspiration for this novel.

Mike and Marie live in Penn Hills, a Pittsburgh suburb. They have five children and are grandparents to ten, and great-grandparents to Tristan, born in 1996.